ARMADRON

The Otherworld Series: Book 1

COREY TATE

ILLUMIFY MEDIA GLOBAL
Littleton, Colorado

ARMADRON

Copyright © 2019 by Corey Tate

All rights reserved. No part of this book may be reproduced in any form or by any means—whether electronic, digital, mechanical, or otherwise—without permission in writing from the publisher, except by a reviewer, who may quote brief passages in a review. This book is a work of fiction. Names, characters, places, and incidents are either the product of the author's imagination or are used fictitiously. Any resemblance to actual persons, living or dead, or to actual events or locales are entirely coincidental.

The views and opinions expressed in this book are those of the author and do not necessarily reflect the official policy or position of Illumify Media Global.

Published by
Illumify Media Global
www.IllumifyMedia.com
"Write. Publish. Market. *SELL!*"

Library of Congress Control Number: 2018966318

Paperback ISBN: 978-1-949021-29-5
eBook ISBN: 978-1-949021-30-1

Cover design by King's Custom Covers: www.kingscustomcovers.com

Printed in the United States of America

To my grandmother, Joan Steenburn

CONTENTS

Acknowledgments   vii

1. The Beginning of Everything   1
2. Rick the Brick   11
3. Ascension   21
4. Having Too Much Fun Can Kill You   28
5. You Must Be Dreaming   37
6. Accelerating   42
7. Bermuda Delta   49
8. The Arcade   59
9. Caged   73
10. Breathtaking   82
11. The Cavern   88
12. The Help   100
13. Come On, Hit Me!   106
14. Seeing Is Believing   113
15. Knowledge Is Living   120
16. Cannibals   127
17. The Infinite Cave   135
18. Into the Hole   145
19. Problems, Solutions . . . and More Problems   155
20. There's No Place Like Home   165
21. One Down, Four to Go!   181
22. Rejoined! Or . . . Maybe Not   199

23.	It All Comes Together	208
24.	Breaking Bonds	215
25.	A Nightmare in a Nightmare	222
26.	Potential	228
27.	The Journey	235
28.	The Final Battle	242
29.	Recharging	257
	Wait! There's more!	267
	About Corey Tate	268

ACKNOWLEDGMENTS

I have many people to thank in the various facets of my life.

My military life. Gung Ho! Brandon Davis—the friend who's been with me from the first day of basic training when I couldn't stay awake, to our last day of being active duty military. Alma Stuldreher, Donny Saetan, Rachel and Phil Atkinson, who watched over my dog Scarlord and me during our awesome time at Airman Leadership School. Eric Matzek, Jeff Evans and Joseph McCoin, who mentored me as I grew up in the TACP career field and picked me up where I fell. Jay Decker, Patrick Miller, Carter, Ashley and Bryan Boyd, the best roommates and housemates that I could have ever asked for, each in their own way. Joel Mathews, for giving me this amazing, humbling opportunity to publish my first book. To my first airmen—Michael Christe, Colton Drye, Luke Grant, Harm Purewal, Joel Fierro and Matthew First—thank you for teaching me the hardships of being a supervisor, and how to overcome them together. Daniel Ritche, I can never thank you enough for giving me faith during my deployment, and for constantly reminding me that there are good people out there who are willing to go the extra mile. Almond, Rumor, Harley and Data, thank you all for being man's best friends, and for filling my life with joy everywhere that I go.

My civilian life. Liam Roberts, Logan Weiss, Nick Goffredo, and Katie Mezzacappa. You all never stopped calling and texting me, even when I was too busy to answer. You always compromised with me, and you always made time to see me when I was home on leave. My jiu jitsu and MMA families at Twin Wolves MMA, Johns Gym and Brazilian Top Team, especially Wilkinson, Leny, Miller, Moore and Toledo: I can never thank you enough for motivating me to get out there and train, even when I want to stay in bed. Your instruction and motivation have been truly invaluable and have never been taken lightly.

My family life. Mom, Dad, Bobby, Leah, Breanna, Katie, Cameron and Dustin. Thank you for adopting me into this family at such a young age. I don't know who I would have been without all of you, and I look forward to spending the rest of my life with this giant family that we have. Mary and Scarlord, you are both the start of my new family, and I couldn't be more excited. I wouldn't want anyone else in the world at my side, which makes me the luckiest, happiest man alive.

My future life. Illumify Media Global has given me the chance to be an author—something I've wanted to be from the moment I wrote the first six-page draft of *Armadron* in Mrs. Fields' tenth grade English class. Karen Scalf Bouchard, Geoffrey Stone, Michael Klassen, Jen Clark, Deb Lewis, Darrin Geisinger and others at Illumify and beyond have given me unbelievable support in completing this book and preparing for the rest of the series as well.

Most of all, my grandmother, Joan Steenburn, who always challenged me to think outside the box, and who always looked at me over my French toast and chocolate milkshake like I was more than I knew.

1

THE BEGINNING OF EVERYTHING

Boom!

Whattheheck?

Instantly awake, Scott Faranger threw his hands up in front of his face to protect himself. After a moment he realized he'd been dreaming and gave a loud sigh.

"Every. Single. Freaking. Morning." The frustration of his voice echoed off every wall in his bedroom.

He rolled to the right and stared at the small digital alarm clock on the nightstand, unable to ignore the fact that his heart was still trying to beat a hole through his chest from the inside out. After blinking and wiping his eyes a few times, he could see the numbers: 6:32 a.m.

"Crap."

Throwing off his covers, he hurried to the corner of the bedroom, stumbling on clothes strewn across the floor. In that corner was the door that led to another world: his personal shower.

Scott opened the bathroom door and stepped onto the white tiled floor. Peeling off his pajamas, he flung them onto yet another pile of clothes.

He looked at himself in the mirror, checking for any signs of the change that had been happening recently. The face that greeted him was that of an average-looking fifteen-year-old boy with blue eyes and sandy-colored hair. He looked tired, with tiny bags under his eyes that gave away the fact that he had been tossing and turning all night. After a few more moments of inspection, Scott grunted, turned away, and started the shower.

The water came out ice cold.

Awesome.

He waited for the water to heat up, occasionally testing it with his finger. The water was so cold, each time he pulled his finger back out he half expected to see it encased in ice.

This was the third day in a row his younger brother had beat him to all the hot water, and it was beyond the point of annoying.

Jared! Scott thought angrily. He balled his hands into fists, already thinking of revenge.

A dull thud came from the water pipes inside the wall, and water stopped flowing out of the showerhead. He leaned over the tub and peered up at the nozzle.

Pssssssshhhhhttt!

A torrent of boiling-hot water erupted out of the showerhead. As the water hit the bottom of the tub, it instantly turned into steam.

Scott yelled and fell backward, shielding his face with his right arm as he hit the wall.

Suddenly the showerhead was ripped from the pipe. The projectile slammed into the cabinet next to Scott's left ear, then fell to the ground.

Tink.

Scott stayed where he was sitting on the floor for a minute or two, and then stood up once his heart slowed down a bit and his brain stopped telling him that he was about to have an aneurysm.

After he picked up the showerhead and tossed it into the trash by the toilet, he took a good look at the nozzle-less pipe. Scott adjusted the temperature, then stepped cautiously into the shower. Water—not boiling, just hot—was now spewing out of the pipe in one thick stream. He could still shower; it just looked like he lived in a third world country now.

Gooood morning, Vietnam, he thought to himself as he showered beneath the impromptu spigot.

When he was finished, he tried to turn off the water—there remained a slow drip coming out of the pipe—and threw on a pair of tan shorts, a white polo shirt, his watch, and a tan belt. He turned toward the mirror to comb his hair . . . and saw it.

Oh. There was a booger in his nose.

He flicked it out into the sink and looked at himself again, shaking.

His eyes were purple.

The change was still happening.

He did a double take. The irises were a deep purple. And the color was sort of . . . moving. Kind of like how water moves in a stream. Whatever was happening to him, it was getting worse. It was also freaky—like something out of a Stephen King novel.

He rubbed his palms against his eyes furiously. Then he slowly removed his hands and looked again.

His eyes were now their normal blue.

Scott continued to stare at his reflection and for the third time this month unsuccessfully attempted to convince himself that nothing was wrong. He remained motionless for several seconds, then eventually turned away from the mirror.

He walked out of the bathroom, past the wall-mounted TV where his gaming console was connected and reached next to his bed for his black book bag. Whatever was happening to him, it was still a school morning and he had thirteen minutes to catch the bus.

Before he could reach the bag, he felt a horrific wrenching sensation in his stomach. He dropped to the floor, gasping and holding back tears from the pain.

He tasted bile in the back of his throat, and his eyes rolled backward. The pain was so great that he went in and out of consciousness for at least a minute. He felt his arms and legs move on their own accord, and his neck felt like it was going to snap in half. His spine ached, and his feet were hyperextended way past where they should have been. This went on for what felt like forever, and he felt tears well up in his eyes.

Just when he thought it was over, it escalated. Suddenly his body turned so that he was on his stomach. It felt to Scott like a bull on steroids was bucking against his heart and ribcage, trying to break through the skin.

"Aaaaaarrrrgghhhh!" Scott screamed and rolled into one of the piles of discarded clothes.

He tried to spit part of a dirty shirt from his mouth, but he couldn't control his jaw. He gasped for breath, but his nose felt scrunched up against his face. Thirty seconds went by. Then a minute.

Scott couldn't breathe. He kept telling his body to move, but it wouldn't listen to him.

The walls started closing in. His vision began shimmering at the edges, and his peripheral vision completely cut out. The blackness overtook his eyes, and even though his eyes were wide open, he couldn't see anything.

Suddenly he felt himself gain control of his body again.

He rolled to the right and spat the shirt out with the last of his energy. He lay on the floor for several seconds, getting his breath back.

"What the hell was that?" Scott mumbled to himself, but his voice was hoarse now.

Eventually Scott was able to stand up. He was shaking as he bent again to grab his book bag. Nothing crazy happened this time.

He slung the bag over his right shoulder and glanced at the alarm clock on his nightstand.

It was now 6:57 a.m. He didn't have much time left to catch the bus to school.

He opened his bedroom door. A familiar shape scooted past and ran down the stairs in white shorts and a red shirt. It was his eleven-year-old brother, Jared.

"Hey, Jared!"

Jared stopped halfway down the staircase and looked up at Scott. "Stop using up all the hot water."

"I didn't!" Jared cried unconvincingly.

"Sure you didn't," Scott said, then added spitefully, "just like I didn't take your Game Boy."

Jared's eyes widened.

Scott swallowed a grin and kept a straight face. The Game Boy was Jared's prized possession.

Jared ran back up to his room, screaming obnoxiously. He came out of his bedroom a few seconds later, holding his Game Boy.

"You didn't take it!" Jared cheered. "You lied!"

"Remember what that felt like, Jared," Scott warned darkly, savoring the moment.

Jared's smile dropped.

"Because if you ever use up all the hot water again," Scott threatened, "you'll suddenly find that your favorite toy is missing."

Jared cringed.

"Or broken," Scott added.

Jared looked like he was going to cry. Scott relished every nanosecond of this torment.

"You got it?" Scott asked.

Jared saw the expression on his older brother's face and decided to hurry down the steps.

"And towels exist, ya know!" Jared yelled once he was a safe enough distance away. "Use 'em!"

Scott looked down at himself and noticed that his shirt was soaked through with sweat.

You've gotta be kidding me, he thought.

He walked back into the room, pulled out another white shirt, and put it on. It was more or less the same as the first one, but he still went to the mirror to take a quick look.

"Scott," a woman's voice called from downstairs, "are you up?"

"Yeah, Mom!" Scott broke away from his thoughts and meandered out of his bedroom to the top of the stairs. "Coming!"

He descended the spiral oak staircase and made for the kitchen. Jared was already at the table, eating a bagel.

"Good morning," Scott muttered as he passed the sink and the refrigerator.

"Good morning," Christine Faranger replied without looking at him. Wearing a gray pantsuit and her fancy watch, her hair in a tight bun, she looked ready to take on the world. She pretty much looked like that every day, and Scott was getting tired of it. She never dressed like an actual mom anymore. She was always a businesswoman first.

Picking up her coffee, she wished her sons a good day, and promptly exited the kitchen—car keys, coffee, and portfolio in hand.

"Wait!" Scott called, "I think I just had a sei—"

"I have to go, Scott!" she interrupted without skipping a beat, shouldering her purse on the way out the front door. "I'm late and I have a 7:15."

"Mom, seriously?! I'm trying to tell you that I—"

"After school!" she yelled over her shoulder.

"Mom!"

The front door slammed shut behind her.

Scott let loose such a stream of profanity aimed at the door that Jared wouldn't have been surprised if it popped off the hinges.

Staring at his brother, Jared jumped up from the table and ran into a corner of the kitchen, trying to make himself a smaller target.

"And then the showerhead exploded," Scott finished lamely and threw his arms to his sides.

"What? Something exploded?! Cool!" Jared suddenly exclaimed, forgetting about Scott's angry outburst. He grinned from ear to ear as he watched his brother grab a box of cereal from the pantry.

"It didn't explode, Jared," Scott lied, trying to cut his brother off before he started asking a million questions.

"Yeah it did. You just said so."

"Yeah, but it didn't."

"So does that mean you're a liar?" Jared grinned.

Scott, standing at the counter pouring milk into his bowl, rolled his eyes.

"It kind of sounds like iiiiit," Jared nagged in a sing-song voice.

Scott grabbed a spoon from the silverware drawer and threw it at Jared's arm.

"Ow!"

Jared pretended to be hurt, but then they both laughed. Jared sat down again and went back to eating his bagel.

Eventually Scott sat down on the opposite side of the table from his little brother, but not before he ruffled Jared's hair a little bit and pulled his right ear.

He knew Jared hated that, but their dad used to do it to them, so Scott felt like that boundary had already been breached. Now it had become a thing.

"Stop, I'm not a kid," Jared mumbled in between bites. "I'm eleven now."

"Yeah," Scott said, smiling, as he ate another spoonful, "as of last week."

There was silence for a few seconds, and Scott's thoughts returned to the seizure. This morning's episode had been the worst, and it terrified him more than he could put into words. What if he had some genetic disorder thingy and Jared was going to get it too? What if the next one killed him? What if it was contagious?

"Scott?"

Jared was leaning forward in his chair, looking into Scott's eyes.

"Hmm?" Scott put aside his dark thoughts.

"I heard you in your room," Jared replied, looking incredibly concerned. "You were yelling. And you were rolling around and stuff. You okay?"

Scott took in a sharp breath. Jared was always catching him off guard. Most of the time, he was just a clueless, annoying kid. But sometimes he reminded Scott of their father. Sometimes Jared seemed a lot smarter than he let on, and it honestly creeped Scott out a little bit. Okay, a lot.

"I'm okay, Jared," he replied unconvincingly, absentmindedly stirring his cereal around in his bowl.

Jared looked down at his bowl and back up. "Well, you've got me. I mean, Mom's always busy, and . . . but you got me. And I got you. Right?"

"Right."

"What's goin' on, then?" Jared pushed. "Is it about Dad?"

"Jared, you're the little brother. I'm the big brother. You're not supposed to worry about me. Let's just stick to our roles."

Jared just stared at Scott without blinking and waited for a real answer.

Fine. Screw it, Scott thought.

"I keep having seizures, I think, and I'm pretty sure I made a fire hydrant blow up the other day and the shower blow up too. I can do things. Stuff that people can do in comics and movies and stuff, but not in a cool way. I can't control it. It's . . . it's stuff that I can't explain. It's been going on for weeks, and I think it's killing me."

After a couple seconds Scott noticed that Jared was just staring at his bowl, not making any sounds.

"Uh, hello?" Scott chuckled and tapped Jared on the head with his finger. "Anyone home? I was being serious, ya know. You're the only person that I've told this stuff to. I'm actually freaking out a little bit."

Jared ignored him, got up, and put his bowl in the sink without looking at Scott. He started to walk toward the stairs and out of the kitchen.

"Jared!" Scott was yelling at him now. "Why are you being weird? I just told you the truth!"

"No! No, you didn't! You never tell me anything!" When Jared whirled around, Scott saw tears in his eyes. "You—you always act so tough and . . . and I never get to really talk to you! And n–now D–Dad's dead and Mom's never around—"

Scott was already on his feet moving toward his brother. Before Jared could react, Scott pulled him in for a hug and let Jared cry into his shirt.

"Shh." Scott brushed back Jared's curly brown hair repeatedly. "Shh."

"It's not fair, though! He just—"

"I know," Scott soothed. "I know, buddy. But Mom's gonna be okay. And so are we."

"How do you know?"

"I just do."

"Then why are you still lying to me all the time?" Jared shot back at him.

"I'm not lying, Jared. I swear," Scott said.

"You swear?" Jared sniffled.

"Yeah." Scott nodded slowly. "I swear."

"Then you're either crazy or a superhero or something," Jared said with a small laugh.

"You believe me?" Scott asked, incredulous.

Jared looked up at him and stared him right in the eyes.

"Yup."

Scott saw something veiled in Jared's eyes, and he suddenly had the unsettling thought that his brother might be keeping secrets of his own.

Scott released him from their hug.

"Go upstairs and wash your face, man. We'll talk later, okay?"

"Okay," Jared said and ran upstairs, leaving Scott alone in the kitchen.

Scott had always suspected that Jared kept some things to himself. There was something different about Jared. Some kind of underlying intelligence. An old-soul sort of thing. Scott wasn't even sure that *Jared* knew what it was. It was almost like there were two people in there. One was an innocent kid, and the other was . . . not.

Scott finished breakfast just as the bus was pulling in. He grabbed his book bag from the kitchen chair and made for the front door.

"Jared!"

"Coming!" Jared called, running back down the stairs with his backpack over his shoulder.

He tried to slip past Scott, but Scott held his arm out to stop him.

"Do you have your inhaler?" Scott asked.

"No, but—"

"Go get it."

Jared looked like he wanted to argue, but Scott pushed him a little bit and he ran back up the stairs.

Jared was only about five two and weighed less than a hundred pounds soaking wet. He had asthma and was always forgetting his inhaler, so it was Scott's job to remind him. Constantly.

Jared came thundering down the stairs, inhaler in hand, and Scott ushered him toward the bus, locking the front door behind them.

2

RICK THE BRICK

The bus doors opened with a hiss.

Jared walked to the back of the bus to sit near the other sixth graders, as noisy and obnoxious as always. In sharp contrast, Jared sat quietly and stared out the window.

He'd once been an outgoing kid, as rambunctious as his buddies. But events from the last few months had left their mark on him.

We'll get through this, Jared, Scott thought, remembering what Jared had just said to him in the kitchen: "You got me. And I got you."

Scott quickly made his way down the aisle and stopped at his preassigned seat, which was next to his best friend, Charlie McEntly. Charlie, wearing a black Metallica T-shirt loosely hung over his skinny frame, looked up at Scott with a tired grin on his face. He looked even more tired than usual, and his thick orange hair was sticking up on the right side where he had been using his book bag as a pillow.

"What up, Scott?" Charlie greeted sleepily.

"Mornin'." Scott slumped into the aisle seat and set his backpack on the floor. "*COD* or *Battlefield*?"

"The new *Battlefield*. Just came out."

Charlie was a gamer. Every night. All the time. Nonstop. He loved it, and he probably would never give it up.

"You ready for soccer tryouts?" Charlie asked.

"I was born ready." Scott grinned.

"Sure ya were, stud," Charlie replied sarcastically as he put his head back and closed his eyes.

"Yeah, buddy." Scott laughed and patted his friend's arm. "You get some sleep. You're gonna need it if you want to make the team again this year."

Charlie shot him the middle finger, and Scott laughed.

The bus accelerated and pulled away from the curb.

Scott loved being the last stop. Now, everyone on the bus had twenty minutes to kick back and relax, because there were only one or two stop signs between the Farangers' house and the school.

He unlocked his phone and inserted headphones in his ears. He listened to a couple oldies tracks, from a playlist Charlie had given him, and several minutes later he turned to ask Charlie if they had a geometry test that day.

Charlie was fast asleep. He was using his book bag topped with his jacket as a pillow again.

Scott shook his head and once again immersed himself in Charlie's music. He watched the streets pass by as the bus drove through his hometown of Glendale, Arizona. The sun had risen above the horizon a little while ago, and as he looked out the bus window, he saw dozens of cul-de-sacs lined with front yards of yellow, dead grass. Kids waited at street corners with parents, and everyone was dressed in minimal clothing in a vain attempt to combat the over-100-degree temperatures that had been hitting them lately.

A ball of paper hit the seat in front of him, and Scott turned around to see who threw it.

He saw three kids in the back of the bus laughing and throwing paper at each other. Jared was sitting a seat in front of them, reading a science fiction book and trying to tune all of it out.

Scott frowned, remembering something his mother had said a couple days ago.

Scott, why don't you take Jared with you the next time you hang out with Charlie? Your brother needs to socialize more. He's by himself too often. Too immersed in pretend worlds. I don't think it's helping him.

Scott wasn't sure he agreed. Reading seemed to relax Jared. Plus, Scott wasn't ready for Jared to act like a full-blown teenager yet. Despite the occasional tension between them, he liked having a little brother who looked up to him.

A couple songs later the bus screeched to a halt behind the line of buses in the front of the high school.

He woke Charlie. Exiting the bus in a crowd of drowsy school kids, they headed toward what Charlie liked to call "the prison." The adults in their lives preferred to call it Glendale High School. Charlie claimed they were one and the same. After all, they both had assigned seats, bells, premade food, cells (teachers called them classrooms), an exercise yard, and a massive lunchroom.

True to form, Charlie suddenly cleared his throat and yelled, "Welcome to prison!"

Scott did a face palm.

"You ready for the trip on Sunday?" Charlie asked suddenly.

"I *can't* stop thinking about it. It's gonna be *awesome!*" Scott replied, feigning overexcitement.

Charlie laughed. Scott was always making fun of the way he went from zero to a hundred in less than a second. He was just that kind of guy, though. He couldn't help it. *Just like electricity.* Charlie smiled to himself at the thought.

"For once, my mom is being pretty cool," Scott commented.

"Your mom's always cool!"

"My mom? What planet are you from?"

Christine Farranger was the CEO of some big company that sold healthy chips. Sometimes her company did fun things, like book executive meetings on cruise ships. In fact, that's exactly what was going down this Sunday. She would be boarding a cruise ship and spending a week at sea—and bringing Scott and Jared with her. She'd even generously purchased fares for Charlie and his parents. Christine and Barbara McEntly, best friends since high school, had always thought it would be fun for the families to vacation together. It was almost too good to be true, but Charlie and Scott were just a few days away from spending a week wreaking havoc on a cruise ship together.

By now they'd reached the front doors of the school, along with the other several hundred school kids. The noise of the crowd was so deafening that Scott seriously contemplated bringing earplugs to school from now on.

A small group of kids was blocking the front door. Everyone seemed to be watching a video on a phone while talking excitedly to one another.

"That dude's lifting a *car*," someone was saying, "with one hand!"

Charlie rolled his eyes at Scott. Charlie believed kids their age didn't need cell phones unless it was an emergency. Charlie also had bright-orange hair, though, so he was a little off-center from the norm.

"Chill, Gramps," Scott told him as they walked past the kids.

Charlie gritted his teeth at the nickname Scott was growing fonder of using with each passing day. Scott just chuckled.

The two went through the main doors and weaved their way through the milling students until they reached the stairs.

"See ya!" Charlie clapped Scott on the back before turning down a side hallway, hollering over his shoulder, "See you at tryouts after school!"

Scott shot him a thumbs-up and headed up the staircase.

Halfway up, his heart nearly skipped a beat. At the top of the stairwell, making her way down the stairs, was the best thing about being in the tenth grade: Molly Clenton.

He took in her curly brown hair, her turquoise blouse with the button gaps caused by an impressive bustline, and cropped jean shorts showing off tanned legs. Molly had these little freckles near the tops of her cheeks that made her look Irish. She also walked so confidently that Scott wondered if she'd ever tripped on anything in her entire life.

He realized he was staring and made himself blink.

"Hey, Scott! Don't you just love the end of the week?" Molly gave a dazzling smile that could melt the sun.

"Alas, Moll-ay, to end is simply to start again," Scott joked, instantly realizing how lame he must have sounded.

RICK THE BRICK

Some nearby kids in the stairwell laughed. He was certain they were laughing at him.

Oh God, that was corny. He mentally slapped himself. *Kill me now.*

He joked with Molly all the time, but she was still eons out of his league. That much was obvious to anyone.

Molly smiled sweetly at his comment and disappeared around the corner.

Scott kept walking up the stairs and took a right at the top, accidentally bumping into someone getting a drink at the water fountain. Scott's backpack slid off his shoulder and landed on the floor with a thud.

Before he knew what was happening, he was on his back on the yellow-and-brown tiled floor with the breath completely knocked out of him. Turning his head, he realized he was eye level with his backpack on the floor, and it was at that moment that Scott knew who he had bumped into.

"Watch where you're steppin', Faranger!"

Scott looked up and groaned out loud.

Rick the Brick, he thought as the color drained from his face.

Rick Levinston. Senior at Glendale High. He'd failed twelfth grade once already, and was the only guy in school who had a full-grown beard and looked like a pro wrestler. He was a super senior. But not of the superhero variety. Rick the Brick tortured any kid in his field of view. In fact, most people took the intelligent route and usually just sat down and pretended not to exist when Rick came near them.

Scott was not most people.

"Sorry, Brick. I didn't see you," Scott said from the ground.

"What'd you call me?!" Rick the Brick snapped.

"Aww geez, Rick," Scott whined in his best *Rick and Morty* impression.

Brick picked Scott up with ease and slammed him against a locker.

"Ohhhhhh!"

It took Scott a second to realize that the sound had not come from him. It had come from several dozen kids who had stopped to watch, and the crowd was growing fast.

Brick was getting a little nervous from all the attention. Scott could see it on his face.

"I called you Brick because I respect you," Scott gasped, "and because you lift a lot, right?"

Rick the Brick thought about this for a second.

"What? Yeah. Yeah I do. . ."

"How much do you bench?" Scott interjected quickly.

Some of the kids in the crowd were trying to cover up their laughter. They knew the Scott/Brick routine. More kids kept gathering around with every second too.

"Well, 245 is my—"

"Warm-up." Scott finished the sentence still pinned against the locker by one of Brick's massive arms. "And then you finish by eating small children."

Laughter erupted among the crowd. Brick's face contorted in a look of embarrassment; he hated all the attention and he wasn't good at thinking on his feet.

"Are you—?" Brick thought out loud.

"Making fun of you?" Scott cut in, faking an appalled expression. "Brick, you're the most popular dad in school. Why would I do that?!"

The crowd laughed and cheered, while Brick stood there, perplexed.

Ohhhh crap. Crap crap crap. I'm getting that seizure feeling again, Scott realized, noting how his head was starting to ache and throb and his stomach was turning into knots.

Brick suddenly looked at him differently, like he was seeing his face for the first time.

"Your eyes," Brick mumbled, "they're purp—"

"Break it up!" a teacher suddenly yelled from deep inside the crowd.

The students quickly dispersed, running in all directions. In the confusion, Scott pushed back against Rick so that he would let him off the locker.

Rick the Brick flew seven feet back, knocking three other kids into the lockers on the other side of the hall.

Scott felt like his head was about to peel like a banana. He scooped up his backpack and just ran.

Janitor's closet, janitor's closet, janitor's closet!

He ran down a side hallway and into the nearest janitor's closet he could find. Scott slammed the door, locked it, and turned on the light.

The closet was just big enough for him to get in a ball on the floor, and that's just what he did. As he half fell and half crouched down, Scott could have sworn that the water in the mop bucket nearest to him floated out, temporarily ignoring gravity and all its laws. It dropped back in again before Scott could blink, though.

Whaaat?

That was all that he could think before the seizure struck.

Scott's back arched like lightning had struck him, and his head slammed back against the metal shelf behind him, knocking him out cold.

* * *

Twenty minutes later Scott jerked awake. As soon as he realized where he was, he scrambled to his feet, grabbed his stuff, and opened the door. There was no one in the hallway outside, so he full-on sprinted to first period.

The uber-vigilant Mrs. Wontsman didn't even notice him sneak in from the back of the class. Smooth.

He quietly took his seat as a couple of nearby girls giggled. While Mrs. Wontsman droned on about the life cycle of plants, Scott's brain raced a million miles per hour trying to process what had just happened.

He experimentally pinched his forearm hard and cried out, distracting the class for a second.

"My bad." Scott smiled sheepishly, and Mrs. Wontsman continued, only slightly perturbed.

When the bell rang, Scott was the first one out the door. He fast-walked to geometry class. It was three doors down on the same floor that he was on, so he was there in no time.

When he entered the room, he found there were only two other people in the classroom: Mr. Eidington and Molly.

It actually wasn't that much of a surprise to him. Scott had noticed over the past couple months that Molly liked to be early to things. He wasn't being creepy, though. Just observant.

He took his seat next to Molly and smiled at her. She smiled back like a supermodel.

"Sooo . . . you goin' to soccer tryouts?" she asked him, leaning toward him a bit from her desk.

"Yeah. You?" Scott asked, leaning back in his chair in a bad attempt to look cool and at ease.

Her hazel eyes were staring into his soul, and that always made him say stupid things.

"You betcha. I'll dribble circles around those girls, and when I'm done, I'm comin' for you." Molly winked at him.

"You won't make it past the girls," Scott snorted.

"Hey," Molly said, her face suddenly changing expression as a thought crossed her mind, "I saw you and Rick in the hallway . . ."

She let the statement hang in the air, and Scott could feel his face getting red. Luckily, kids started filing into the room, so he was saved the response.

When everyone was seated, Mr. Eidington started "tweaching." Someone had come up with the nickname because whenever it got completely silent and all eyes were on him, Mr. Eidington would twitch his neck and his voice would vibrate from nerves. It happened all the time. It used to be funnier, before it happened so often that everyone got used to it—and especially before last year's talent show when one of the students performed an impression of him and he had taken it extremely personally.

Scott couldn't hold on to a single piece of information that the tweacher had been tweaching. His thoughts of Molly—and of Rick the Brick slamming him into a locker for sport—drove the entire lesson out of his head. More than that, though, Scott kept trying to think of someone he could tell about the seizures. Jared already knew, but Scott probably needed to tell a doctor or his mom or something. Or Charlie.

The bell rang.

He gathered up his books and slid out of the classroom as fast as he could, pointedly dodging Molly's gaze. He didn't want Molly to question him again about how he kept getting his ass beaten by the human-gorilla-hybrid test subject known as Brick. Not right now anyway.

Scott walked down to English class and opened the door to find that a lot of his friends had gathered in a circle in the middle of the classroom, with Charlie at the center of the circle. Scott overhead the last few words of the story Charlie was telling.

"Knocked him flat on his ass!"

Everyone laughed, and all heads turned in Scott's direction. When people saw him, they fell over laughing, clutching their stomachs and clapping their hands.

Scott was instantly embarrassed, assuming Charlie had seen what had transpired between him and Rick the freakin' prick.

He made his way to the center of the group, trying to save face.

"Hey, McEntly, you hallucinating again?" He feigned coolness, all the while shooting Charlie a look that said, *come on, man, let this one go.*

"Yeah," Charlie said, not seeing Scott's expression, "I was telling 'em about the time when you were riding your four-wheeler and ran over that vine, and it got caught up in the tires! You flew off . . . into that little creek!"

A lot of people doubled over laughing and came up with watery eyes and red faces. Scott relaxed, convinced Charlie hadn't seen anything.

"Did you happen to mention that you tried to help but tripped over your own big feet?" Scott grinned.

"Yeah, well," Charlie started, pretending to be embarrassed, "I was too busy laughing at you!"

"Sure you were," Scott laughed.

Charlie grinned wickedly as he leaned forward on the desk. "But we had to walk back to the house so I could get clothes for you, and you had to wait outside, remember?"

"Yesss, I remember." Scott shook his head and smiled.

He knew exactly where Charlie was going with this one.

Charlie now addressed the rest of the kids and shook with laughter as he told the rest of the story.

"When I came back with the clothes, a chicken from the Hekinsals' farm was tryin' to eat his shirt! He was cryin' bloody murder and screamin' 'Charlie, Charlie! This turkey's tryna eat me!'"

Everyone doubled over again in laughter.

"That's not exactly what happened! And I had never seen a live chicken before!" Scott cried out in vain, laughing in the middle of his own sentence.

Once Mrs. Fields came in, it took her five whole minutes to get the class to quiet down.

It had been a rough morning, but Scott was finally feeling like things were getting back to normal.

Little did he know that normal was a long way away.

3

ASCENSION

Scott was feeling focused during soccer tryouts. He wasn't thinking of Molly on the other side of the field practicing with the girls, or how her unnaturally shiny, curly brown hair moved when she ran. Definitely not.

For the drill they were doing, Scott's teammate Devan was on his left. Their teammate Howard was on the right. Scott, in the center with the ball, sprinted up the field.

He passed the ball to Howard as a defender came near. Howard trapped the ball and faked left. As the defender tripped, Howard danced to the right. He shot the ball at the goal.

The goalie dove for the ball, and it hit his left knee. It rebounded toward Scott. He used his stomach to stop the ball and passed it to Devan, and Devan passed it back to Scott when the defender was away from him.

Scott immediately trapped the ball and kicked . . . at empty air.

At the last possible second, a defender had come from the right of Scott and slide tackled him in the ankle. Scott almost did a flip to the side and landed on his head and right shoulder.

The defender, a lanky kid named Johnny, jogged off with the ball.

Scott got up angrily and ran after the defender. The boy was about ten feet ahead of Scott and pulling away fast.

Scott ran as fast as he could. As he caught up with the kid, tiny white lines appeared everywhere in his vision, colliding with each other.

They disappeared as quickly as they had come, and Scott kicked the ball away from Johnny, who then tripped and crashed to the ground.

Scott took a second to catch his breath before kicking the ball to Devan, who was now right by the goal. Devan trapped the ball, juked the remaining defender, and scored.

"Yes!" Scott cheered, grinning from ear to ear as he slowed to a jog.

"Well done, Group E!" Coach Ghentelle clapped from the bench, staring at Scott. "Very well done."

The coach was staring him down, and Scott had a feeling the burly middle-aged man had seen something weird.

Scott jogged off the field with his teammates, heading toward the bench. He grabbed a water bottle.

"Dude, Scott. That was awesome!" Howard, wide eyed, gave Scott a knuckle touch.

"Seriously," Devan agreed behind raised eyebrows.

"Thanks, guys." Scott took a sip of water. "What's the deal with the deer-in-the-headlights look, though?"

Devan and Howard shared a nervous glance.

"When you was out there . . . somethin' . . . weird happened," Devan said. "The ground under yo' cleats, like . . . like, moved, 'n the ground under Johnny's cleats kinda like, stuck him there 'er somethin'."

"Funny." Scott chuckled and reached to give Devan's shoulder a playful hit.

Devan flinched and turned away. He jogged down to the other side of the bench and started to talk to Johnny, who had a look of utter confusion on his face.

What the hell is going on? Scott shook his head.

He smiled nervously at several players who had been watching the exchange from the other benches.

He took his cell phone out of his book bag next to the bench and opened the camera app, switching the screen so that it faced him. Peering into the screen, he saw a sweaty teenager with dirty-blond hair and a dimple on his right cheek. Except that his trademark dimple was not showing, because he was not smiling at all.

My eyes are purple again, he thought as he stared at himself in disbelief.

He closed his eyes and tried to relax, and then opened them after few seconds.

The irises were back to blue.

Scott shook his head and blew out the breath that he'd been holding. He put his phone back in his bag and wiped sweat off his forehead with the back of his hand.

He tried to watch a group of boys kicking the ball around on the field near him. Instead, his gaze was drawn to Molly on the other side of the field. She was bobbing and weaving around the competition, making it look easy.

Scott watched Molly easily pass the ball, get it back, and shoot it at the goal. Her words suddenly came to mind:

I'll dribble circles around those girls, and when I'm done, I'm comin' for you.

He smiled. The ball was flying right toward the arms of the goalie, though. The goalie was obviously going to catch it. Even his cousin Henry (who was five years old) could probably catch it.

Just before the goalie touched the ball, Scott noticed Molly tilt her head slightly, but deliberately.

Scott slowly stood up, getting a very weird feeling.

The ball gained much more speed and curved midair. It whistled just past the goalie's left ear and plowed into the net. The net became stretched where the soccer ball collided with it, barely holding the ball inside the goal.

Immediately after she scored, Molly cheered and high-fived a couple girls before she jogged over to the girls' bench and picked up her water bottle.

Molly drank some water and wiped her mouth with the back of her hand. After replacing her bottle on the bench, she looked up and saw Scott.

Molly took in Scott's jaw that had basically dropped to the ground, along with his raised eyebrows and look of utter disbelief.

She quickly averted her eyes and took a deep breath.

"Great goal!" Scott yelled at her across the field, playing dumb. "That was amazing!"

He put both of his thumbs up and smiled. Molly did the same before wriggling her eyebrows and looking relieved.

But it was too late. He'd seen her curve the ball.

Scott heard Coach Ghentelle calling the team in. After a quick wave to Molly he joined the other boys in a circle around the coach. Coach Ghentelle was hunched over, talking in his low, dramatic voice.

"You showed great effort out there today. There was a lotta great teamwork goin' on. Still, I gotta make some cuts. Don't sweat it. If you don't make the cut, I might ask you to be on JV. And for those of you who were on JV last year, I may put you on varsity."

Charlie winked at Scott from the other side of the huddle and mouthed, "That's us!"

"Put your hands in," Coach Ghentelle instructed, adding, "On three we say 'Glendale.' One! Two! Three!"

"Glendale!" the boys shouted in unison, their sweaty hands stacked in the middle of the circle.

The tryout team dispersed, and Scott jogged up to Charlie, who was walking toward the school with a confident grin on his face.

"You do okay?" he asked Charlie.

Scott and Charlie hadn't been near each other the entire tryout, due to Coach Ghentelle's alphabetical way of doing things.

"Better than 'okay!' I did great! I couldn't have done any better if you paid me!" Charlie enthusiastically replied. "And I *should* get paid for this!"

"I think we'll both make varsity."

"Make it?! Are you kidding me?! I saw you schooling Johnny back there on the field. That was sick!"

"Yeah, well, it's what I do," Scott joked, but his heart wasn't in it. *Maybe I should tell him what really happened.*

"Yeah, well, so why aren't you using those *suhweet* moves against Brick?"

Scott shot him a look. So Charlie *had* seen his run-in with Brick. Apparently he'd just been saving the verbal ammo to mess with Scott in private. What a . . . well, what a Charlie McEntly thing to do.

Scott glared at him. "You're an asshat."

"Oh, stop it," Charlie grinned. "You're making me blush."

They both laughed at that one.

"Hey," Scott said suddenly, "did you see what Molly did?"

"What?"

Scott looked at Charlie for a moment and instantly thought better of it. Maybe he'd tell him another time. He'd play the Charlie game on this one and keep things close to the chest. He hesitated before saying simply, "I thought she played a mean game."

"You're a weirdo. And a stalker."

By then they had walked through the gym to the locker room. There were a couple people inside changing back into regular clothes, and Scott and Charlie did the same.

After changing, they walked past a red brick planter filled with yellow blossoming brittlebush and headed to a patch of grass next to the late bus area. They plopped onto the grass next to their gym bags, sore from running. A few other kids waiting for the buses were scattered around waiting as well.

"Aah," Charlie said, "this feels good."

"It's definitely a lot better than getting slammed against a locker."

"Yeah, you would know." Charlie's eyes were closed, face turned toward the warmth of the sun.

"Yeah I would." Then Scott added pointedly, "And so would you if you had a set of balls."

Charlie opened his eyes and turned to look at Scott. "Yeah . . . except that I know when not to talk, and I'm not dumb enough to go against Brick." He poked Scott in the chest. "You're not invincible."

"Don't poke me," Scott said, rubbing his chest. "That dude's a bully who needs to be taken down a notch or two."

"He's all that and more. But you're my friend. Just . . . walk away next time."

"No," Scott said, shaking his head. "And I don't want to have this conversation again, dude. If I get my ass beat, then that's honestly fine with me. At least he won't be picking on someone like Carl again. I can't take that. And he got away with it because Carl's too much of a freakin' scaredy-cat—"

"Scott," Charlie said, growing serious, which was rare for him, "lighten up on the kid. Carl is in the *hospital*. With a broken arm and a shattered kneecap."

"All the more reason he needs to tell the truth," Scott answered with a scowl.

"Scott, come on, relax—"

"No! Dude, I'm not gonna relax!" Scott jumped to his feet. Charlie just shook his head and stayed seated as Scott continued his rant. "Carl didn't want to snitch on him because he's scared. Plain and simple. And I hate Brick for that. I hate people who make other people feel like that. I hate him. And I hate not being able to do anything real about it. It sucks."

"If you could hurt Brick, would you?"

Scott looked at his friend with utter confusion.

"What, like if I could bench cars before I get on the bus in the morning? Yeah, I'd hurt him if I could," Scott answered. "In a freaking heartbeat."

"And then?"

"And then?" Scott repeated, like a parrot. "And then . . . then I'd tell him to . . . I dunno, honestly. I'd come up with something, though."

Charlie didn't say a word. After a moment, Scott sat back down and stared at the ground, mad at himself. He never got anywhere talking to Charlie about this. Charlie just always wanted to take the nonviolent route. The safe route. He wanted to hide.

They both sat in silence for a minute and gazed at the passing cars on the other side of the street.

"Yeah, I got video too."

Scott heard the unfamiliar voice. He looked around. He didn't see anyone talking who would have been within earshot, besides Charlie. There was just a huddle of three kids talking a couple hundred feet away by the far side of the school.

"Did you see Faranger running? Weeeirrd," someone else said.

Scott's vision suddenly had wavy white lines overlapping everything that he saw, and he blinked a couple times, trying to get the problem to go away. He shook his head from side to side, and the lines began to subside until a third voice was heard.

"Wait! Pause it there! Dude, it looks like he's *floating!*"

His vision now had white lines traveling every which way, colliding with each other and causing overlays of color on everything that he looked at.

What keeps happening to me?! Scott thought as his heart rate increased dramatically.

"Scott!"

Scott flinched, and his vision returned to normal. He glanced next to him and saw Charlie staring right at him.

"I called your name like four times." Charlie laughed nervously. "You all right?"

"Charlie, did you see anything . . . weird happen to me at tryouts?" Scott asked bluntly.

Charlie made a face, pretending to think about the question for a minute. "Define weird. Weird is basically your level of normal."

Scott rolled his eyes. "Okay, fine. What about anything strange?"

"What are you talking about, dude?"

"Nothing," Scott caved, dropping it.

"You sure it's nothing?"

"Yeah, I'm good."

"Okaaay . . ."

"Hey guys," a girl's voice said cheerfully from behind them.

4

HAVING TOO MUCH FUN CAN KILL YOU

"What the fudge?!" Charlie jumped up, and Molly covered her mouth with her hand to stop laughing at him.

Scott instantly felt like his vocal cords were being force-choked by Darth Vader.

How long had she been standing there?

"Wow! That Diet Pepsi finally caught up with me," Charlie lied while holding his stomach. "Excuse me while I go drain the sea monster."

Scott shook his head at the lame excuse.

Molly said simply, "*Dodgeball*. Nice."

"It's Scott's *favorite* movie!" Charlie shot back with a grin.

Charlie jogged toward the front entrance of the school, leaving Scott sitting alone on the grass, with Molly standing beside him on the sidewalk. A couple seconds later Scott spotted Charlie hiding behind the nearby brick planter and flowering shrubs, giving him a thumbs-up sign with a wolfish grin and crazy eyes for dramatic effect.

He turned his attention back to Molly to see her staring at him questioningly.

"What was that?" Molly asked with an amused smile and a raised eyebrow.

"What was what?"

"You had a funny look on your face when you saw me standing behind you." She shrugged and suddenly changed the direction of the conversation. "Never mind about that. I wanted to ask how you did during tryouts."

"I did alright. You?"

"Well . . . I did great. Except all the girls on the varsity team think that I'll make a perfect midfielder, but I love playing forward. And Coach wants me to play forward too." She nervously chewed her lip.

"Wow. Sounds like a tough choice," Scott commented dryly. "They're talking to you about varsity. First world problems."

"Jerk." She smiled at him, showing her perfectly white teeth.

"Bigger jerk."

Molly looked hurt by that comment.

"I'm just kidding," Scott explained quickly. "I'm sorry, I was just—"

Molly suddenly laughed. "You're gullible."

"Oh, now who's the jerk?" he asked.

"You still are," Molly joked, pushing him in the shoulder. "And being gullible isn't a bad thing. It means you trust people."

Scott was looking at her. Suddenly he blurted, "You wanna sit down near me?"

One side of Molly's lips raised in a little smile.

"I mean, sit down on the grass. Where I'm sitting. On the grass," Scott corrected.

Molly's smile kept growing, and she covered her face with her hand, stifling giggles.

"I mean . . ." Scott stopped himself and made an exasperated sigh. "Molly, please sit down. It feels weird talking to you like you're the overlord of the sidewalk with you standing up there and me sitting down here."

"Sure." Molly dropped her books and sat down next to him. She picked at a piece of grass. "I think you have a future as a stand-up comedian."

"I think you have a future in modeling," Scott said before he could filter the thought.

Molly stared at him, and his face instantly turned the color of a tomato. So did hers.

Crap, Scott gulped. *Totally creepy. That was a totally creepy thing to say. Why do I even—*

She smiled and leaned in toward him almost imperceptibly. Almost.

"What else do you see in my future?"

Scott knew a lifeline when he was being thrown one. He thought back to the silent promise that he had made himself earlier in the year: *I'm gonna get Molly Clenton to go out with me.*

"Scott?"

He mentally slapped himself. He had been zoning out again. He cleared his throat. "What do I see in your future?"

Molly nodded.

"Your future is . . ."

Out of nowhere, his throat seemed to turn to dust and his lips to stone. He couldn't get it out.

She just kept looking at him with those bright hazel eyes.

"With me?" he lamely finished.

That last little bit had come out as a high-pitched question.

"BWAHAHAHA!"

Scott and Molly swiveled toward the burst of laughter. There was Charlie laughing hysterically and rolling around in the grass. Apparently, he'd laughed himself right out from behind the planter from where he'd been spying on them.

Molly looked over her shoulder at Charlie, who picked himself up and sauntered off, embarrassed for both himself and Scott. Probably more for Scott, though.

Molly turned back around and stared at Scott for a couple seconds. He held her gaze, terrified and completely red in the face.

She broke the silence. "You really think you're something, huh, Scott?"

Get me out of here! I'm such an idiot, he thought, then stammered, "M–m–m–maybe?"

"Yeah . . . well . . . keep trying." Molly grinned mischievously and patted his knee.

She didn't take her hand off his knee.

Scott looked down and instantly blushed. Molly started to slide her hand away, but Scott reached down and held it, with his own hand shaking a little. This was the girl he'd been chasing since the fourth grade. Today was the day he was going to kiss her. He could feel it.

Her gaze flickered up to Scott questioningly. There was no backing out now. He nervously leaned in, put one hand on the sidewalk, and . . .

"What are you doing?" she asked.

Scott quickly realized that his eyes were closed. He opened them as he leaned back and fumbled over his words.

"Were you trying to kiss me?" Molly asked quietly.

"Yuh—no. No. Definitely no." Scott was really confused and was practically shaking out of his skin in embarrassment.

"What the what . . . ?!" Scott heard Charlie whisper loudly. He was behind the planter again.

"Oh. Good." Molly smiled.

Scott was mortified. He felt like he wanted to cry. His dreams had been utterly shattered in one fell swoop. An unpleasant chill ran through his body, rattling his bones to their core.

"Because I wanted to kiss *you*. It's always the guy that does it, but women can initiate too, ya know?" Molly smiled again.

She leaned forward to kiss him, and he held his breath, inching his face toward hers.

Suddenly they heard the rumble of an engine, the squeal of brakes, and the hiss of hydraulics as the late bus pulled into the parking lot.

Scott and Molly both jumped up and grabbed their bags.

Scott noticed that on the edge of the sidewalk near the road where his hand had been, the ground was warped and mutilated. It looked like a hot lump of iron ore had sunk into the cement.

He quickly looked around, but it didn't seem like anyone else had seen it.

He looked at his hand, but nothing seemed wrong with it. He went to go pull out his phone and check his eyes, but Charlie jogged up in front of him and turned around, walking backward. Charlie gave a big grin and a wink and then turned back around.

On the bus, Scott took a seat next to Charlie, and Molly sat with a few of her friends in the back. The bus rumbled out of the school lot. Charlie turned to push Scott's buttons a bit more, but Scott was sound asleep. He'd fallen asleep almost as soon as his body hit the seat.

The next thing Scott knew, he was jerking awake to discover himself almost falling into the bus aisle. The bus had stopped, and Molly was standing up and getting her bags.

"Later," she said. She smiled at him and waved from only a foot or two away.

He still felt unnaturally sleepy. The best he could muster was a nod.

Molly got off the bus and turned around. She waved good-bye to Scott from the sidewalk. He waved back sluggishly.

* * *

Shortly after, Charlie got off the bus and Scott was left alone with his dreams. The only other person on the bus was the bus driver now.

"I don't mind if you stay on this bus, kid, but don't you have a life to get to?" the driver joked.

Hearing the voice, Scott struggled to pull his brain out of the fog. The bus was stopped, engine idling, in front of his driveway. Scott picked up his bags and mumbled a half-intelligible apology to the bus driver. The driver pulled the lever to hold the door open, smiling and shaking his head as Scott climbed out of the bus and headed up the driveway.

Halfway up, Scott groaned. He'd hadn't even asked for Molly's number.

He finished walking up the driveway and opened the front door to find Jared in the kitchen doing math homework.

"Hey man, how was your day?" It took effort, but Scott managed to ruffle Jared's hair and pulled his ear like he always did.

"Good!" Jared said excitedly. "How was soccer?"

Christine opened the front door just as her oldest son was about to respond.

"Hi, boys," she greeted as she stepped in the house.

"Hi, Mom," they said in near unison.

She walked over to the kitchen table and deposited her coffee cup and her work folder. She sat down with a heavy sigh and looked at Jared and Scott.

"So how was your day?"

Jared spoke first. "Mine was great! I got three touchdowns playing football at lunch!"

"You have asthma," Scott reminded him.

Jared glared at Scott. "Oh yeah. I forgot for a second. Thanks for telling me."

"I bet you didn't get three touchdowns. I bet you got two at the most."

"I really did get three!" Jared yelled, rising out of his seat and leaning forward on the table. "Seriously! It was awesome!"

"That's great, Jared." Christine smiled and patted his hand. "You should be proud of yourself."

But he wasn't anymore. He shot both of them a look of contempt and slunk back into his seat with his arms crossed.

"Stupid," Jared muttered. "Everyone treats me like I'm a child."

Christine turned to Scott. "How about you? Anything interesting happen at school today?"

Scott looked at Jared and frowned.

"I got a good grade on a math test, and I think I did really good at soccer tryouts," Scott replied, knowing that she would be satisfied by this and leave him alone.

Suddenly the pain started up again in Scott's head. He tried not to panic—outwardly.

"That's great!" Christine said distractedly. She looked at her watch, then stood to leave, the kitchen chair scraping loudly on the tile floor. "I've got to wrap up a few things. I'll leave you guys to it, then!"

She was humming as she walked out of the kitchen.

"Actually, Mom," Scott blurted, suddenly remembering something, "my shower head broke upstairs. I don't know how but there's a problem with the water. It's . . . it's kind of broken now."

"Okay." Christine stopped and looked at her son. "I'll have a plumber come check it out tomorrow."

"Thanks."

"Alright, well, I'll see you boys in a bit!" She beamed at them and then walked away.

The boys heard her bedroom door open and then close shortly after.

Jared's shoulders slumped. She was always there one second and then gone the next.

Jared immediately got up from the table and ran out of the kitchen. He sprinted up the stairs to his room and locked the door behind him.

Scott followed him upstairs, but then turned and went to his own room. He closed the door and locked it, just as his brain felt like it had exploded.

"No, no, no!"

That was all that he could get out before the seizure started.

He writhed on his bed back and forth, knocking books and papers every which way. His vision flickered to the white lines again, and Scott could see them coming from outside, underneath the door, from his alarm clock and many other places. They were everywhere now, and they weren't stopping.

Scott couldn't think as he rolled and jerked back and forth like a possessed voodoo doll. He couldn't feel his limbs anymore. He screamed inside his own head, trapped within his own body and unable to do anything about it. Except that the layer of sweat that had formed on Scott's body as he twisted suddenly rose and was now floating around him, about two feet off the bed. The vague glistening form moved around the room wherever his eyes looked.

He suddenly felt his left leg again. He could move his toes, but nothing else. That's when something about this started to finally click.

Scott concentrated on the floating sweat and thought of one word: *Help.*

Even before the thought had fully formed, all the sweat droplets combined into different letters to form the word *Help*, which was now suspended in midair a foot in front of his TV.

Just before Scott passed out, the feeling return to his right arm and hips.

* * *

He woke up to a wet bed, and papers and books on the floor everywhere. The word *Help* was gone, and there was a small puddle of water under the TV on the floor.

He cleaned up the water with a used towel from the bathroom. Scott looked at the floor when he was done and saw some drops of water he'd missed. He stared at the drops, trying to make them float again.

After about twenty minutes, Scott just gave up. He had tried squinting his eyes, moving his hands up and down, physically throwing water from the sink and snapping his fingers—all to no avail. The water didn't float, he didn't get a headache, and his eyes didn't change color.

"This is so stupid!" Scott finally yelled at himself as he threw himself into his desk chair.

He decided to concentrate on his homework, since being a magician/superhero/Bible figure didn't seem to be in the cards for him today.

After finishing some math assignments, American history, and an English essay, Scott was now free and clear to try his hand at being a water bender again.

"Dinner's almost ready!" Christine called up from the kitchen.

"Aaargh!" He threw himself dramatically on the bed and closed his eyes for a second, with the intention of hopping up, running downstairs, wolfing down dinner, and retreating to his room as quickly as he could.

5

YOU MUST BE DREAMING

He was standing in a vast open plain. There were no trees in any direction as far as the eye could see. It was sunny with few clouds, which struck Scott as odd since all his recent nightmares had been set at nighttime.

"Hello, Scott."

Scott startled and yelled like a little girl. He slowly turned around to find an old man dressed in a long purple robe sitting barefoot and cross-legged on the ground. He looked like Merlin from a dime-store picture book.

"Won't you join me?" the man asked politely.

Yup. He's a wizard, Harry. Scott smiled to himself in the dream.

He sat across from the old man and waited until the man spoke once more.

"This is temperamental magic even for me, but I will try to shed some light on our situation during our limited time together. I will be brief and direct." The old man looked Scott up and down.

There was something unnerving about him, and it took Scott a moment or two to realize what it was.

The man looked like he was made of glass, but not in the fragile sort of way. Depending on the way he turned, either his skin reflected the light or Scott could see his bones and his veins very clearly for a fraction of a second. His fingernails also reminded Scott of a rat's teeth. They were chipped and worn and cracked and looked like the old man had been using them to pick locks.

"I have a theory that the acute brain cancer and seizures that you are experiencing are caused by molecular displacement," the old man stated as if they were discussing lunch plans. "Come to Armadron and we can help you. It's where you need to be, or you'll die in weeks. You'll be fine after you Accelerate for the first time, but no one has ever done that on Earth."

"Who . . . who *are* you?" Scott asked, perplexed. "Is this another nightmare? And *what* about brain cancer? And why do you look like you—"

"I have had hundreds of names in my time. You may call me Artam. This is most certainly not a nightmare, and yes, you are developing brain cancer every time you use your curse before you have learned how to Accelerate. If you come to Armadron, I can help you."

Artam paused, letting his words sink in, before continuing.

"I am what is known as a Conjurer. I've been instructed to help you, because we need you. My appearance is that of transparency because I come from a different place than you. On Irri, you are the one who looks strange. "

"Oh." Scott nodded slowly, then stared at the old man. "But seriously, though, what was that about me having freaking *brain cancer?*"

"Listen closely," Artam said, suddenly appearing as if there were some unnamed urgency. "According to our intel, Terminus is in possession of a young boy. A portal creator. In a few days, he will use the boy to create a portal through which he will send his Conjurers to retrieve you. We are covertly sending one of our operatives in that portal behind them, with the hope that our operative can get to you before they do. We need to get you to Armadron to keep you safe."

A bottle of water appeared out of thin air, and the old man paused to remove the cap and take a long drink. When he was finished, he returned the cap and tossed the bottle behind him, where it blinked out of existence.

"As of now, you will not receive any further help from me," Artam continued. "But I will tell you this: To the best of our knowledge only *your* curse works on Earth, Scott. No one else's. At least not yet. You are different from the Conjurers, and even from the test subjects who are under Terminus's control. Still, you need to be careful. If Terminus is smart, the Conjurers who come for you may look and act like normal humans in order to get close to you and prevent mass panic—but, Scott, you are more powerful in ways you cannot yet understand."

"What the hell?! What the hell are you even talking about? You are telling me that I have *brain cancer*, and that I have a curse? Or abilities or something? And on top of that jambalaya, you want me to blindly just—"

"Yes. To all," Artam interrupted, tapping his hand on his leg impatiently. "All you have to do is get on the ship, make it to the Bermuda Triangle, and let our operative take care of the rest. My best guess is that the boy Terminus has acquired can handle only a fraction of the energy required to keep a space-bridge open for a sustainable period of time. We suspect our operative will have just enough time to use the portal to get to you but will need to bring you to Armadron using other means."

"Which is what? A Star Trek beam-up thing?" Scott commented dryly. He couldn't take any of this seriously. Nothing was making sense, and he honestly couldn't remember half of the stuff that this guy was saying anyway. A bunch of stuff about someone named Terminus, Conjurers, curses, and Armadron or something.

"That would be convenient," Artam said. "But no. It is the naturally occurring Gateway generated by Halley's Comet, which will open on your side very, very soon. You must get to us through that Gateway and let us help you, or Terminus will kill your family, your friends, and everyone that you hold dear. He is coming."

"When?"

"As you near the Bermuda Triangle, Terminus nears you," Artam answered.

"So I just won't go." Scott laughed. "Then this Terminus guy can't get to me, and all isn't lost, or whatever you said earlier. I'll just wait this one out."

Artam was already shaking his head.

"Terminus has the means to get to you. He will capture you, he will experiment on you, and he will torture you beyond what you are currently mentally capable of perceiving. You will be brought to Armadron, one way or another. I would prefer it to be our way, so that we have a chance. You are the key, Scott. Our only hope is getting you through the Gateway so that we can help you fight—and you can help us—once you get here."

"Fight who?" Scott was rubbing his forehead back and forth.

"Everyone," Artam replied with a frown. "You are the Mediator for Earth, and that comes with a lot of responsibilities. There are only a few Mediators for each of the six planets, and you have some, shall we say, unusual qualities, the precise advantages of which are still unknown. We need you on Armadron. We need to keep you alive, and we need your help."

There was about a minute's pause while Scott attempted to process all this information.

"Nope. I'm out." Scott shook his head. "Even if this were for real, I still wouldn't do it. I have my little brother to think about. And school. And my mom. And I'm not into stranger danger. You look like you should be driving a magical ice cream truck at Comic-Con. Plus, I don't want to go to a different planet anyway. I'll leave that crap to the astronauts."

"You're lying to yourself, and I see right through you. And like it or not, you're coming with us so that Terminus can't use you to finish what he started. This is bigger than you, boy."

Scott shrugged his shoulders. "I'll think about it. Sounds pretty dangerous, so I'll have to talk to my mom about it once I wake up and realize that this isn't real. Maybe get a permission slip."

Artam snorted. "Then think about this, boy. In two days the Gateway will open and allow people from Earth to travel to Armadron. You're going to make that journey one way or another—willingly with our operative, or unwillingly with Terminus. When it reverses in roughly a week, things will get *really* interesting. I say this because people from Armadron will travel to Earth unchecked. Those people will be able to keep their abilities, and Terminus will have the means to—"

Artam's eyes flashed a brilliant white for a second. Suddenly he said, "I must leave you. He's tracking me somehow."

"Who? Who is tracking you?"

Suddenly, Artam's expression shifted to a slightly more cheerful one.

"Also, in thirty Earth seconds your mother will call you down for dinner. Do not worry, and enjoy the hamburgers. I'm sorry that you're out of ketchup. We'll get you to Armadron. Leave it to her."

"You didn't answer my question!" Scott yelled at him. "And leave it to *her*? To *who*?!"

Artam's body evaporated with a hiss like water hitting a hot surface, and Scott awoke from the dream.

He was on the floor by his bed, lying on his back. He opened his eyes and laughed to himself for several seconds.

Ha! That was a load of bull—

"Boys, dinner time!" Christine called up the stairwell. "I made burgers!"

Scott's face instantly turned the color of computer paper.

"We're out of ketchup," she added, "so you'll have to use barbecue sauce!"

"Coming!" Jared yelled as he raced out of his room and down the stairs.

"Coming," Scott mumbled distantly to himself.

He turned on his side and slowly stood up, groaning. He opened his bedroom door, went downstairs, and ate dinner with his family. He thought of Armadron, Irri, Conjurers, and Mediators the whole time.

6

ACCELERATING

After dinner, Scott returned to his room, closing the door softly behind him as he sidestepped a pile of dirty clothes. He glanced over at the clock on his nightstand. It was 8:47 p.m. Without hesitation, he flopped down on the bed again, crashing the back of his head into the pillows and sinking blissfully into them. He was too tired to practice with the water. Plus, he wasn't sure if he should do that anymore.

For the next hour or so he responded to text messages from Charlie and some other friends and played some games on his phone. After a while, though, he tossed his phone next to him, laid back, and folded his hands over his stomach, thinking about the day.

A place called Armadron. Mediators. Accelerating. Conjurers, and everything else. And what else was that guy talking about? Molecular displacement something? And how did a dream-guy know about dinner?!

He sat up and put his head in his hands, finally starting to see some of the pieces coming together. He was connecting the dots, slowly but surely.

His heart was beating faster and faster, and he couldn't get himself to relax. He was too wound up. The vision problems. The seizures. The perfectly convenient trip that he was already going on to Bermuda. Together they raised a big question.

What if the dream wasn't just a dream?

He wiped his palms on his legs and blew out a big breath, fighting the thin film of sweat that was starting to accumulate all over his body.

"I got one of your pairs of pants in my laundry!" Jared shouted at Scott from the other side of the closed bedroom door. "You want me to leave them here?"

"Gah!" Scott jumped.

His heart rate skyrocketed, and he could feel every pore on his body physically moving like ants crawling all over him.

"Thanks," he struggled to speak, "I'll just see you tomorrow, Jared."

"Okay, whatever. I'm dropping them in front of your door, then," Jared called. "Night!"

His chest was now tightening up, and Scott quickly changed his mind about sending Jared away.

"Jared, wait! Hel—"

He tried to take another breath, but his lungs couldn't hold in any air. It was too late anyway. Jared had already shut his own bedroom door across the hall.

Craaaack!

Every bone in his body twisted and jerked out of place, and Scott thought that he could hear multiple splinters and cracks reverberating throughout his entire body.

The pains and aches that had been coming from the inside of his stomach the past few days immediately intensified.

Ziiiip!

He could hear and feel his stomach rip on the inside of his body like a zipper.

He would have been screaming in pain from all this had he been able to hold a breath in. Rivers of tears flowed down his face and absorbed into the comforter, making it damp. He fell off the bed and was abruptly forced into unconsciousness for what had to be the millionth time that day.

* * *

He bolted upright from his spot on the floor, drenched in sweat. He rubbed his bloodshot eyes and stared at the clock. It was now 1:55 in the morning.

He got up and turned off the large overhead light that he had left on, or at least he tried to. He flipped the switch down, but oddly the light stayed on.

More than a little freaked out, Scott flicked the switch up and down, over and over again. It didn't matter if the light was on or off. His vision remained perfect. With the switch in the on position, he could see an additional halo of light around the bulb that wasn't there with the switch in the off position, but that was about it. He could see everything in the room just as clearly either way.

He turned the light off because he didn't want Jared seeing light beneath his door and knowing that he was still awake.

Now Scott looked around the room and noticed that every item (including himself) was pulsating with slow, white waves, like the ones he had been seeing lately, only much clearer than before. It reminded him of a documentary he had once seen about dolphins. The waves looked like sonar blips on the monitor of a ship.

"Wow," he said out loud.

Instantly it looked like a nuclear bomb of sound had gone off in his room. The waves crashed into each other and accelerated, all moving either toward Scott or away from him. He could feel individual pores all over his body moving as well, responding to the waves like they were speaking to one another.

Scott stumbled backward away from the pulses and fell onto the floor, involuntarily closing his eyes.

He quickly realized that he could *feel* everything in the room without actually touching anything.

He had been hesitating to do this, but he crawled across the floor and peered into full length mirror on his closet door.

His eyes weren't his natural blue. However, they weren't the deep purple color he'd been anticipating either. They were somewhere in between, changing from a dark blue to an extremely light purple every couple seconds. Something was also different about his joints, but he couldn't figure out exactly what by looking at his body.

He rolled his wrist in a circle and immediately saw a difference. His wrist could now rotate much more in any direction. He could easily touch his thumb to his forearm now as well, which he was pretty sure should have been impossible unless he was a master gymnast or something.

Next were the fingers. He tried to move them around in circles, but he had the same mobility as before. Nothing had changed, except he still felt a tingling kind of pressure in each of them.

Maybe . . .

He pulled his right pointer finger.

His finger popped and quickly unfolded like an accordion to grow an extra few inches in length. The finger unfolded out of its sockets, which felt only slightly discomforting. He did the same process with most of his other fingers. As each of his fingers unfolded, his hand grew slightly bigger as well. He looked down at his feet and had another thought.

Responding to his thoughts faster than he could have imagined, Scott saw his toes and his feet grow the same way that his hands and fingers had—except that he didn't need to do anything to them this time. The rest of the fingers that he hadn't yet pulled out became elongated by themselves too.

It probably would have been painful if he had been wearing socks and shoes.

His feet "unfolded" their bones until Scott guessed that he was could wear a size 16 or 17 shoe instead of the size 10.5 that he usually wore.

He looked at his body in the mirror and could now very clearly see the white pulses of light coming off everything, sharper than ever before.

Sheeeeeeeeek!

Scott heard an earsplitting white noise reverberate inside the walls of his skull. The noise progressed and broke off into separate noises. They came in pulses, coming and going in the same way that the sonar waves were coming and going. They didn't stop, and they kept getting louder, like when someone accidentally clicks on the AM radio when they disconnect their phone from Bluetooth in the car.

He fell to the floor on his side, silently moaning, realizing at the same time that he still hadn't taken a single breath.

Wincing with each white noise, Scott looked at his body to see if he had any gills or any other weird mutation that could allow him to breathe, because his lungs and mouth were choosing not to listen to him at the moment.

His neck quickly bulged outward in all directions and his chest expanded. The pain that accompanied this particular transformation was excruciating.

In another moment or two, though, his neck and chest returned to normal.

"Wow." Scott breathed for the first time in a while.

The splitting headache stopped, and so did the white noise. He stood up and looked at himself in the mirror again, sizing himself up and moving back and forth, testing whatever his body had turned itself into.

His feet were now angled so that when he stood up, he was immediately balanced on the balls of his feet. He was about five inches taller because of this, making him roughly six foot three, and he was willing to bet that he could now run a lot faster as well. He could somehow feel it.

"Scott?" Someone called timidly from outside the door. "Are you okay?"

It was Jared. Scott could see the sound waves from Jared's voice flowing toward him from under the door. He had less than two seconds before his little brother barged through the door and saw him.

Now would be a good time to change back, Scott thought, silently willing himself.

Jared reached for the doorknob and turned it quietly. Cracking open the door, he peered into the darkness, looking around Scott's room.

Scott stayed absolutely still. With his new vision, he could see everything clear as day.

Jared looked around the room for a minute, but he obviously couldn't see anything. He eventually just sighed and closed the door. Scott heard him walk back down the hall and return to his own bedroom. Once Scott heard the door shut, he slumped onto his bed, releasing all the tension he had been holding in.

After a minute, he realized that the white waves had gone away. He couldn't see them anymore.

He looked in the mirror.

He was looking at his old self again. Even his eyes were now their normal blue.

He grinned. He had no more stomach pains, and he felt a lot better now. It was like his body had just been stuck in a cocoon, and he had now evolved. He felt better, he didn't feel weak anymore, and somehow he knew with absolute certainty that he was not going to have another seizure. He was beyond that now. Whatever had been holding him back didn't apply anymore.

You will be fine after you Accelerate for the first time, but no one has ever done that on Earth.

Scott mulled over those words. The words that Artam had said.

He had just Accelerated. He had changed, which meant that he didn't need to go to Armadron anymore. He didn't need the cure for cancer, because Scott could just *feel* that he didn't have it anymore. His cells had purged it.

Okay, so all this stuff is real. Still, whatever Artam needs from me, I'm not giving it to him, Scott thought. *Or any of them. It's honestly not my problem. I'm not about to just go to a whole different planet so that I can fight some bad guy and his experiments and probably get killed. I don't even know any martial arts, and I've never even held a gun before! Plus, Artam's probably just like . . . him. Terminus. Artam's not telling me everything anyway, and he's not answering my questions, and I'm not trusting someone like that. They can figure this out on their own.*

Scott laid back on his pillow and shut his eyes, ready for sleep to take him.

Except that he wasn't ready. He kept tossing and turning and repositioning his pillow, thinking about something else that Artam had said:

You're lying to yourself, and I see right through you. This is bigger than you, boy.

BERMUDA DELTA

Sunday morning arrived quickly.

"Wake up, Scott!"

He shot up in his bed, ready and alert. He looked in the direction of his open door and saw his mom dressed in jeans and some kind of orange-and-red short-sleeved shirt. She also had a flimsy hat on that had palm trees and sandy beaches decorated all over it.

"I'm up," Scott replied as he rubbed his eyes.

"I made breakfast. Eggs, ham, and bacon. It's downstairs whenever you want to eat it. You might want to do it quickly, though, because we leave in thirty," Christine said with a smile on her face.

She left his room and walked down the stairs. Scott could hear her giggling with excitement all the way down. That's when he realized that he hadn't heard her laugh in a while, and it all finally fell into place.

WE'RE GOING ON THE CRUISE TODAY!

He was so excited that when he jumped up from his bed, the water from his goldfish tank in the far corner of the room hyper-evaporated, coating that part of the room in mist.

Luckily, his goldfish had died a couple weeks before.

He felt his body immediately start to Accelerate. His arms got longer, his breath caught in his throat, and the white sonar waves began to—

"Scott! You better not be going back to bed!"

"I'm getting ready, Mom!" he yelled down the stairs.

His body returned to normal, and the waves dissipated as his bones settled back to their regular size.

He checked his phone for messages and found a couple social media notifications that he quickly dismissed. He also had a message from Charlie about the trip.

Once he texted Charlie back, he remembered that he hadn't quite finished packing his suitcase, so he got to it.

In about fifteen minutes, he had taken a shower under his brand new showerhead and was fully dressed in tan shorts and a blue V-neck T-shirt. His suitcase was ready to go, and so was he.

I wonder what Molly's doing today, Scott thought, silently cursing himself, for perhaps the hundredth time, for never getting her number.

He ran down the steps to the kitchen, after seeing Jared jumping up and down in his own room as he went. He noticed his mother wasn't in the kitchen either, so she was probably getting ready too.

He poured himself a glass of orange juice before sitting at the table and starting to scarf down his now-cold breakfast. Halfway through his breakfast, he dropped his fork and clutched his stomach in agony.

You've got to be effing kidding me, he thought.

The stomach pain was back, sharper than yesterday.

Scott closed his eyes and waited for the pain to recede, rocking back and forth.

Actually . . . He began to form an idea.

Scott opened his eyes and concentrated. He focused on the sounds around him, and soon something began to happen.

His eyes shifted, and he could see the white lines everywhere. He could hear his mother somewhere in the house now talking to a coworker on the phone, and he could hear Jared upstairs as well. He slowed his breathing and didn't Accelerate all the way, this time only allowing his eyes to change and his hearing to improve.

He held that for a couple seconds, remaining perfectly still.

Scott breathed out slowly and relaxed, trying to revert to normal.

The lines disappeared from his vision, and so did his stomach pain and his headache.

"Yes!" Scott cheered out loud, grinning wickedly.

"You okay?"

It was Jared. He was standing behind Scott in the kitchen entryway.

"Yeah." Scott turned in his chair and flashed Jared a smile. "I'm actually great."

"Hmm," Jared responded, disbelief all over his face. "Looked like you were gonna go throw up."

"I'm good, Jared. Thanks, really. I'm good, though."

He rose up from his chair quickly, and Jared flinched obnoxiously in response, trying to make it look like Scott was being aggressive.

Scott just rolled his eyes and put his dishes in the dishwasher. He paused as he stood over the dishwasher, thinking about Artam and the dream.

I don't know whether to tell Mom or not, he thought. *I don't want to die . . . and I don't think that I'm going to anymore. I'm getting better. Still, I don't want to go to Area 51 or something like that. Plus, Artam did say that it'd go away if I could Accelerate. He just didn't think that I could do it here. But . . . can brain cancer really go away? Just like that? I mean, it's cancer!*

Scott was still lost in thought as Jared slipped past and disappeared around the corner into the living room. Christine appeared in the kitchen with her bags.

"You ready to go?" she asked cheerfully.

"Yep. I just gotta brush my teeth and get my bags," Scott said, taking the fear out of his head by putting excitement back into his voice.

"Jared and I will be in the car then. Hurry, Scott. The McEntlys are already on their way to the airport."

Christine left the room, and having heard the conversation, Jared took his cue and followed his mother out of the house with his bags. As his mom started to put their suitcases in the rental car in the driveway, Scott ran upstairs and a moment later ran back down with his bags. The engine was running. He hopped in the car, and they were off, just like that.

"I have to go to the bathroom!" Jared cried from the backseat.

"You can't hold it?!" Scott turned around in the front seat and looked at his little brother.

"No."

"You should have gone before we left, Jared," Christine told him as she swung the car around.

Three to four minutes later, they were ready to go with Jared back in the car again.

As they backed out of the driveway—again—Scott remembered the feeling of his bones moving and his ears popping, and laid his head back onto the leather headrest. They drove out of town and then got onto the highway, and the GPS said they had an hour drive ahead of them. Scott looked out of the window and happily watched Arizona slowly fade into the distance. He closed his eyes for a second and went right back to thinking about the events that happened in his dream, and what was to come. He wasn't going to go to Armadron, so *that* was settled. But something else Artam said kept nagging at him.

I'm a Mediator, he thought dully as tiredness quickly overtook him. *I'm a Mediator.*

* * *

"We're here!" Christine cheered from the driver's seat, lightly shaking Scott awake.

Scott whipped open his eyes and felt a surge of excitement hit him at the same time that his eyes began shifting.

No no no no! he thought, feeling something powerful rise to the surface.

Come on, relax, he told himself, keeping the power at bay. *Relaaaaax.*

Once his heart rate slowed down enough, he realized his eyes were squeezed shut again. He opened them and looked outside the window.

They were already at the airport. It was huge. To Scott, it seemed larger than life.

He'd never actually been in an airport before. He'd only seen them in movies. This one looked to him like it could house all the residents of Canada.

They all stepped out of the car, got their bags, and entered the building. An employee from Mrs. Faranger's company came and took their rental car for them. The three passed through the bag drop-off and quickly made their way through security.

They found the McEntlys waiting for them at the Subway restaurant near their gate, just as Christine had arranged.

"Hello, Tim, Barbara, Charlie." Christine dipped her head like a foreign diplomat with each name that she spoke. "Are you ready?"

"I'm always ready for a vacation," Tim, Charlie's father, said with a smile.

Scott pulled Charlie to the side as the grown-ups started talking about trip logistics and grown-up stuff. They found a couple seats by the gate entrance near Jared, who was already immersed in his Game Boy.

"You're gonna think I'm crazy, but I have to tell you something," Scott said, looking Charlie in the eye.

Charlie raised an eyebrow. "Okaay. Crazier than usual? This oughta be good."

He had decided this morning that he would tell Charlie about what was happening to him. Charlie would understand. Maybe. Or he'd laugh at him.

Still, Charlie was clearly not getting the gravity of the situation.

"Charlie, focus," Scott told him impatiently. "I'm serious right now. This is important."

Charlie promptly shut his mouth and raised both eyebrows this time.

"Charlie, something happened last night. I don't know exactly what, but something happened."

"What happened?" Charlie asked, already beyond interested.

"I . . . changed," Scott explained, awkwardly avoiding eye contact.

"What do you mean?" Charlie asked. "If you're fooling with me, I'll get you back. This is a lame joke anyway, dude."

"I already told you. I'm not kidding."

"Okay," Charlie nodded and waited for his best friend to get his thoughts in order.

"I . . . changed into something else. I . . ."

Scott looked at Charlie.

Charlie looked at Scott, waiting.

Scott realized Charlie would never believe him unless he had some proof.

"I'm serious. Here. Watch my hands," Scott ordered.

He pulled his right pointer finger and the bone popped. Nothing out of the ordinary happened, though. It didn't grow this time. The bone just clicked.

"You're going to show me the world's most serious fart?" Charlie asked.

"No!" Scott exclaimed, confused. "It grows!"

"I hope it does," Charlie sighed, mockingly patting him on the back. "Because some of the guys in the locker room the other day were saying that you've got a small—"

"Charlie, please," Scott stared at him, unwavering. "This is big. Like . . . 'different planets in the universe' big."

Something in Charlie's eyes shifted. He looked like he might know something.

"Okay, bud. I think I know what's going on," Charlie smiled.

"You do?!" Scott was relieved.

"Yeah. You've waited so long to go out with Molly, and now that you can't see her, it's obviously screwing with your head," Charlie explained. "Plus, you never got her number. 'Cause you're half idiot and other half weenie."

"No!" Scott argued, "It's like, when I get nervous or something, I change!"

"Into what?" Charlie mocked. "One of those Teen Wolf dudes?"

"No! I—"

"Dude," Charlie cut in, "stop yellin' so loud. People can hear you over the freaking planes."

"Yeah," Jared agreed without looking up from his Game Boy.

"Okay." Scott lowered his voice and took a deep breath, coming to a realization.

He looked at Charlie in his Rolling Stones T-shirt, his orange spiky hair, and his slouched appearance. He knew Charlie better than anyone else, and he knew that Charlie wouldn't entertain this.

"I'm just gonna stop it here." Scott pretended to be embarrassed and suddenly threw up his hands. "I don't even know where I was going with this joke anymore. I just wanted to mess with you."

"Well, thanks for wasting five minutes of my life, dude. Now I've gotta figure out a way to get you back when we're on the plane."

"Yeah," Scott agreed, then gave a wicked grin, "unless your narcolepsy kicks in and you fall asleep on me after two minutes, Gramps."

"You little bastard," Charlie replied, shaking his head. "If I had a—"

"Crutch?"

"If I had a brother like you, I'd go nuts. I honestly don't know how Jared does it."

"Please don't bother me," Jared called from three seats away, waving them off at the mention of his name. "I'm on the last lap of the Zelda map in Mario Kart."

They both laughed at that, and Jared repositioned himself in the seat and tried to block out their annoyance.

Scott wiped tears out of his eyes and Charlie held his own stomach as they kept laughing. Jared was the kind of little brother who would often do funny things at his own expense without even realizing it.

"This trip is gonna be awesome," Scott said.

"Yeah," Charlie agreed, still chuckling. "You ready to wreak some havoc on the ship?"

"I think they have a game room," Scott announced as a form of approval, grinning from ear to ear.

"They do. I went on the website. They also have two pools, hot tubs, a wave machine, and a slip 'n slide."

"A *wave machine?!* Holy crap, that's awesome."

"Holy crap, I know."

They both relaxed back in their seats, listening to the sound of Jared losing on the final lap and laughing hysterically at his reaction.

Eventually, the parents ended their own discussion and bought them all five-dollar footlongs from Subway, which Charlie called twenty-dollar foot longs because he was Gramps and complained more than the average person.

As soon as they all finished their meals, their flight to Ft. Lauderdale, Florida, was called. The group of six picked up their carry-on luggage and headed toward their first-class flight.

Sure enough, when they got on the plane, Gramps fell asleep in less than two minutes, and Scott took a video of him snoring to use as ammunition in future arguments.

After landing, they got off the plane, took their bags, and rode in a limousine to the cruise ship that would sail them to Bermuda and back. As they stepped out of the limo, Scott took in the bright gold letters on the side of the ocean liner. They read BERMUDA DELTA.

The smell of the ocean was in the air, and there were people everywhere. People were on the cruise ship on the upper decks waving to them and cheering. Families were hooting and hollering and letting the world know that they were finally going on vacation.

Scott tried to hear what this one man on the upper deck was yelling, and he rotated his head so that his right ear was pointed toward the man.

His vision flashed, and the sonar waves all came at him. As usual, there were thousands of them. This time, Scott quickly got over his initial shock and tried to concentrate on one thread, like when someone tunes an FM radio to the right frequency.

"You're gonna love it here!" the man cheered at the top of his lungs.

Why, yes I am. Scott smiled to himself. *I get eight days to practice—*

"Beautiful, isn't it, boys?" Mr. McEntly's voice made Scott jump.

"I just hope it doesn't go Titanic on us," Mrs. McEntly joked.

Oh lord, Scott thought in mock prayer as he shared a look with Charlie, *please kill me before super-Gramps and super-Grandma do with their corniness. Please. Not today.*

Everyone else but Jared laughed awkwardly, and Mr. McEntly spoke again, welcoming the attention.

"Oh, come on. There aren't any icebergs near Florida. We're more likely to hit a giant floating tree."

They all chuckled awkwardly again, and Mr. McEntly went on, pointing at the ship. "There, you see, boys. This old ship is named *Bermuda Delta*. 'Delta' is obviously another word for triangle. I kinda like the name."

Scott gave a goofy smile and a wink to Charlie, pointing his thumb covertly at Charlie's dad. Charlie rolled his eyes dramatically. Everyone above the age of five already knew that delta meant triangle. Mr. McEntly just liked to talk. And talk.

And talk.

He also was the nerdiest human being on the planet Earth.

"Thanks, Dad. Can we get on the ship now?" Charlie responded in a deadpan voice.

"Yes"—Mr. McEntly frowned at his son—"and you can lose the attitude, mister."

"Yessir," Charlie told him, faking seriousness to his father. "I'm leaving it on dry land, and I'll have a new one on the ship."

"Alright then, have it your way," Mr. McEntly said, slipping back into his cheerful demeanor.

"Burger King," Jared mumbled to himself, tapping his fingers over his Game Boy faster than Bill Gates programming a computer.

They got their luggage out of the limo, and Christine and Mrs. McEntly both tipped the driver, who drove off without a backward glance.

The cruise ship employees gave them all a warm welcome. That is, if you count a warm welcome as going through an X-ray machine, taking your shoes off, and having to watch your bag being searched.

"Just keeping everyone safe, folks," one of the security guards told them as he ruffled through Mr. McEntly's bag.

After that they were shown to their cabins, which were right next to each other.

Scott unpacked his bags while Christine left to meet with someone from her company.

Company meetings would begin tomorrow. This afternoon, however, she'd be tied up overseeing a commercial they were shooting on board the ship.

That meant that Jared and Scott were alone for most of the late afternoon, and Scott was tasked with playing babysitter once again. Christine had agreed to give each of her boys sixty dollars to spend each day, so Scott and Jared went to get Charlie. Charlie always had "good ideas" when it came to spending money.

8

THE ARCADE

An hour later the ship set sail. Scott, Charlie, and Jared were swimming in the pool, and at first there were no lines and very few people to stand in their way for anything. However, their fun shrunk when people started coming out of their cabins and into the pool area. By the time they left, the pool had more people in it than water. They were all old people too.

The boys dried themselves with the ship's complimentary towels and walked to the arcade. When they got there, there were about ten or twelve kids playing various games. Scott, Charlie, and Jared started doing the thing that comes naturally to all boys: raging against the machine.

Jared was particularly good at *Dance Mania 2* (well, pretty much any video game ever), and Scott and Charlie were playing *Buck Hunt* over and over again until they were interrupted.

"Hey, can I get a turn in?"

They both stopped and turned around to see a teenage girl with short white shorts, a white tank top, and sandy-blonde hair staring back at them. Her legs were tan and toned, and she looked like she was a little older than they were. Maybe sixteen or seventeen. She had a fist-sized scar on her left shoulder that looked like she may have lost a fight to Wolverine a while ago, but besides that she looked amazing. She was staring at Scott with a playful smile on her face, and her bright blue eyes were looking hopefully at him.

Holy mother of God, Scott thought, gulping.

The boys were both still wearing just their swimming trunks and standing there awkwardly.

"Sure," Scott smiled as he stepped back from the machine and handed the girl his plastic rifle.

"Thanks." The girl smiled back at him.

Their hands touched, and Scott instantly felt a familiar tingling sensation in the back of his skull somewhere, but the feeling went away in less than a second. He looked at the girl's face to see if she had felt something too. Her face showed that she hadn't—or she was a good actor.

Now where have I had that feeling before? Scott pondered.

He looked over at Charlie to see how he was taking all this.

Charlie kept looking at the girl, barely paying attention to the game screen. He was staring at her, not even trying to be subtle.

Geez, Gramps, Scott thought, *at least blink.*

She started the game again and played against Charlie, beating him on every level.

When they finished, Scott engaged the girl in conversation. Charlie sat down in a game chair quietly and basically just watched the two talk. That wasn't like him at all.

"So. You like to play video games?" Scott asked.

"They're all right. Real life's more fun, though." The girl gave him a dazzling smile.

"So I've heard. Hey, what's your name?" Scott asked.

"Sam."

"Last name?"

"Not important." Sam smiled.

"Well, I'm Scott Faranger and this is Charlie McEntly," he said, gesturing to Charlie.

"Sup," Charlie greeted from his chair.

"Charlie?" Sam playfully chewed her finger, then pointed at him. "You look more like a Seth to me."

"I can't look like a name," Charlie replied dryly, looking away from her.

Is he mad at something? Scott thought. *What in the hell is going on? Is he that much of a sore loser?*

"Oh, well, you're probably right." Sam smiled like a movie star. "Hey, I'm sorry you had to lose, Charlie."

Scott started to get the feeling that she was one of those kinds of people who could mess with someone right to their face and never crack a smile because she was so confident. Damn.

"I'm sorry too," Charlie said, not sounding bothered in the slightest. "I'll get ya next time."

"Keep tellin' yourself that," Sam replied. Scott didn't expect her to be that cocky.

"So . . . do you guys feel like going to the wave machine?" Scott interjected, trying to cut the tension.

"Yeah," Sam agreed.

"Sure," Charlie answered after a moment's hesitation.

"Alright!" Scott excitedly exclaimed, clapping his hands in finality.

They all did a slow walk, heading to the other side of the *Bermuda Delta*. Scott couldn't help looking at Sam's curves on the way and the way that her long blonde hair moved. She was so confident, and she held herself very high. Really high. She was almost his height, and she had long legs that connected to a perfect—

Suddenly his heart dropped.

How can I think of that when I like Molly?

When they were nearly at the wave machine, Charlie's cell phone rang.

The three stopped walking and stood in place while he took his phone out of his pocket.

"It's my dad," he told them quickly as he answered the phone.

Sam looked really confused for a second, but she wiped the look off her face. Scott saw it, though.

What is going on with them? They're both so weird! Scott couldn't even think straight.

"Hello?" Charlie said into the phone.

There was a long pause.

"Wow," he said, taking the phone away from his ear and looking at the screen, "I didn't even realize the time, Dad. Sorry. It *is* almost seven."

There was more talking coming from the other end of the line.

"Yeah, Dad, I'll be right there," Charlie concluded. "Sorry."

He ended the call and slid his smartphone back into his pocket. He looked at them, shielding his eyes from the sun with his hand.

"I have to go eat dinner. I'll meet both of you guys by the wave machine in a half hour." Charlie waited for a response. "The wave machine, right?"

"I'll be there," Scott replied as Charlie stared at him with a strange intensity. "How about you, Sam?"

"Yeah. Me too. We'll be there."

"Are you sure you'll be at the wave machine in half an hour?" Charlie pressed.

"Yes, Mom." Scott laughed. "Relax."

"Promise me, Scott," Charlie pressed. "I just want a good meal right now. I'll be right back."

"Charlie, what's going on?" Scott asked him. "Why are you both acting weird? What the hell is going on?"

"Alright. Cool," Charlie said, ignoring his questions. "See you guys later then. Take care of him!"

Charlie turned and jogged down the ship, quickly disappearing out of view.

"Scott, we need to go. Now," Sam told him the second that Charlie was out of sight.

"What?! I don't know who you are, but Charlie—"

"Charlie's fine. He'll be at the wave machine once he gets a good last meal. There are more important things for you to worry about right now," Sam replied.

"What?! Hey, Charlie's not—"

"Scott! Scott!"

He turned around to find Jared running down the deck toward him. He stopped right in front of Scott and took a deep breath.

"I thought I lost you! There were tons of people in the game room, and I couldn't find you at the pool, and you didn't tell me you were leaving!" Jared cried.

"Look, Jared. Why don't you go swimming again in the pool," Scott suggested, trying to send his little brother away so he could process what Sam had just said about that final meal.

"Why? So you can stand here and flirt with your giiiirlfriend?" Jared mocked. "Plus, Mom says I have to stay with you today anyway."

"Aaargh! I don't care what Mom said! You're being annoying," he lashed back angrily.

"Big deal," Jared mocked him, "deal with it."

"Deal with it?! Let's see about that." Scott took a step in the direction of Christine's commercial shooting on the other side of the ship.

Sam watched impatiently, crossing her arms in front of her.

"Okay fine, I'll go," Jared said, caving, then teared up. "I just hate being by myself all the time."

"Jared," Scott exhaled, "I'll hang out with you later. I just don't have time for this right now. I'm busy."

"You always say that!" Jared screamed, tears freely running down his face now. "You—you're the worst!"

He turned and stormed off, and Sam and Scott both watched him in silence. Suddenly Jared turned around and addressed Sam.

"Do—do you want me to leave?" Jared cried, wiping tears from his eyes.

"I think it would be for the best," Sam answered without a moment's hesitation.

That made Jared angry.

"Fine! I don't even care! You guys are lame as hell anyway!" Jared shouted and ran away from them on the deck of the ship.

After running for about a hundred feet he turned around again and yelled at Scott.

"You're the worst brother ever, stupid! I hate you! I hate you!"

Scott felt his eyes dilate, and he started to pick out thousands of thin sonar waves propagating through the air that were being generated by the sound of the ocean. He felt his stomach split in half, but there was no pain this time.

A long whip of water rose up out of the ocean and appeared on the side of the ship. It slapped Jared's feet and slammed him on his back, evaporating into steam a moment after it touched him. A second whip of water rose up out of the swells, and that's when Scott realized that he was the one controlling the water.

Scott was still frustrated, though, and before he could stop it, the water sliced toward Jared from above.

The water impacted Jared with the force of a large wave at the beach, and Jared cried out in pain and surprise. He slowly stood up after a second, limping on his left leg. He looked at Scott, and Scott looked back at him from across the deck, completely dumbfounded.

Jared slowly backed away, petrified. His wide eyes mirrored Scott's own, except that Jared looked like an animal that had just realized it wasn't safe out there in the world.

Scott took a half step toward him. He tried to make words come out of his mouth, but he didn't know what to say.

Jared bolted in the other direction, running as fast as his legs could carry him. His inhaler dropped onto the deck of the ship, and Scott walked over to pick it up for him by force of habit. He picked up the small blue life-saving device and put it in his pocket.

Suddenly, he remembered that Sam was there.

He slowly turned his head to look at her. She must have followed him when he walked to get the inhaler, because she was still standing next to him. Her mouth was hanging open, and her eyes looked like they were just about ready to bulge out of their sockets.

"He's a pretty clumsy kid?" Scott feigned nonchalance.

"You can use your curse on Earth? So *that's* why Terminus and Artam want you so bad! I thought it was just because you were a

Mediator, and we don't know much about them. But you can use your . . . oh wow, this is nuts."

"I don't know what you're talking about," Scott said, his brain still processing the fact that she had just mentioned Artam and Terminus by name—*and* she had called Scott a Mediator.

Plus, Scott's head was still swirling with what had just happened to Jared. His little brother. His little brother who had trusted him . . . until Scott slammed him onto the deck of the ship with a whip of sea water.

"Okay, let's cut the crap." Sam changed gears from excited to dead serious. "I'm from Armadron. Artam snuck me through a portal behind Terminus's cronies and sent me here to get you to Armadron safely. They're going to be here any second. You need to follow me. Now. Every second that we waste is another second that the Conjurers could beat us to the Gateway. It's another second that my people are enslaved, tortured, and experimented on by that psychopath."

Right there, right then, Scott would have turned around to go find his little brother. He would have ignored whatever was happening, because he didn't care anymore. His whole body felt numb. Detached. He had hurt and scared his little brother. He was like Brick. He was just a bully, and Jared had probably felt like a toy doll being thrown around.

Scott was already halfway turned around with tears welling up in his eyes, ready to run away from Sam and never look back. Then the deafening sound of popcorn popping erupted from everywhere at once, and Scott was abruptly pulled back into the moment.

Something whizzed past his head. He crouched instinctively and turned around to see what was going on. That's when everything started happening faster than he could mentally process.

Three men standing together. Black hooded cloaks. Big guns. Shooting everywhere. Killing people. Screaming. Crying. Begging. So many people. Dying too fast.

Sam yanked his arm and forced him to run behind her as the man on the left of the other two raised a shotgun at them from thirty feet away. She was yelling at him loudly, but Scott couldn't hear anything she was saying. He just ran behind her and followed blindly, completely terrified.

Where's Mom and Jared?! That single thought made its way to the forefront of his mind, and he almost stopped, then thought better of it.

Bullets were flying everywhere, people were falling, and the ship was pure chaos.

Still running, Scott followed Sam into a storage hallway bordered by racks of towels and several doors. Suddenly Sam stopped dead in her tracks. Scott slammed into her at full speed, and they both went down hard.

"What the hell is your problem?" she demanded angrily as she stood up quickly and kept her eyes looking in front of her, scanning ahead for threats.

"The guys"—Scott desperately sucked in air—"with guns. The three men. And I don't know where my mom and brother are right now!"

"Three?" Sam responded without moving her gaze. "Yeah, well, now there are five."

He looked ahead of Sam. Now he knew why they'd stopped. Several yards away two men dressed in black cloaks were blocking their path.

Sam and Scott turned around to see that three more men had appeared behind them. All the men slowly walked threateningly forward and, within moments, had formed a wide semi-circle around the teenagers.

The two backed up against a rack of towels. Scott noticed that the men had transparent hands, just like Artam did in the dream. Their eyes were grayed out and looked distant, though. Like a dead person's. And they smelled like crap.

Sam was saying something to him.

"Make a move. I need you to run out one of the doors. If you can, I need you to Accelerate in less than a half second. Reacting at a human speed will be too slow for you. Can you?"

"Accelerate, yeah. Half second, no." Scott gulped.

The men all took leg-sized guns out of their cloaks and pointed them at the two teenagers.

"Do it now."

Suddenly a man burst through one of the side doors into the hallway, frantically juggling an armload of bloody towels. The flung door knocked aside one of the men dressed in black.

"Oh, I'm so—"

The man stopped midsentence, seeing the guns. He screamed, threw the bloody towels up in the air, and ran back out the same door as fast as he could.

Two of the men emotionlessly raised their guns and shot through the doorway. The sound of the bullets hitting the man in his back followed by the sound of his body crashing on the deck of the ship would be imprinted permanently to Scott's memory.

Amidst the chaos, Sam sprung into action. She knocked a rack of towels over two of the men while pulling Scott along, and they both ran out the door as fast as they could. The sound of bullets raining down on them was terrifying to Scott, and he screamed in uncontrollable fear.

"Scott! Accelerate! Do it now! Now!" Sam was screaming at him while running.

As they were running, Scott's form shifted, faster than ever before. In the span of two steps, Scott had changed completely. He was several inches taller, he could breathe better, he could see the sounds flying through the air now, and he felt a hell of a lot deadlier.

Sam just kept on running down the ship as fast as she could, and they eventually came to a stairwell leading to the lower deck.

She ran down the stairs, dangerously skipping steps and almost falling. Scott was still at the top of the stairs. He hesitated, thinking of going to look for his mom and Jared.

There's no way in hell I'm leaving them.

A bullet went through a painting in front of his face. Without thinking, he jumped down.

He didn't even have enough time to think that could break his legs before his feet touched the ground at the bottom of the long two-story staircase.

As Scott landed, all his weight was balanced perfectly on the balls of his feet, and without even trying his body bounced back up, an inch or so in the air.

He heard more bullets not too far away and kept on running. There were multitudes of people running everywhere, getting in his way. He looked for Jared and his mom but didn't see them among the faces. He saw Sam, though, waiting for him impatiently in the large dining hall a hundred feet away.

When Scott caught up to her, she ran with him, and they zipped through the dining hall. Scott noticed that she hadn't changed like he had, so she was a lot slower at running. He had to dial down his new speed a bit for her to keep up.

Still, she seemed to be running a lot faster than usual for a normal human. She was just breathing a lot harder than he was.

As they were running, an alarm sounded throughout the ship.

Beep! Beep! Beep!

"Attention all passengers and staff! Attention all passengers and staff! We are now in full lockdown mode. Go to your cabins and lock all doors immediately. Do not come out until you are instructed to do so. This is not a drill."

The alarm sounded repeatedly. Sam pulled Scott under a table, and she stopped to catch her breath, so he started asking questions.

"Those guys are with Terminus, right? Why do they want to kill us? How come they can't change like me—"

"Scott, shut up," Sam told him, slightly out of breath still.

"No! What the freaking hell is going on?! My brother and my mom—"

Slap!

Scott, still kneeling next to Sam, was stunned.

She had just slapped him harder than he had ever been slapped in his life.

"There is no point asking questions right now," she said, slowly lowering her hand. "It will only delay us getting to the Gateway. Now, we need to get to the front of the ship before they do!"

"What the hell do you mean, get to the Gateway?! I need to get to my family! I'm not going anywhere! My mom and my brother need me! I can do things, and I can help them!"

"First off, stop yelling." Sam rubbed her temples impatiently. "We're hiding under a freaking table for a reason. Secondly, those guys don't want your family, and they haven't had the time to figure out who your family even are. They want you. They want your brain, your DNA, bone matter, or whatever the hell else Terminus is after," she told Scott. "And you're not good enough yet to fight them. They'll just shoot you and take you and you won't be helping anyone except Terminus. Now let's move, genius."

Sam slipped out from under the table and started running. Scott copied the motion, and soon they were both running down the ship again.

As they were running, he realized that he could feel bullets going through the ship, traveling near him. He could feel everything else, too, and it was way too much.

One bullet almost hit Sam in the back, but Scott's 360-degree sonar vision had picked up the vibrations of one of the men in black robes raising his gun. Scott could somehow *feel* the friction of the gun moving against the air and being aimed at Sam.

The gun fired, and Scott pushed Sam by the shoulder to the right slightly so that the bullet would go in between their torsos. Sam nodded her head in thanks, somehow knowing what had just happened without seeing the bullet or being able to feel it.

They ran up another flight of stairs and onto the main deck.

Scott's ears started to bleed, the blood falling from his earlobes in a slow drip. His vision started to get fuzzy at the edges. The amount of sound that was reaching his ears was overpowering. He stumbled for a second, but he wouldn't slow down because even though Sam was slower, she was running at a pace that would have put an Olympic sprinter to shame.

"Why aren't you changing or whatever or using your curse?" Scott asked her while running, closing his eyes for a second to fight the pain in his vision and ears.

"It's called Accelerating. And I can't on Earth," she huffed. "No one can. Except you apparently."

They ran to the front of the ship, and Sam once again stopped dead in her tracks. Scott almost ran into her for the second time.

"Would you stop doing that?" she hissed.

He stopped, and his ears suddenly made a high-pitched popping sound. Now he could hear a lot less and the bleeding had stopped. Still, his sonar hearing could pick up the vibration of multiple sets of feet on the ship running toward them not too far away. They were running in unison, like they were in the military or something. He rotated his jaw and instantly was bombarded by the noises from the sonar waves. His ears felt like they were splitting in half again.

Aaarrggh!

He rotated his jaw slightly, and most of the sounds died away and his ears stopped hurting.

He concentrated on two of the waves that seemed familiar. Somehow, he knew from those two waves that Jared and his mom were in their cabin on the other side of the ship. They were hiding under a table being yelled at to stay quiet by one of the crew members.

Tears welled up in Scott's eyes and he looked at Sam.

Sam pointed down into the waves. There was a small whirlpool developing in the water on the left side of the ship.

"I can stop them," Scott said to her, setting his feet and looking back down the length of the ship. "We don't need to go in."

"You can't stop bullets with water, dumbass." Sam rolled her eyes as she turned around to look at him.

Her eyes suddenly widened, and she reached for him as fast as she could.

"Scott!"

Scott was thrown bodily over the railing like a football, without seeing who threw him, and he plummeted toward the water. As he was falling, he heard and felt the sound of gunshots on the ship deck.

He hit the water and immediately gasped for breath.

The water was freezing! The ship was already slowly pulling away. He had to get back to the ship. Sam was wrong. People were being slaughtered like cattle up there.

He heard a yell and looked above him. Sam was falling toward the ocean with her back facing the water.

She hit the water a few feet away from Scott with a resounding crash and sank below the surface, unconscious. With his sonar he could see her perfectly under the water, floating downward. He could feel her heart beating slowly too. Dangerously slowly.

He tried to dive in under the water after her, but the whirlpool was just too strong. It pulled him around and around in a circle and sucked the air right out of his lungs. The last images Scott saw were the five men in black cloaks diving toward him, and a person on the edge of the ship who looked a lot like someone he knew giving him a thumbs-up.

The whirlpool sucked Scott under the water before he could process that last part, forcing the last bit of air out of his lungs. He fought against the freezing water and the pressure, holding his breath for as long as possible. Suddenly, he felt his whole body go numb as darkness set in.

He shut his eyes, waiting to die.

He ran out of air and spasmed, trying vainly to kick toward the surface as he was pulled down further and further.

He took a big gulp of water and coughed.

It happened again, and he coughed again.

He took a deep breath and tried to concentrate on not swallowing any more water.

Wait . . . I'm breathing! Scott opened his eyes and gave the biggest smile that he ever had given in his life to date. I'm breathing.

As he got pulled down further and further, he eventually realized that his pores were moving. They were his medium for breathing somehow.

He saw a flash of white in the water around him and felt a wave of weightlessness overcome his body—only to be replaced quickly by a growing pressure. The pressure grew until he thought that his eyes would pop out of his head and his ribs would crack, and then it settled.

* * *

He opened his eyes and noticed that he was on his back on the ground. He was lying on hard-packed pure-black dirt. The sky was overcast and had what appeared to be purple lightning shooting out of it. There was constant lightning, and the air smelled like burnt toast, or at least Scott thought it did. It could have just been him.

He sat up slowly and blinked a few times. All around him there was nothing. Just dead wasteland, no trees and no people. There wasn't a single sound coming from anywhere, except his own breathing and someone lying next to him.

He turned to the right and saw Sam. She had a bullet wound in her left leg that was slowly oozing blood, and another from a bullet that had grazed her right shoulder. She looked slightly worse than the way that Scott felt at the moment.

He dug into his pockets and pulled out his phone. It still had 10 percent battery left, and somehow the LifeProof case on it had worked better than advertised. He looked at the top of his phone, though, and saw that he had no service. Scott groaned.

The five Conjurers from the cruise ship appeared. They came out of thin air, faster than he had time to blink.

That's when he noticed that everyone was dry, including himself.

One of the men bent his knees, cocked his arm back, and punched Scott dead center in the face. Someone else came out of the air behind the men in cloaks just before Scott lost consciousness, but things had already gotten too blurry to make out who it was.

9

CAGED

Drip. Drip. Drip.

It was all a dream. He was sure of it. As long as he didn't open his eyes, he could convince himself of that. He could just lie here forever and relax.

Drip. Drip. Drip.

Yup. Just forget everything. He probably was stressed about soccer. That was it. Molly too. She was beautiful. Well, Sam was beautiful too, but she was probably way out of his league.

Drip. Drip. Drip.

He reluctantly opened his eyes, already knowing that things had changed for the worse.

He was trapped in a very small red cage that had a weird, oily smell coming from it. Rusty liquid that looked like blood dripped off the bars and collected on the floor. He also was trapped in this cage by himself, with no one to talk to in a smelly, damp cave. Plus, his forehead really hurt. A lot.

"Hey!" Scott yelled, "Can anyone hear me?!"

"Yes," a man's voice answered hoarsely.

He looked in the direction of the voice and saw nothing. The cave was too dark. He looked harder and saw a gangly, skinny man in a similar cage come into focus, not ten feet away from him, grinning evilly through the darkness.

His heart rate soared. The man looked dangerous: he had a cut-up, ugly face and had been branded all over his body. He had mangy brown hair and probably liked it that way.

Scott Accelerated and his sonar vision illuminated the cave for him. Sort of. It was turning off and on like cable TV with a bad signal. His body didn't change at all like before either. His bones stayed the same, and his headache immediately got worse.

"What's going on? Am I dreaming? Please tell me that I'm dreaming," Scott pleaded with the man.

"Sadly, no. You are not dreaming," the man solemnly replied. "You are really here."

"Where's here?"

"The Coliseum."

"The what?!"

"The Coliseum! Terminus's Coliseum," the man repeated.

"What the hell is the Coliseum?"

"You don't know?!" the man exclaimed, clearly surprised. "Are you stupid, boy?"

"No!"

"The Coliseum is where Terminus makes people battle to the death. You win, Terminus takes your curse and you're home free, at least until one of his Conjurers kills you. They always kill you. They find you. You lose, though, and you're food," the man explained as he licked his lips.

"So either way, you're dead?" Scott pressed on, ignoring the chilling feeling he was getting.

"Yup."

Scott fell silent for a moment before asking, "What's your 'curse'?"

"You already know that answer," the man replied glumly. "You really are stupid, boy."

"What are you talking about? How long have I been here, anyway?"

"Nine hours." The man rubbed his hands together gleefully. "I can't wait to kill you and get outta here."

"Kill me?!"

"Well, yeah. Terminus's probably gonna make us fight each other," the man went on, "or it might be a tag-team match. I know they got two other prisoners in the other holding room. I heard one of 'em's a girl." The man smiled at the thought of killing a girl. "Easy prey for me."

Oh no. Sam.

"Is one of them named Sam?" Scott shouted.

"I don't care about no names," the man said, waving off his question. "I care about blood."

Scott clenched his teeth. "How long until we have to fight?"

"How am I supposed to know? It could be an hour, could be a day, could be a coupla' minutes," the man whined. "Relax."

"Why do we even have to do this?!"

"'Cause Terminus has all the power," the man stated, as if it should be a known fact.

"You keep saying 'Terminus.' Who is he?"

"The ruler of the planet," the man said.

"The ruler of the planet?" Scott repeated like a parrot.

"Yeah, idiot. The ruler of Armadron," the man chuckled.

Scott felt chills go through his body. He wasn't on the cruise ship anymore. No, he wasn't on Earth anymore. His last hope of this whole thing being a hoax was diminished.

"You still haven't told me what a 'curse' is. You said it like it was a thing," Scott said.

"I ain't tellin' you what mine is, you little funny-talkin', lyin', silver-tongued demon!"

"Who *are* you?" Scott was thoroughly confused. "Whatever, well, screw you."

"Go cry to your mommy, kid." The man laughed, showing his yellow, broken teeth.

Scott yelled and tried kicking the bars for a while, but they didn't even vibrate. There was also no lock in sight, so obviously no key either. He also felt something coming from the bars. An emotion of sorts. A malice, like the cage itself wanted to kill him. But that was impossible. They were just bars.

Scott whimpered and wrapped his arms around his legs, rocking back and forth. He lay curled up like that for another several hours, listening to the man taunt him and make crying and boo-boo sounds at him. He fell asleep some time later when exhaustion finally overtook him.

* * *

Gray waves of light came into the cave as part of the rock wall slid aside. It revealed a huge earth-made Coliseum with thousands of people sitting in the stands. The roar of the crowd was overwhelming, and there were things being thrown in the stands everywhere.

Two men stepped toward them. Both were wearing black robes like the men on the cruise ship. They simultaneously raised their hands, and Scott's sonar vision went ballistic, giving him a fresh new headache.

He noticed that one moment there were doors on the cages, and the next there weren't.

"Get into the arena. You two are next," the men both said at the same time in a low dialect.

Oh, hell no. Scott ground his teeth together.

He slowly rose out of his cage and walked toward the men. The man in the other cage did the same.

"What's your name?" Scott quietly asked the man. "We need to work together."

"Bernard," he replied in a weak voice. "And I'm gonna eat you."

When they had almost reached the two cloaked men, Scott turned around and tried to run back into the cave. At that moment, both of the men chanted something unintelligible. Scott's left foot hadn't even touched back down when he was frozen in place, suspended above the ground like time itself had stopped.

One of the men dressed in black walked behind Scott and touched his back. Scott "unfroze," landed on his feet, and began to be pushed along by the man. The other black-dressed man walked behind Bernard.

Scott couldn't even process what just happened.

As soon as they stepped out of the cave, he noticed purple moonlight was coming from the clouds overhead. It lit up the Coliseum with a pale glow and reflected off the shiny black soil that was the floor of the battlefield.

Battlefield.

That word sent shivers down Scott's spine.

Another captive was walking toward them out of a cave on the opposite end of the field, goaded along by a Conjurer dressed in black. Seconds later, someone else emerged, also pushed along by a cloaked goon.

She was hopping on her right leg, trying not to put any pressure on her left one.

"Sam!" Scott yelled.

The man in a black robe behind Scott jabbed him with his elbow between the shoulder blades. Scott stumbled and barely caught himself. He lost his breath and waited a couple seconds to get it back.

"I'm going to kill you like you killed all of those people!" Scott yelled at the ground, too afraid to turn around.

"Hey! Just relax! I'll get us outta this!" Sam yelled back, trying to force a smile from the other side of the Coliseum floor.

Sam was dealt with in a similar way by the man forcing her along.

Scott shouted when he saw this and was hit in the back of the head. Once he stopped seeing stars, he noticed that they were nearing the center of the arena.

A minute later Scott, Sam, the two other prisoners, and the men dressed in black arrived in the center of the field. Scott hadn't failed to notice that there were a lot of blood marks on the field. That wasn't the worst of it, though. Animal bones littered the field everywhere as well.

Except that they weren't animal bones. Scott was just telling himself that.

A man's voice was heard over the roar of the crowd, and everyone instantly fell silent.

"Welcome, ladies and gentlemen, to Terminus's Coliseum. My name is Kane. I hope that all bets have been placed and that all food has been eaten. I must remind any plant growers here this evening that this is strictly a no-grow area. Whatever food you have must have been grown outside the Coliseum. I like to keep the Coliseum area free of roots, and if I see anyone henceforth growing plants, my master's guards or I will kill you on sight. We will make it slow and painful. Thank you for your consideration," Kane said.

The man known as Kane cleared his throat and spoke again.

"Today we will be having a classic-style fight to the death. There are four opponents, each with unknown curses. Any and all alliances may be made, but ultimately there will only be one winner. I will let you all take your seats while my guards explain the rules to the challengers. We will begin in five minutes."

The crowd grew loud again.

While the speech was being given by Terminus's herald, Scott had been looking for him in the stands. He hadn't seen anyone stand up or otherwise look out of place, though. He just saw thousands of ragged-clothed people yelling and pumping their arms. It looked like something out of a *Mad Max* movie.

Sam gave Scott a knowing glance, leaning on her good leg.

"He's probably invisible," she rasped to Scott. "Terminus gives those close to him more curses."

"Are you all ri—"

"Shut up and listen," one of the guards said in a mechanical voice. "The rules are as follows: One, if you possess the curse of healing, no healing anyone other than yourself. Two, any direct contact with anyone in the audience will result in immediate termination. Three, guards will be placed around the arena. All attempts to escape will also result in immediate termination. Four, you must kill your opponent to survive."

As he was talking, Scott noticed his hands. Then he looked at the hands of all of the cloaked guards. They all had chipped, broken nails, and it looked like they'd had their hands in the dirt their whole lives, which almost covered up the fact that they were transparent.

They were Conjurers. Just like Artam.

The crowd was chanting the rules at the same time. Some people in the stands were cutting themselves and dripping blood in front of them.

Scott felt nauseous. He could barely stand.

The guards suddenly vanished into thin air. Scott noticed that the arena walls were somewhat black now, when before they were a coppery color. He looked a little closer and realized that it wasn't the arena walls that were black; it was about a hundred or so guards spread out in front of the wall, blocking any means of escape.

All the guards had different heights and different looks, but they all had the same emotionless expression on their faces and the same dirty, animalistic-looking hands. Their eyes were grayed out too—like the Conjurers on the cruise ship.

The two other men on the field and Sam stood stock-still, looking at the ground. Sam lifted her head up and tried to hobble over to Scott. He met her a little more than halfway.

"Sam, I don't understand any of this," he cried helplessly. "This is Armadron, right? Why did I have to come? Am I gonna die? I don't see how we're going to live through this, and I don't even know—"

Sam took her pointer finger and put it to Scott's lips.

Scott blushed despite the dire situation at hand.

She beckoned to Scott, and he leaned forward. Then she softly whispered to him.

"Listen. We only have a minute until battle time, so I'll make it brief. You're only half-Armadronian, so some curses may or may not work on you. I'm like a power cell. I can control light and dark and neutralize powers that are near me. Don't tell any of them that. From what I've seen, you can control water. Hopefully you're powerful enough to generate it too. That's at least two powers. If we can last just a couple minutes, we have a way outta here," she explained. "And don't tell anyone your name. The only reason that you're not in his lab right now getting split in half is because he expected that hunting party to come back with one boy. He probably found out that they came back with two Armadronians, so Terminus might be still waiting for the 'right' group of Conjurers to get back. They're not great on executing specific orders. Just generic ones."

"That's your plan?!" he whispered fiercely. "We *might* have a way outta here?"

"It's better than what you came up with," she retorted.

"What did I come up with?"

"Nothing."

He glared at Sam.

"Fine. You got me into this, so I guess I have to trust you to get me out," Scott said.

"Or you have no other options," Sam argued hotly.

"Whatever. Just tell me what to do and I'll do it." He put a determined face on.

"All right! The time to battle is at hand!" Kane's voice shouted over the roar of the crowd.

Once again, everyone in the Coliseum grew silent.

"Opponents, take your positions in the center!"

Scott, Sam, and the two other men faced each other in the center of the field. The two men weren't anywhere close to each other, so they hopefully weren't acting as a team.

He let Sam lean on him for support. She looked like she was about to pass out. Her leg had barely stopped bleeding, and there was a trail of dried blood from the bullet hole to her shoes.

How did my life get to this? Scott thought. *How?*

Sam slowly closed her eyes and . . . evolved.

She instantly grew larger hands and feet, her stomach bulged outward and then moved back into place, her bone structure changed to become more aerodynamic, and her eyes changed to a dark, burning red color.

The transformation was extremely odd for Scott to watch. Even though he had already Accelerated a couple times himself, seeing someone else do it made him uneasy.

"I thought you couldn't Accelerate," Scott asked her.

"Not on Earth." She winked.

"And your eyes—"

"Good point. Don't Accelerate until you need to. They'll see your eyes and it'll be all over."

Scott nodded.

"Opponents, take your positions in the center!"

The two men also Accelerated and stepped closer to Sam and Scott. Scott stepped back instinctively.

The man who wasn't Bernard chuckled, eyed Scott, and made a slicing gesture with his thumb across his neck. He continued to glare at Scott, licking his dry, cracked lips like a deranged lunatic.

Scott felt like he was going to pass out again.

10

BREATHTAKING

"Go!" the announcer bellowed.

The crowd instantaneously became a screaming frenzy. Both men started to make a move toward Scott and Sam.

Before Scott had time to breathe, his vision went completely black. It stayed that way for about two seconds, and then light filtered in.

He could see again. He noticed that Sam was still next to him—and that they were all the way at the other end of the Coliseum!

Sam started to fall, but Scott caught her before she hit the ground.

"My leg," she hissed through clenched teeth.

"Hold on a sec, Sam," he said, trying to reassure her.

Scott pulled off his gray T-shirt and wrapped it around the bullet hole in her leg. She cried out as he tied it tighter.

"Better?" he asked.

"Much. Thanks, Scott," Sam said. "And nice move, slick."

She smiled weakly and Scott's heart skipped a beat. He was suddenly self-conscious, realizing that his shirt was off and Sam was staring at him.

Think of Molly, think of Molly, think of Molly!

He quickly scanned the arena for the two other prisoners and saw that they were preoccupied, fighting each other.

Good. He and Sam still had a moment to catch their breath.

He was the first to break the awkward silence. "Did you do that?"

"Yeah. Shadow travel." She paused. "Can you see them?"

Scott nodded.

"Good. Keep your eye on them in case they try to pull anything."

The one on the left was Bernard, the man who had been in the cage near Scott. The one on the right had on a maroon T-shirt and white shorts. He was wearing a huge grin but no shoes.

"No shoes" shot a bolt of blue lightning as thin and straight as a pencil out of his outstretched hand at Bernard. Bernard created some kind of invisible force field the size of Captain America's shield, and the lightning bounced off it in all directions.

Holy mother of God, Scott thought, *I'm in a comic book—and I'm never gonna live to see the last page.*

"No shoes" wasn't finished. He moved his hand slightly, and all the lightning collected into one tiny mass of electricity the size of a softball right above Bernard's head. Bernard dove to the ground and created another force field around him as he was falling.

The lightning exploded with a soft pop, and every spot of dirt within a thirty-foot diameter of the explosion was incinerated. There was a large crater in the place where Bernard had once stood.

"No shoes" smiled and started to walk toward Scott and Sam.

"Get me up!" Sam yelled to Scott, "quickly!"

He lifted her up, and she leaned on him for support.

"No shoes" started to jog, and soon he was only about a hundred feet away from them.

Suddenly, "No shoes" stopped jogging and clawed at his eyes, which were bleeding profusely. Then something seemed to hit him hard in the chest. He flew back twenty feet and landed on his back, dead.

"Craaap," Sam groaned.

"What?" Scott asked, none too calmly.

Sam didn't answer, and she didn't need to. Bernard became visible right next to the no-shoes guy and placed his hand right on his chest. Green light flowed into Bernard, and he stood up and closed his eyes. He reopened them a moment later and looked directly at Sam and Scott. Bernard smiled a very creepy, chilling, horrible smile. His eyes were the color of blood, indicating that he had already Accelerated. Then he vanished.

Scott started to freak out and spin around, frantically looking for the man he could not see.

"Hey," Sam said calmly, "stand still and listen for him. He's going to target me because I'll move slower. Use your sonar if you can but keep your eyes under control. He'll appear in a little bit."

Scott rotated his jaw, and his normal hearing turned into the white noise of the sonar hearing. He winced and tried to concentrate with his sonar, but the crowd was too loud. Sonar waves were bouncing off everything, hitting each other and creating loud, obnoxious static. He dialed it back a bit, because he could feel that familiar *hum* in his eyes that told him they were changing.

A couple seconds later Bernard appeared not twenty feet away from them, completely visible. He looked down at his body with a very confused expression on his face. Scott was also confused.

"Remember," Sam explained to Scott quietly, "I'm like a power cell. My neutrality power is keeping him from becoming invisible when he's near me. Stay close."

Bernard thrust out his palms. Nothing happened.

He tried it again. Nothing.

Finally realizing that it was either Sam or Scott who was causing his powers to deactivate, he stepped backward three steps. On the third step, Bernard once more became invisible.

The millisecond that Sam and Scott could no longer see him, a thin bolt of electricity came rocketing toward them.

Scott's vision had flashed in the split second before the lightning was thrown, warning him of the incoming danger. He pulled Sam down to the ground, and they both landed on their stomachs. The bolt of lightning shot past them, making all the hairs on both of their bodies stand up. The crowd yelled in need of bloodshed, and the air suddenly smelled like burning rubber.

A woman's terrible scream was heard in the crowd. Someone had just been struck by the lightning.

Another bolt of lightning aimed at Sam came out of nowhere, and this time they had no room to dodge. When the lightning was just about to hit them, Scott instinctively Accelerated and shielded Sam's face with his hands, closing his eyes and tensing his body.

The lightning collected in his huge palms, and Scott was flung back ten feet. His hands knocked Sam in the temple, and she screamed in pain, rolling to the side from the impact.

He landed hard on his back. He felt his hands grow unbearably hot and began to yell. The lightning arced out of his hands, turning into a deep purple color, and immediately followed a narrow path in the air, hitting Bernard in the chest and knocking him down.

He looked at his steaming hands, then at Sam.

"You know what they say about men with big hands," she teased as she tried to stand up.

She cried out again and collapsed to the ground, holding her leg. It was gushing blood out of the bullet hole now, turning Scott's gray shirt maroon.

Bernard was about to shoot three more bolts of lightning as he rose to stand again. With his sonar vision Scott could see the energy building inside Bernard's hands.

But Scott was too far back. He couldn't stop it.

Sam didn't see Bernard aiming at her—she was still holding her leg and putting pressure on it.

No! Scott thought, anger and determination welling up from somewhere deep inside.

A low grinding noise was heard coming from the ground. A wall of solid rock rapidly rose up from the dirt just in time to be blasted by the waves of electricity.

The lightning didn't make it through the rock, but Scott felt it hit the ground and leave an imprint. A fresh round of adrenaline shot through him like cold water on a blazing summer day.

As soon as Bernard's lightning hit the barrier, two more jolts of electricity wormed around the left and the right side of it.

"No, Scott." Sam was wheezing. "You can't . . . use . . . too much . . ."

Scott waved his right arm away from his chest reflexively, and three minivan-sized pieces of rock broke from the ground and floated in midair. He flicked his wrist, and one of the rocks sped toward one of the branches of electricity. It hit the electricity, exploded, and landed far off on the other side of the field. He copied this technique with the other branch of electricity. He prepared to fire the third piece of rock, aiming it at Bernard.

Suddenly he felt extremely weak, like he had just run a marathon. His shoulders sagged, and it was all he could do to keep from falling to his knees. The rock that Scott had been floating in midair dropped to the ground with a resounding crash. Scott dropped to the ground, too, on his hands and knees, sweat dripping everywhere.

"Hey," Sam said, tapping Scott on the shoulder and reminding him that she was there, "as soon as you . . . see another shot of electricity coming . . . close your eyes for a second and . . . hurl a smaller rock as hard as you can . . . at the spot."

He didn't know if he could, but he nodded his head in agreement, still looking at the ground.

The next bolt of lightning came from Scott's far left. As soon as he sensed it coming, he closed his eyes and threw a fist-sized hunk of rock out of the ground as hard as he could.

The second Scott let go, the insides of his eyes lit up as if the sun itself were inside them. He gasped, and his first initial thought was that he had missed and gotten hit with lightning.

Within the same second, though, the light became dim again, and Scott reopened his eyes. The crowd became almost completely silent, save for the people in the stands yelling, screaming, and complaining about their eyes bleeding.

The rock was hurtling toward Bernard, who was now visible and screaming at the top of his lungs. He was covering both of his eyes and thrashing while standing in place. When the small rock was about to reach him, he raised his head and the rock bounced off an invisible force field. Still, it was a very fast-moving rock, and the power of it hitting the force field around his head knocked him flat on his back.

Scott used the last remains of his strength to walk over to Bernard.

"Kill him! Kill him! Kill him!" the crowd roared.

Scott fell to his knees for the second time, next to Bernard.

He looked back at Sam. She was lying a good distance away on the ground now, completely passed out.

Bernard was mumbling something about "the light," and he was writhing on the ground. The crowd just grew louder and louder, calling for Bernard's head and laughing at Scott. Scott would have cried in frustration, but he was too exhausted.

"This is your fault!" Scott yelled down at him.

He punched the squirming, defenseless Bernard in the face, using all his enhanced Accelerated strength. In one punch he took out all his confusion, sadness, and anger from the past few days on Bernard, who was now knocked out cold with a screwed-up-looking nose.

As soon as his fist connected, Scott experienced a familiar feeling. His hand tingled, but it went away in a second, just as it had done the previous times.

"Aaargh!" Scott screamed, staring at his hand. "What is happening?!"

The crowd roared at the violence, and they all just kept chanting for Scott to kill him.

Craaaaaaaackkkk!

A familiar old man dressed in brightly colored blue-and-black robes appeared next to Scott through a rip in the universe.

Scott started to have a seizure at that exact moment. He fell to his side. His body was no longer under his control, and his mouth tasted like bile and filled with saliva like a racoon with rabies.

Just as his vision was getting dark, the old man grabbed his shoulders and lifted him up onto his back. Scott once again felt the odd tingling feeling in his limbs, and the man gestured at Sam and mumbled something in an old, archaic language. She flew toward them, and a second later they all traveled through the space rip.

"No!" Scott heard Kane yell from somewhere in the Coliseum right before he lost consciousness.

THE CAVERN

Scott woke up to find himself back in his bed at home. He was in his favorite pajamas, lying with his head propped comfortably against a pillow.

"Scott! Get up! It's time for school!" his mother called from downstairs.

He grinned and threw off his covers. He threw his feet over the side of the bed and stood up.

Thick hands emerged from under the bed and pulled his feet completely out from under him. He slammed his face on the floor, cried out, and kicked his left foot into the face of whoever was under his bed. A man grunted angrily, and the grip on Scott's ankles lessened. Scott kicked three more times with both feet to break the grip, then scrambled to his feet and whipped around.

"Mom, call the cops!" Scott screamed the first thing that came to mind.

The bed suddenly shot up to the ceiling, and the frame splintered into pieces across the room. A big portion of the ceiling fell onto the floor, and he shielded his face with his forearm.

The man under the bed was already on his feet. He reached out a hand and laughed at Scott.

"No," Scott gasped as he saw white sparks dance across the man's outstretched fingertips.

It was Bernard.

"Die, boy." Bernard laughed, showing his yellow, crooked teeth.

Lightning blasted into Scott's face, and he screamed.

* * *

"Aaaaaahh!"

Scott fell backward against the white sheets of the hospital bed. There were machines by the walls and a needle in his arm.

He lifted his head and looked around the room. It was a medium-sized space that was completely white, except for a set of neatly folded clothes placed at the foot of his bed.

He tried to slide out of the bed but quickly returned to the haven under the covers.

He was naked. Why was he naked?

He made a move to reach toward his feet to get the clothes, but a sudden noise made him jump.

"What's your name?" someone asked bluntly.

He looked over at the direction of the voice and, by doing so, realized that his sonar vision was gone now.

Scott glanced at the rest of his body—he had returned to normal. He finally lifted his head to look at whoever had spoken.

Leaning in the doorway was a tall, powerfully built young man, around eighteen or nineteen years old. His jet-black hair was cut short, military-style, and he was wearing black shorts, a tight, light-gray muscle shirt, and what looked like a permanent scowl. His arms were crossed in front of his chest.

"How long have I been asleep?" Scott said, dodging the question. "Where's Sam?"

"Twenty-three hours. Answer the question."

"What's *your* name? And where is Sam?"

"I don't have time for games. Now answer the question!" the stranger spat.

Scott told him his name.

"Just great," the young man muttered to himself, "Scott Faranger. Why did you come here?"

"I got pushed over a boat," he replied glumly.

"What? How?"

"I dunno who it was." Scott looked at the angry newcomer as he said this, waiting for a reaction.

The stranger's body language gave away nothing, other than that he was an arrogant jerk.

"Hmmm . . . I see," Mr. Attitude said thoughtfully, eyeing Scott. "Do you want to go home then?"

"Hell, yes!"

"Well, sorry to burst your bubble. It doesn't matter how much you scream for your mommy in your sleep. The portal isn't open on our side yet. You're gonna have to wait a few days."

I screamed in my sleep? Scott thought. *Great.*

"Artam?" Scott started to remember. "He was in a dream of mine!"

"Cool. Well, he likes you. Says you're the key to getting our world back," the stranger huffed. "That's pretty much the only reason why you're here."

Scott closed his eyes. "I don't care about being a key for whatever crusade you're on—"

"Neither do I."

"—or this whole planet-ending thing. If you could somehow make it possible for me to get back to planet *Earth*, that would be great. I just want to go home, finish the cruise, go back to school, and see if I made the soccer team. You can do all this superhero stuff yourself. I'm done having seizures. They suck."

Scott opened his eyes to find his verbal sparring opponent wearing a big fat smirk.

"What's so funny?"

"Make the soccer team? You're like a two-year-old who can't see over a counter," he scoffed.

"Look, bro," Scott said impatiently, "as you can clearly see, I've barely lived through all this craziness. You're kinda crazy too, dude. And I'm clearly not in Kansas anymore, so just let me—"

"Shut up!" The young man Accelerated and suddenly a stretcher near the wall flew across the room. It slammed into the opposite wall with a thundering *boom* and crumpled to the floor, dented in multiple areas.

Scott stopped talking.

"Are you serious?!" the stranger bellowed angrily, walking slowly toward Scott. "You don't get it, do you? This is just the beginning! It's gonna get a lot tougher from here on out, so get used to it! Oh, and another thing. You are not going home. What you used to call a normal life has ended, *bro*. So man the hell up and make the best of the situation. This isn't about just you anymore . . . it's about our worlds. They've both pretty much turned to complete crap." He took a breath. "Get yourself changed and meet me outside the door. If you're gonna be here anyway, then you need to understand a few things."

As he reached the doorway, he Decelerated, once again looking like a regular Joe, although one with an attitude. Without turning around, he added sarcastically, "Nick is the name. Welcome to Armadron."

"Wait!" Scott cried.

"What?"

"What do you mean, it's about *our* worlds?"

Nick glared at Scott for a long moment before speaking.

"Terminus says he's trying to evolve *everyone*, and that he's tired of ruling just our failed planet. So when Halley's Comet comes around in a couple days on our side of the Gateway . . . he's gonna colonize your planet too."

Nick left the room.

Scott reached for the clothes at the foot of the bed. He had never dressed so slowly in his life. When he was finished, he saw that his cell phone and Jared's blue inhaler had been placed beneath the pile of clothes. He picked up the inhaler and stuffed it in his pocket. He tried to turn on the cell phone, but it was dead. Scott grunted and slid the phone in his other pocket. Then he walked silently across the room and through the door.

* * *

Scott was now dressed in dark-green shorts and a light-brown T-shirt. Also, he was wearing a pair of sleek black shoes that were somehow the perfect size for his feet. He noticed that Nick was wearing the same shoes.

"What happened to my old shoes?" Scott asked him.

"When your feet grew because you Accelerated, your shoes were shredded. I'm guessing you didn't notice because of the adrenaline."

Scott looked down at his new shoes.

"Why won't these rip?"

"They expand with your feet," Nick answered. "Now come out here and take a look at all this."

Scott took one step and then retreated. Nick turned toward him and looked him in the eye.

"What's wrong?" Nick asked.

"Where's Sam? Is she . . . okay?"

"She's at the place where we are going," Nick answered, unblinking.

"And where is that?" Scott crossed his arms.

"Where we are about to go."

"You know what I mean."

"Who cares?" Nick dodged the statement and walked away from Scott.

Scott stood there for a moment and watched Nick walk away. Eventually, Scott gave in and jogged to catch up to Nick. He didn't want to be alone in . . . wherever this place was.

As he jogged toward Nick, Scott took in the most amazing sight of his life.

All around him was a huge cavern that looked like it was a mile wide. It looked never-ending lengthwise, which made him think that he was maybe in a mountain of some sort, or maybe underground. The ceiling of the cavern looked like it could easily have been thirty stories high.

He turned around, jogging backward, and noticed that they had just exited a small white square hut that read Healing Room 37 on the top of it.

THE CAVERN

Throughout the Cavern were huge buildings of either brown, black, or gray color, each probably at least four stories tall. There were also thousands of shops and other small buildings made completely of hard-packed dirt or metal scattered throughout.

A huge river—about five hundred feet across—ran through the middle of it all. Scott saw young people surfing, running, and even walking on top of the river like Jesus, as if it were solid ground. The only light that he saw was artificial, but he didn't see any power lines. He could hear laughter in the distance. This place was definitely better than being in the Coliseum. It felt like a sanctuary.

He saw little kids wrestling good-naturedly with each other—at least until one of them accidentally punched the other in the face. The kid started bleeding and crying, but when the one who did the punching lightly touched the other kid's bleeding face, it was completely healed.

The kid who was crying wiped the blood off his face with his shirt, and they continued wrestling like nothing had happened.

Jared, Scott suddenly thought. *These kids are about his age.*

"What do you see?" Nick asked once Scott finally caught up to him.

"What do you mean, what do I see? I see what you're seeing," Scott replied as he switched from jogging to walking.

"What's the weirdest thing you've seen so far?"

"Well, there was a little kid who completely healed his friend's wound over there."

Nick chuckled.

Soon they reached a young boy who was probably nine- or ten-years old standing near a red circle in the ground marked "Transport." He was also standing by the bottom edge of one of the bigger buildings (or cavescrapers, as Scott was starting to think of them). The boy turned around, and Nick immediately spoke to him in an authoritative voice.

"Library. Civilian and an Icranu."

The boy shot an uneasy glance at Nick.

"You'll be able to take me," Nick reassured the boy. "I can control my curse."

"Wait," Scott interrupted, "what d'ya mean 'transport'? What's he going to do?"

"He's going to get us somewhere," Nick answered.

"Where? And how?"

"Over there," Nick pointed somewhere behind them to the left.

Scott looked over in the direction where Nick had pointed. He didn't see anything that stood out.

Something hard tapped Scott's right temple. His eyes closed, and he was knocked out before he hit the ground.

* * *

He opened his eyes to find Nick walking briskly away. He got up to follow, vaguely remembering something about falling.

As far as Scott could tell, they were now in an entirely different part of the Cavern. Farmland seemed to stretch on for miles, and the only buildings in sight were some ravaged-looking purple structures. The buildings looked like they had survived a nuclear explosion. Barely. There were holes in roofs, corners of buildings missing, and rubble all over the ground.

Scott blinked, and all the buildings instantly became beautiful structures, unblemished at every angle.

What the hell?

But his curiosity dissipated quickly as images of the ravaged buildings were overwritten in his brain by images of unblemished structures. The truth disappeared from his memory.

He ran to catch up to Nick. Even before he got his breath back, he shot off questions.

"What the heck did you just do to me?"

Nick ignored him.

"Did you hit me? I remember something touching my head and now I can't remember stuff."

"What can't you remember?" Nick asked.

Scott thought about that for a second.

"I don't remember."

They walked in silence for several more steps.

"Where are we going, again?" Scott asked.

More ignoring from Nick.

They kept walking for another five minutes or so. Eventually Scott spoke up again.

"So why doesn't anyone on Earth know about Armadron? It seems like everyone here on Armadron knows about Earth."

Nick remained silent.

"How come everyone here has cool powers?"

Nick kept his mouth firmly shut.

"Okaaay . . . what's your power?" he asked blindly.

"Shut up and stop asking people what their curses are," Nick answered as he turned under an arched sign that read LIBRARY.

"Of course," Scott grumbled to himself.

They entered the coolest library that Scott had ever seen in his entire life. There was not a single book in sight, and it was jam-packed with loud, obnoxious people.

There were also hundreds of columns of shelves with small black circular devices stacked in rows across them. Each one looked like a small donut with buttons on it.

Nick walked over to one of the shelves and picked up a black device that was roughly the size of a fist. He walked back over to Scott and quickly went over some instructions.

"You're definitely going to need one of these," Nick yelled over the chatter of the crowd milling around the Library. "It's called a Bastum and it has multiple purposes. For starters, we use it for recon. It functions as a sort of log, recording information about everything you're seeing or experiencing within a ten-foot radius. You can also use it as a weapon. It morphs into a pretty wicked looking sword. I'd show you, but once you activate that function, it takes a while to put it back into place. It doesn't collapse back automatically."

"It doesn't what?!" Scott yelled back to Nick, battling the noise of the people in the Library.

"Just take it." Nick pressed the Bastum into Scott's hand. "It's also a communicator. It's how our teams talk to each other."

Scott put it in his pocket next to his cell phone.

Nick turned and continued walking briskly through the Library. Scott hurried to catch up.

"Who came up with that thing?" Scott asked.

"Me and a friend," Nick said, pride creeping into his voice.

"*You* came up with this?"

"Shhhhh." Nick put a finger to his lips.

And we're back to you being a d-bag, Scott thought.

They walked to a big metal door. Nick waved his hand slightly, and the door opened to allow them in. They walked into a smaller room, and Nick flicked his wrist at the air. The door shut behind them, and the deafening noise of the Library was abruptly silenced. Scott looked past Nick to find a tall, well-built man, most likely in his early forties, with premature gray hair. He was in the middle of scolding three teens who seemed to be between Scott's and Nick's ages.

"Is this what you call a *recon* mission?! What the hell were you guys thinking?! Your job was to follow the shifter—that's it!"

"Excuse me, sir," Nick stated boldly, "you asked to see us?"

The room became deathly quiet, and Scott instinctively held his breath.

"Yes, yes, Nick," the man responded, without taking his eyes off the teenagers in front of him. "Take a seat. Scott too. He can sit. And don't interrupt me again."

How does he know my name? Scott thought.

Nick made his way to the front of the room with Scott in tow. The three people sitting in the front row of thin, metal chairs looked up at Scott.

The first person Scott noticed was Sam.

A mess of emotions ran through him. Initially he was concerned about her well-being, but he immediately saw that she was now in pretty good shape. There wasn't even a wound where the bullet had been shot into her leg! He was so relieved that she was okay that he just stared and smiled at her.

Nick took his shoulder and thrust him into the seat next to Sam.

Scott took an agitated breath and breathed it out slowly. Sam looked at him with puppy dog eyes and smiled. He smiled back.

There was also another girl and a boy. Each looked about sixteen or seventeen years old, maybe a little older than Scott. As Scott looked at the boy, he noticed that he was grinning back at him without blinking. Creepy.

The boy was wearing white shorts with a black sleeveless shirt. He had spiked orange hair with small blue and yellow currents of electricity running through it. When he noticed Scott's eyes move up to his electric hair, the boy grinned madly, and a spark shot off the top of his head, making Scott jump.

Scott tore his gaze away and looked at the third teenager, the other girl in the room. Whoever she was, she was looking at Scott with disgust and disapproval. She had purple hair down to her shoulders that clashed with her light-brown eyes.

The girl was wearing a tight orange tank top and black shorts. She looked like the poster girl for *Halloweentown*.

—*What the hell are you looking at?*

Scott jumped up and looked around the room wildly. He could have sworn he just heard a voice. In his head. A thought passed through his mind, and he looked at the girl again.

—*Yeah. It's me, dumb ass. The girl who's the poster girl for Halloweentown.*

Before he had time to gasp, say something, or widen his eyes any more, Nick sat next to him and coughed loudly.

"Thanks to Nick working in the healing rooms and Sam in the field yesterday, we have secured Scott," the gray-haired man explained, gesturing welcomingly at Scott. "Artam believes that he will do great things for our world. He has told me much about Mr. Faranger's curse as a Mediator, and we may just be able to win now."

"Who is he, really?" asked the girl with purple hair. "He doesn't seem to have a clue what's going on."

"Why don't you have a look inside his head and find out for yourself, Claire?" the man challenged her politely.

Claire shifted slightly in her seat, embarrassed about something, although Scott couldn't imagine what.

"For some reason, I can project plenty of things *to* him, but getting information out of him is a little harder," she mumbled, then asked, "Is that the advantage of being a Mediator?"

"Not the only one, Claire," the man said, holding his chin. "Although I suspect that Scott may be partially resistant to your charms because he's only *half*-Armadronian."

He continued, his eyes suddenly half-lidded, evaluating Scott coolly as he spoke. "Scott's real importance to us lies in the fact that he shouldn't exist. He's a Mediator *and* half-Armadronian, according to Artam. An impossibility. Or at least nothing we've ever seen before. As a Mediator, he will probably have more than one curse. That is to be expected. What we cannot yet discern is the full impact of his mixed blood on those curses. Artam has already observed some promising anomalies. Can Scott tilt the balance of power—and victory—in our favor? We believe this may be the case. And judging from how tenaciously Terminus has been pursuing our friend here, I believe Terminus thinks so, too."

Scott was getting tired of them speaking like he wasn't in the room.

"Well," Claire said, "this kid just looks like he's—"

"This *kid* has a name," Scott interrupted Claire, speaking for the first time.

"Like it matters," she retorted.

"It does. My name is Scott, and you're Claire. Now that we know each other, you can stop calling me *kid*."

Claire raised her eyebrows and whistled mockingly

Scott ignored her and pressed on. "What are your names?" he asked, pointing at the orange-haired boy and the man.

"My name's Seth," the boy grinned.

"Thaught is my name," the man said.

"That's your name too? You're both named Seth?" Scott looked confused.

Everyone busted out laughing, cutting the tension that had been building in the room.

"No," the man smiled. "Not *that*. And not *thought*. Thaught. As in T-h-a-u-g-h-t."

"Oh," Scott nodded. "Sorry."

"Alright, Scott," Thaught leaned forward and clapped his hands, effectively silencing the room. "Let's talk about what you can do for us."

THE HELP

"Say what?" Scott looked nervous.

"You asked Nick earlier how come we all have such 'cool powers,'" Thought said.

Several of the others snickered, and Scott shot a quick glare in Nick's direction.

Thought continued talking. "For many years, it has been believed that we Armadronians can access the energy within Armadron. Think, for lack of a better phrase, 'human antennae.' We suspect that each person vibrates at a slightly different frequency, so that is why the 'cool powers,' as you call them, manifest differently for each person. Without receiving energy from our planet, we would seem *normal* to you. In fact, on your planet, Scott, our powers—which we call 'curses,' by the way—do not exist.

"Scott, what makes you different than us—and different from everyone on Earth, too—is that, according to Artam, you operate on two different frequencies. This is why you are so unpredictable and powerful. One of these frequencies is from Earth, the other is from Armadron. And Artam suspects that you may also be able to tune in to the infinite frequencies in between them."

"I don't understand how that's supposed to help—"

Thought held up his hand, cutting Scott off.

"We have recently acquired intel that Terminus has synthesized a new set of 'cool powers.'"

Scott winced.

"These powers are not tethered to the energy of this planet. That means these curses are functional on Armadron *as well as on Earth*." His voice suddenly turned grave. "Terminus has created an army of people thus endowed. We are still trying to discern the full extent of his plans, but we know that his lust for power is unquenchable, and his army of upgrades gives him access to a great and dangerous level of power."

"Terminus is just one guy, right?" Scott asked. "How is he doing all this?"

"Of course, he has help. Five years ago, Terminus learned of a race of people from the planet Irri known as Conjurers. They were a mystical, peaceful people who traveled the universe, helping others. Terminus captured an entire nomadic tribe of them in one fell swoop—how he managed this is still a mystery to us. He has enslaved the minds of these people and is using them—and their magic—to do his bidding."

Scott furrowed his brows. "But isn't Artam a Conjurer?"

"Artam, the Conjurer who saved you from the Coliseum, escaped from Terminus with the help of others from his planet, and fled to Earth. They created a magical portal for him, and he arrived around your year of 1135, living there for several centuries under the name of Merlin until he felt that it was safe to return.

"Terminus wisely decided not to go after Artam because even though Terminus is immeasurably powerful here, he is still an Armadronian and cannot use his curse on any other planet," Thought explained. "That means on Earth he is weak, just like the rest of us. On the other hand, Artam is from Irri and draws his power from the Chaos Dimension, so he retains some of his magic everywhere he goes."

"So how did Sam get to me?" Scott asked, looking over at her.

Thought furrowed his brow and leaned back in his chair. "What do you mean?"

"How did she get on the cruise ship?" Scott closed his eyes, trying to remember something. "Artam told me something about a Gateway that turns into some sort of bridge, and people from Armadron traveling to Earth . . . but he said the Gateway wasn't open yet. So how did Sam get on the cruise ship?"

"Ah," Thaught smiled, "we snuck her through a portal generated by Brandon, someone Terminus captured but who is still loyal to our side and willing to risk his life for us. Brandon's curse is being able to create portals, and Terminus used him to open the way for Conjurers to travel to Earth on a mission to find and capture you. Brandon alerted us to the plan, and we were able to sneak Sam in behind them. Within hours, the Gateway from earth to Armadron opened, Brandon's portal disappeared, and she brought you back with her through the Gateway."

Scott closed his eyes. It was coming back to him, now. Brandon's portal. The operative. Sam was the operative Artam had told him about.

"There's more," Thaught said.

Scott huffed. This guy was long-winded. He was worse than Charlie.

Claire shot him a look, and Scott rolled his eyes, sitting up straighter in his chair.

"Whenever Halley's Comet is in the right orbital area, it crosses between Earth and Armadron for ten days, activating the wormhole, which we know as the Gateway. On the first seven days, the people of Earth have a one-way ticket to Armadron. On the last three days the direction of the wormhole reverses polarity, and the people of Armadron have a one-way ticket to Earth. When the Gateway reverses and opens the path from Armadron to Earth, Terminus will be ready. His army of Upgrades will be ready. And life on your planet will never be the same."

"And you're saying this whole ten-day-open-wormhole-Gateway thing has already started?" Scott asked incredulously.

"Yes. Two days ago, when you arrived from the cruise ship. The Gateway from Earth is already open. We now have roughly five days remaining until it reverses."

The room was silent for a beat; then Scott looked at Thaught.

"So you all think that I'm The One?" Scott asked.

"The One?" Thaught looked puzzled.

"Yeah, The One. Like in *The Matrix*. You know, Neo . . . The One. He stops bullets and stuff."

Seth laughed, but everyone else just squinted at Scott, trying to understand. Sam scratched her nose.

"Scott," Thought shook his head slowly, "we do not know what that means. Is that something from Earth?"

"Yeah!" Scott explained to everyone, "it's a movie. He's the guy in the prophecy, and there's this whole digital world, and he takes the blue pill and goes there and saves everyone because he's different."

"Yeah, except . . ." Nick chuckled, "you're more like the help."

They all laughed, and even Thought couldn't help himself. He still covered his mouth out of respect though and pretended to cough.

Scott frowned, then turned to Thought, addressing him directly.

"Alright. So where's this Halley's Comet Gateway? What's the plan? And how do we stop this guy?"

"You're on board?!" Seth asked.

"Sorta," Scott shrugged his shoulders. "I don't really know. All I know is that it sounds like I still have to wait awhile to go home. And you *still* haven't actually told me why you need my help."

He's just the help, Nick mouthed to Seth, and a brief spark went through Seth's hair as he chuckled.

Claire frowned and pointedly ignored them. Scott followed her gaze and just waited for a response.

"Scott," Thought began, "as I said earlier, the Gateway to Earth will appear on our side when it is operational in five days, in a different location from the one that you came out of. We do not know where yet, and we do not know *exactly* when. As for the plan, we need to kill Terminus. It's that simple. If Terminus dies, then the Conjurers are free of whatever control he has on them, and we have them on our side. That will give us the firepower that we need to go against the rest of Upgrades created by Terminus that he will use to try to kill us. We have caves like this all over Armadron, but we only have a few hundred Icranu teams to fight against these new enemies who can seemingly use their curses with no consequences."

"Consequences? So you guys get seizures too?" Scott looked around the room.

Everyone nodded.

"Scott," Thought said softly, "I told you that we believe Armadronians are like antennas. If you channel too much power through yourself at one time, you'll die. That's why we call it a curse. Even for you."

—How did you not figure that out already? We've been talking for nearly an hour.

Scott jumped up at the mental intrusion and looked over at Claire to see her looking at him.

—Stop doing that! He thought back.

Claire's head snapped back abruptly like she'd been smacked. She toppled and fell out of her chair without crying out.

She got back up and sat down in the chair again, looking bewildered.

Everyone looked at Scott. Seth raised his eyebrows, and Sam pursed her lips.

"Um . . . what just happened?" Scott asked. "Did I do that to her?"

"Yes." Thought answered shortly.

Scott slowly nodded his head, staring down at his hands. They were getting slightly bigger, and his vision was pulsing again.

He took a deep breath and relaxed, willing his eyes to become blue again and his hands to return to normal.

There was still one question that had been bugging Scott.

"Why are you and Artam the only older adults that I've seen so far?" he inquired.

"Scott," Thought said, "Armadronians are always transmitting energy from our planet. In time—by the time we reach middle age—it takes a toll. A devastating, fatal toll. We have more seizures as we get older. We wear out. Only beings such as myself, Artam, Terminus, and the remaining Conjurers under Terminus's control have the ability to endure through the ages, in myriad ways."

"Yeah, they didn't look so good to me," Scott noted, remembering the cracked fingernails and dirty hands of the Conjurers.

"That," Thought said, shaking his head sadly, "is because of Terminus. He has them hunting around the clock for us, the Icranu. Plus, he makes them dig into people's homes, sometimes literally, so he can snatch up young kids to experiment on. Many of the Conjurers are occasionally pushed past their physical limits, so seeing their veins pop or their bones snap is not uncommon."

"Oh." Scott nodded his head and swallowed back his disgust. "Terminus must have some crazy curse then. If he's that strong, I mean."

Scott reached into his pocket and felt for Jared's inhaler. It was there, safe and sound. Hopefully Jared was too. And his mom.

"He was born a Carcan, Scott," Thought explained, interrupting Scott's thoughts. "Roughly four percent of Armadronians are. No curses. Defenseless. He has managed to acquire unnatural abilities somehow. Be wary, though. He is the most vicious creature that you will ever meet, and he is the smartest opponent I have ever gone up against. And you are going to help us kill him."

13

COME ON, HIT ME!

"So what d'ya think?" Seth grinned as they walked out of the Library.

"Wow," Scott answered.

"Well, get ready for more 'wow,'" Seth laughed.

Nick, Scott, Claire, Sam, and Seth were walking toward a place in the Cavern known as the Training Grounds. They were all nearly shoulder to shoulder, with Scott in the middle next to Nick and Seth. Thaught had assigned Scott to their team, and Scott needed proper education and training. He had no experience in any kind of fighting, so the others had been instructed to run him through the basics. And with only five days until the Gateway opened in some random location on Armadron, there wasn't any time to waste.

Scott turned to Nick. "Are we gonna walk this time?"

"Yes," Nick answered quickly.

Claire glanced at Nick, and Nick met her eyes with his. Something brief passed between them, and Nick glanced away, ashamed.

"What?" she suddenly shouted and stopped walking. "You jumped him to the Library? Nick, we don't know what his curses are yet! You could have disrupted a spatial field or done serious damage to you both! What were you thinking?"

"I was thinking that since time is of the essence. I needed to get him trained—fast," he stated with authority. "We need to kill this guy."

"What do you mean, time is of the essence?" Scott cut in.

"Just because you're here doesn't mean Terminus has stopped hunting for you," Seth explained. You're safer here than on earth, but still . . ."

"I still don't understand why he thinks I'm so important."

"Terminus has been waiting a long time for a Mediator from Earth to come along. He probably thinks that with your DNA he can solve his problem," Sam interjected.

"What problem?" Scott asked.

"Terminus has created an army with a new generation of abilities—he calls them Upgrades," Sam reminded Scott. "There's a drawback, though. He can only put one upgraded ability in each person. These are physical abilities, and if a person receives more than one at a time, it will kill him."

"So this army of people, with these upgraded abilities—they're not unstoppable?" Scott asked.

"No," Sam answered. "They're not. But they're incredibly powerful. They don't have curses, like we do. They have *abilities*. There's a difference."

"But hey, as long as we can get past Terminus's Conjurers, his castle, his right-hand man, Terminus himself, and then sever his connection with the Conjurers, " Nick said dryly, "we're home free."

Sam smiled and shrugged. "Who knows, we might be able to do it. We have Scott, now."

Claire rolled her eyes.

"What's jumping?" Scott asked, trying to change the mood.

"Teleporting," Seth answered. "It's a pretty rare curse, and it's easy to mess yourself up if you get too jumpy."

They continued walking down the edge of the Cavern while Scott's brain went to work. He watched the underground city go about its everyday business. There were people everywhere doing various tasks. Planting, building new buildings, getting water, you name it. Scott spotted a merchant bazaar filled with chaos and color, and couples walking and holding hands near the edges of the Cavern. But something was still off.

"When I look at everything, sometimes things look blurry. Why is that?" Scott asked. "It's like . . . it's like some things have a haze covering them."

For some reason, everyone turned and looked at Claire. She returned the stares coolly.

"You probably just need glasses," she suggested. "Let's keep walking."

Scott didn't think so. He'd never needed glasses before. Plus, his head kind of hurt if he looked at anything shimmery for too long.

Weird.

Another question popped into his head.

"I've seen plenty of water, but no animals. What do you guys eat on Armadron?"

Everyone gave him a funny look.

"Haven't you guessed?" Claire questioned.

"Well, I've seen a lot of plants, but that's about it. And I haven't seen any supermarkets or food stores, so I dunno. Unless . . . that is, unless if you guys . . ." He stopped in the middle of his sentence and stood still. The rest of the group immediately stopped walking.

"Unless if we . . . eat our dead," Sam finished with a grim smile.

He looked at each person in the group. They all wore straight faces. This was not a joke.

"Scott, listen," Nick said, "we—"

Scott bent to the side and dry heaved. Eventually, once the disturbing images snuck in, he threw up yesterday's lunch.

"It makes a lot of sense if you think about it," Sam explained between Scott's gasps.

He stood up and wiped his mouth. Seth glanced at him, and the vomit evaporated off his shirtsleeve and off the corner of his chin. The smell was still there, though.

He took a second to look at what Seth had done, then turned back to the five people standing before him.

"So everyone on this planet is a cannibal?"

"No—"

"Yes," Nick interrupted Sam and stared at Scott. "But that's not important. We're here. Let's teach you how to fight so we can kill this bastard. We've just got a few days, and we need to focus. I'm tired of talking."

* * *

Nick was covered head to toe in metal and running straight at Scott. It wasn't exactly like he had put on a metal suit—more like the metal was an extension of his determination to hurt someone. The protective armor somehow seemed as aggressive and angry as Nick himself. It didn't follow the lines of his body, nor was it aesthetically pleasing. It clearly was designed for one purpose.

Nick's accelerated form also made the metal look twice as threatening, because his body was bigger and longer than usual. It made the armor appear sharper, too.

"Come on, Scott," Seth cheered, "let's see what you got."

Seth's voice snapped Scott back to reality. He had to fight, and he had to figure out ways to use his curse that wouldn't cause a seizure. That was the point of the training.

When Nick was ten feet away from him, Scott thrust out his hands. A thin wall of flame-colored rock protruded from the ground and hit Nick square in the chest.

He ran right through it, and the rock harmlessly smashed against his metal without a scratch, breaking into pebbles.

Scott jumped to the side, and Nick narrowly missed him.

Nick went thundering past, chuckling inside his armor.

"You have to feel the earth, Scott," Sam called as Nick ran by. "Reinforce it with your energy. Don't just stick a target out so Nick can smash through it."

There were people watching now. Hundreds of them.

"They're watching *you*, Scott," Sam said, smiling at him. "They believe in their Mediator."

Nick stopped and turned around about five feet from Scott. The metal bent around his mouth to form a crooked smile.

"That's what I thought, Scott," Nick mocked. "You don't have the stones."

"Doubt it," he lashed back.

He kicked his foot straight into the ground, and Nick was shot high into the air. He went up so high that he almost touched the ceiling of the Cavern.

Four seconds later, he started falling back down to Armadron. Right before he crashed, he moved his hands, stopping the fall abruptly. Nick just hung there in open space. His body turned toward Scott until he was levitating about two feet in midair, twenty feet away from him.

"That was a neat trick," Nick said in his metallic voice. "Got any more? You're gonna have to do better than that to kill Terminus."

They had already been at this for three hours, and Scott had lost all eight rounds so far, incurring the wrath of two seizures in the process. He grit his teeth together. Nick was toying with him.

—*Come on, Scott,* Claire projected inside his head, *you have to think! This isn't a pissing contest. How can you use your curses in the most efficient, energy-saving way?*

—*I'm trying!* he thought back to Claire, defending himself. *But he just keeps breaking everything down—wait! That's it!* Scott interrupted his own thoughts. *Break it down . . .*

"Hey, Scott," Nick taunted, "Just go run back to Mommy and Daddy. You're no good to us. I've had my curse for four years. You've had yours for four minutes. There's no competition here. You're a liability to this operation. Terminus is going to kill all of us, because of *you*."

Scott didn't respond. He was too busy concentrating. He narrowed his eyes, and the ground under Nick's levitating feet began breaking apart, then turning into the consistency of pudding. Suddenly a wave of mud rose up and, before Nick could react, it swallowed him up.

Scott felt the ground transport Nick lower and lower under the surface. Scott kept concentrating and forced Nick lower still. He could feel Nick thrashing all the way down.

Above the surface, Sam, Claire, Seth, and the rest of the onlookers were silent. They each looked at Scott and waited for his next move.

"Well," Scott said, turning toward them, "looks like round nine goes to me."

Rrrrrrrrhhhhhhh!

Scott looked at the ground, and his sonar vision went ballistic. It was Nick. A moment later he rose up out of the ground. His hands had combined with his metal to form a large drill. He landed on his feet, and his hands separated from each other as he let all the metal fall off him onto the floor of the cave.

The metal filling in one of Scott's molars vibrated violently and shot out of his mouth, carrying a thin trail of blood behind it. He yelped loudly and covered the left side of his jaw. Red-hot pain built up in his mouth.

"You need a wake-up call, Scott. You're not on safe little Earth anymore. There are no rules here. Do you know why we brought you here in the first place?" Nick scowled.

"Why?" Scott groaned, backing away as Nick strode confidently toward him. "Why the hell would you do that? Are you *insane*?"

"Because we thought that you could save us. I guess we thought wrong. All you want to do is go home, have a happy little life, and play by the rules while innocent people die. You're a coward, and you always will be."

Nick spat at Scott from twenty feet away. The spittle landed in the center of Scott's chest.

Scott yelled and kicked his foot down at the ground again. A copper-colored boulder the size of a large couch was ejected out of the ground and into the air. The boulder began to fall and, before it hit the ground, Nick struck out with his foot, nailed the center of the big rock and sent it hurtling toward Nick's face.

Nick dove to his stomach and threw his arms out. The rock harmlessly sailed above Nick's head as two smaller metal lumps rose up from the ground. He stood up and waved both arms, and the metallic boulders flew toward Scott.

Water shot from Scott's hands and made two long missiles at Nick's eyes. The water found its mark just before the metal chunks hit

Scott, and Nick howled and covered his bruised retinas. Both metal pieces crashed into each other, and Scott was gone.

Into the air.

He had crouched on top of a large ellipsoid-shaped rock just before the metal lumps thrown by Nick made impact. By manipulating the rock with a few instinctive hand gestures, Scott easily gained twenty feet, riding the rock.

Nick wiped his stinging red eyes and glared at Scott through slits.

Even while Scott was still in the air, Nick was on the attack. He willed a large piece of metal out of the soil and psychically crushed it until it was the size of a basketball.

Scott landed back on Armadron, letting the rock smash into pebbles beneath him. Nick fired a gigantic wall of sharp, dense shards of metal from the ball at unimaginable speeds, straight at Scott.

At the same time, Nick cried out and held his arm, fighting the seizure that was threatening to overtake him.

Scott couldn't react fast enough. As soon as the first shard grazed his skin, he knew that he had lost.

14

SEEING IS BELIEVING

"Thaught has finally instructed me to lift the protective field over your senses," Claire was saying.

Scott was lost in thought, mulling over the events of the afternoon. He had lost to Nick, and then Claire and Sam had sparred. As the women had been training, Nick had given Scott some pointers and even a few compliments. Now they were all done, sitting on stone chairs in a circle on the edge of the training ground, and Claire had just said something to him.

"What?" Scott said abruptly, looking at her.

"I covered them up slightly," Claire explained hastily. "I made it so that in your subconscious you didn't really believe any of this now, so that ultimately you could accept it more easily later. Thaught wanted to take this particular COA—"

"COA?" Scott asked.

"Course of action," Seth answered.

"He wanted to take this course of action," Claire repeated, "because he said it would keep you from going into shock or having a panic attack or heart attack or . . . something. If you had tried to process everything all at once it would have overloaded your senses, and your mind and body would have been compromised. We need you right now. We can't have you breaking down."

"What are you talking about?" Scott asked, rising to his feet and eyeing Claire.

"Sit down, Scott," Nick ordered. "This is going to be a lot to wrap your head around."

Scott sat back down slowly, still warily watching Claire.

Claire widened her eyes, and Scott felt a sharp ping in his forehead. He closed his eyes and quickly recovered from the pain.

When he opened his eyes again, he knew instantly why he had been having the dreams back on Earth. If anyone needed help, it was this planet—or at least these people.

Claire's legs and neck were covered with bruises, and her left pointer finger and thumb looked broken.

Sam still had a large bandage on her left leg and shoulder from where she had been shot on the cruise ship. She also had some new cuts on her arms and legs, probably from sparring with Claire.

Scott couldn't believe it. He'd thought Sam had made a full recovery, but it had just been Claire the whole time, messing with his mind for "his own safety."

Seth. He was hiding behind Claire, looking extremely nervous.

"Seth, step forward," Claire ordered him, reading Scott's mind.

Seth stepped in front of Claire.

"Scott, you now see everything as it really is, except for Seth. Prepare yourself. It will be a bit of a shock," Claire warned.

He felt another ping in his forehead. Scott blinked the dizziness away from his eyes and focused on Seth again.

The boy standing in front of him was not Seth. It was Charlie.

"Charlie! You're . . . you're *what*? You're Armadronian?"

Charlie gave a sheepish grin as Scott stared, open mouthed.

"So what happened was . . . I jumped into the water after I saw a couple Conjurers go in after you. I had no idea that you were a Mediator, or why Sam was there. I just knew something was up."

There was silence for several heartbeats. They could hear the shouts and sounds of training going on in the distance.

"So tell me, Charlie. Seth. Whoever you are," Scott finally said angrily. "How did you get to Earth if this is your home? And why did you go to school with me and become my friend?"

"Scott, I didn't go to school just to—"

"Or was that just another big coincidence in my happy-go-lucky life?" Scott crossed his arms.

"It wasn't a coincidence, Scott. I—"

"You *what*?"

"Okay, Scott. You want answers, you got 'em," Seth said, stepping into the challenge. "I am a full Armadronian. I lived on this planet until I was thirteen years old. Shortly after my thirteenth birthday, both my parents died in front of me. I was mad at the world and wanted a way out. I was secretly planning to commit suicide the next time Nick, Claire, Sam, and I went on a search-and-rescue mission together. Turns out, I found a better alternative. We found this eleven-year-old kid on the mission who could generate wormholes."

"Wormholes?" Scott repeated. "You can't come up with anything more original than that?"

Seth ignored him. "One night, he and I sneaked out of the Cavern, and I sort of bullied him into making a wormhole to get me to Earth, even though he'd never done it before. When I jumped inside, I heard a shout, and the wormhole started to close behind me. I turned around before it closed and saw the kid get taken away. Before I could catch a glimpse of who had taken him, I was whisked off."

"Okay," Scott said, shaking his head. "But that doesn't explain why you went to school with me, why you became my friend, and how you got the McEntlys to be your parents on Earth. And it doesn't explain why you lied to me. Me. Your best friend."

"What happened"—Seth took a deep breath, then continued—"when I emerged from the other end of the wormhole will explain a lot. The end of the wormhole was right in their living room. The McEntlys. Right between their couch and the TV. By a stroke of luck, they were watching TV at the time. They freaked out, turned off the TV and ran behind the couch to watch. I saw all this through my end of the wormhole."

Scott wasn't convinced.

"When I came out," Charlie continued, "it started to close slowly behind me. I remembered what Thaught had told us about Armadron. He'd always said we don't have real power, that the planet was the source of our power, we're just the antennas. Once the wormhole closed, I figured that I wouldn't be able to use my curse anymore. So I ran over to the couple and used my electricity to reform their synapses. Their new memories would tell them that I was an orphaned kid living on the streets, and that they wanted to adopt me. After I fixed the wife's memories and finished with the husband's, I lost my curse. I turned around to look at the wormhole and saw that it was closed. Then I noticed there was an envelope on the carpet next where the opening had just been."

Charlie stopped talking.

"Go on," Scott prompted.

"So," Charlie continued, "as I had arranged, the McEntlys gave me the good news that I was going to be adopted. In the meantime, I went up to a room they told me I could sleep in that night, taking the envelope with me. When I got upstairs and opened the envelope, I found a piece of paper that had two instructions: one, find Scott Faranger and protect him with your life, and two, if I protected you, there would be a time when I would need to follow you back home. I could tell from the handwriting that the note was from Thaught. Apparently, he'd figured out that I was gonna take the portal, but he didn't stop me. He used me. He didn't want anyone else to know, though. He doesn't trust anyone. Ever.

"There was only one thing to do," Seth went on. "I had to find you and befriend you. Luckily, it wasn't that hard. Turns out, you're a pretty likeable guy."

Scott smiled before he could stop himself.

"So I went to school, and my new parents paid for everything I needed. Almost immediately, I found you and we became best friends, *Step Brothers*-style. After a while, I got a visit in the dream-realm from Artam telling me to go with you on the cruise. He said that you and my team would need me in the battle to come. That's it."

There was silence for a long time. Enough time for things to feel awkward.

Scott tried to say something, but his voice was hoarse. He cleared his throat.

"I feel like I don't know you anymore, man." He shook his head glumly. "I mean . . . all of these secrets. You're like . . . I don't know you," Scott repeated.

"Au contraire. Yes, you do," Charlie insisted. "I didn't develop a fake personality on Earth. This is who I am. You saw the real deal. You and I were best friends then, so why can't we be best friends now?"

"Because you lied to me," Scott said quietly. "Over and over again."

"Yeah, but I was just waiting for the right time to tell you the truth, dude. I know you the best out of anyone on this planet. We're bros," Seth finished weakly and let the idea hang in the air.

The two sat there for over a minute.

Nick coughed and shuffled his feet, and Claire slapped him in the chest, reminding everyone that others were present for this personal conversation.

"Let's give them a minute," Claire said as she practically dragged Nick away, while Sam followed them wordlessly.

The three of them walked off, leaving the two former friends alone.

Seth looked to Scott for approval, but Scott was looking at the floor with a dead, meaningless stare.

"I understand, Scott. It looks like I only became your friend to get myself back home. Well, it was like that at first, because I was homesick as hell, but then I just didn't care anymore about Armadron. I had a good life on Earth. You and I became best friends. We did cool stuff. We went to parties, played on the soccer team, hit on girls, watched movies. Jared sort of became my little brother, too. Bro, we've hopped fences together. Remember that dumb lemonade stand we ran all summer that made zero money? Your family took me snowboarding for my first time. And we always had each other's backs. In my book, all that meant something." Seth almost whispered the last sentence.

Scott stood up. Seth followed suit.

"What's your name?" Scott asked, still avoiding eye contact.

"What?" Seth was confused.

"What's your name?" he repeated, this time looking Seth right in the eye. "They call you Seth. Is that it?"

Seth hesitated for a moment, then replied, "It's Seth. Yeah."

Scott held out his hand to shake.

"Hi, Seth. I'm Scott Faranger. I've heard so much about you."

"Oh, have you now?" Seth grinned, blinking away a few tears as he shook Scott's hand. "What have you heard?"

"Actually, Rick the Brick was just having a wonderful conversation with me about you," Scott said with a smirk.

They both laughed at that one.

"You know what?" Seth mused aloud.

"What?"

"Nick would beat the ever-livin'-crap out of Brick."

"Agreed." Scott laughed imagining the grudge match.

After a brief pause, Scott broke the silence.

"Why'd you change your name to Charlie?" Scott asked.

"I was a kid. Seemed like a fun idea at the time." Seth grinned.

"YOLO."

"You're still a kid."

"Not on this planet." Seth winked.

They both laughed again and then hugged it out.

Dropping the embrace, the two friends stepped back and looked at each other, and something in Scott's mind finally settled.

"All right, let's do this," Scott said, nodding. "Let's get this over with."

"Wait . . . what? Just like that?"

"Yup. Just like that. We've got five days, right? Until the Gateway reverses?"

"So you're all in?"

"You guys need to teach me what I need to know, and I'll learn what I can. Like you've all been saying," Scott stared at him, unwavering.

Seth grabbed him by the shoulders, grinning from ear to ear. "That's what I'm talking about, Faranger."

He released Scott and turned around.

"Hey guys!" Seth called everyone over. "Let's go!"

Nick, Claire, and Sam appeared almost immediately—they hadn't gone far—and Scott spoke to them once they were all in a circle.

"I've read books about kids my age getting superpowers, traveling to other worlds, to other dimensions—and whining about it. I never understood it. I always thought that if I got a choice, I'd choose the superpowers and say good-bye to my family. But when it really happened—like, *really* happened—it's a tougher choice than you'd think, and I didn't want to be here. But I *am* here. And now I know what I have to do, what I was maybe even born to do. I'm going to do all that I can to save this planet with you guys so that I can get back to my mom and my brother. I'm done talking about the past. I'm done feeling sorry for myself. I could have stayed on Earth if I really wanted to, even if I probably would have gotten shot."

Nick chuckled at that, and it was Sam's turn to glare at him.

"I made a choice, and I'm sticking by that choice," Scott continued, ignoring Nick. "This isn't a time for talking anymore, it's a time for action."

Everyone looked at him in amazement.

Nick brought his hands together, trying to start a sarcastic slow-clap.

Seth Accelerated just his hands and eyes. He rubbed his hands in his own hair and pointed at Nick.

A thin, white bolt of lightning shot toward the middle of Nick's close-cropped black hair. The hair collected the charge and *poofed*, making Nick look like he had a mohawk.

Nick looked up at his hair with a frown, and Sam giggled.

Scott's stomach grumbled.

Everyone laughed. Seth was holding his gut and almost falling over, tears streaming down his face. Even Claire was doubled over with laughter. Once they all finally stopped laughing, it was Sam's turn to address the group.

"Let's go get some food!"

15

KNOWLEDGE IS LIVING

They'd been walking for about half an hour when Scott spotted a boy totally immersed in blue fire. It seemed as if the intense flame had no effect on him, which was probably the case. Scott averted his eyes quickly, as the boy didn't appear to be wearing any clothes, almost as if the fire had *become* his clothes.

Farther ahead Scott saw six kids, four boys and two girls, who each looked to be about nine years old. They were all wearing ragged clothes and no shoes. He looked down at what he was wearing in contrast. He then looked around at Sam, Seth, Nick, and Claire.

"Are clothes hard to get here? How come we get decent clothes but those kids don't? And what does the symbol mean?"

For the first time since Claire had lifted the protective filter on his eyes and mind, Scott took a good look at everyone's clothing. They were each wearing some form of sleeveless or short-sleeved shirt and black, tan, or white shorts. Each of their shirts had a strange symbol that looked like a severely curved line with two circles at each end. The line was cut in the middle by a turned hourglass. They also each wore black shoes that seemed to be made from some form of enhanced rubber.

"We are all wearing the same symbol because it means we are Icranu. Protectors of this barbaric world," Claire explained. "As for the clothes, they are not hard to come by if you know the right people with the right curses."

Scott nodded and resumed looking at the six children moving up ahead. The children were playing a game of keep-away from the child in the center. The boy in the center was helplessly trying to get the ball as the five other children kicked it around him. He noticed a few things about the game. For one, the ball was made entirely of ice and black dirt. Secondly, one of the boys on the outside would kick the ball toward the boy in the center, but when the boy in the center would dive for the ball, the boy on the outside would twitch his hand and the ball would change its path toward another person on the outside. Thirdly, one of the girls on the outside would close her eyes if the ball got too close to the boy in the center, and the boy in the center would move very slowly. It looked like he moved in slow motion or like he was stuck in Jell-O.

Scott smiled. These games were probably normal for Armadronians, just like soccer was normal for humans. He was about to turn away and suggest that they keep heading toward some food when the boy in the center made a move. He stretched his hand out toward the ball, and red, pulsating lightning shot out of his fingers. The ball burst into fragments, and ice rained everywhere. The boy cheered.

One of the boys on the outside was not so happy.

"You cheated!" he screamed.

"No I didn't!" the boy argued.

"Yes, you diiiiiid!" the boy on the outside of the circle bellowed back.

His voice sounded much louder and more amplified than a normal voice. The boy in the center was thrown off his feet and landed on the dirt five feet away on his head.

"Jon, stop it!" one of the girls cried in vain.

Jon looked over at the girl but acted as if he hadn't heard her. He waited for the boy with the slightly bleeding forehead to pick himself up.

"Not so hot now, huh, Andrew?" Jon mocked.

Jon went to clap his hands together, but he never got that far: his hands stopped just before they touched, and they seemed to move on their own accord. They intertwined behind his back, and he fell to his knees. He was staring down open mouthed at his body.

"That's quite enough, Jon," Claire told him.

Claire was standing right next to the boy when Seth, Nick, Sam, and Scott were all still about thirty feet away. Scott couldn't believe it.

"How did she do that?" he asked Seth.

"Claire either made us all forget that she moved over there, or she tricked our minds into not seeing her," Seth explained. "Or something."

"Wow," Scott said, breathless.

"But I didn't start it!" Jon argued with Claire.

"You were sure going to finish it, though," she said, glaring at him.

The boy lowered his head.

"Andrew, will you please come over here," Claire said, more as an order, not a question.

Andrew slowly made his way over to them.

Seth, Sam, and Nick watched in silence. Scott looked at each one of them in turn.

This is amazing, he thought.

—*No, Scott,* Claire answered his thought, *it's normal.*

"Jon, apologize," Claire commanded out loud.

"Sorry," Jon mumbled.

"Not good enough. Look Andrew in the eye and apologize," she ordered.

Jon lifted his head and sighed. "I'm sorry for hitting you with a sound wave, and I'm sorry for calling you a cheater."

"It's okay." Andrew shrugged.

"Now go on and see a plant grower," Claire told the kids. "You all look tired, like you could use something quick to eat."

With that, the kids dispersed, and Claire walked back to the group.

"Why aren't any of their parents around? Do they just let their kids roam free?" Scott asked as Claire neared them. "They're nuts."

"No, Scott," Sam answered. "Remember? Most adults don't live to be that old with Terminus running the show. We grow up on our own usually from around age twelve."

"No way. That's crazy," Scott huffed. "You mean you get your own food and your own clothing when you're that young? And fend for yourself? With Terminus on the loose and abducting people?"

"Yes," Nick answered dryly. "Now do you want to eat, or not?"

Scott's stomach chose that moment to grumble again.

"It's like that thing has a mind of its own," Sam joked.

Nick started walking again, and everyone followed behind him.

"Do you guys know what all the curses are?" Scott questioned.

"No," Sam told him. "Just the most well-known. There are hundreds more."

"Hundreds?"

"Yeah," Sam explained. "More than eighty percent that we encounter are low-level, though."

"Low-level?" Scott repeated.

"Yeah," Seth interjected, "like having a faster metabolism, way better hearing, shapeshifting into one thing, having camouflage, resistance to temperature spikes, growing horns, or some other weird stuff, blah blah blah."

They walked for a while, deeper into the Cavern. It seemed to stretch on forever, and once again, wherever Scott looked he saw life. People of all different colors, shapes, and sizes. Scott decided the architecture was just as diverse as they passed what looked like an old West trading post, adobe buildings sporting Southwestern décor, and ornate manicured gardens out of an English storybook. Sometimes the group found themselves navigating through crowds of people, and when they did Scott could hear a multitude of languages and dialects.

"There are so many different ethnicities here," Scott said. "Do you guys not have race wars, World Wars, Hitler, that sort of thing?"

Everyone looked confused, except for Seth.

"Dude, we've got Terminus. The good news is, nothing unites people more than a common enemy," Seth answered for everyone.

They kept walking, trudging over loosely packed dirt as they got further into the Cavern.

"There are so many languages here. Why is it you guys all speak English?"

"Because, Scott," Claire replied, "English is the universal language. As far as we can tell, every planet speaks English. We speak other languages too, but English is the most common."

"Here we are!" Sam cheered.

Scott looked at their surroundings. In front of them were miles and miles of plants and farmland. There were hundreds of people scattered throughout the endless fields, some harvesting plants, others causing new stalks to grow by merely waving their hands. Still others were shooting water out of their hands and coating crops of plants with mist.

They were still in the Cavern, though. The rock ceiling loomed high above them, blocking out the dark skies and purple lightning Scott had seen through the roof of the Coliseum.

"I just thought of something," Scott stated.

"That happens sometimes," Nick responded.

"Do you always have to—"

"Interrupt?" Nick said as he grinned at Scott.

"Yeah, I'm ignoring you," Scott said good-naturedly.

Nick didn't know how to react to this. Scott could act like a little prick, but sometimes the kid was alright. *He bounces back quick,* Nick silently admitted.

—*Good,* Claire agreed, mentally eavesdropping. *Because we need him.*

—*Claire,* Nick thought, agitated, *what did I say about getting inside my head without—*

—*Okay, okay, I'm out.*

"How can those people and I generate water?" Scott said, bringing Nick and Claire back to the present.

It was Seth who answered. "All atoms are made up of the smallest particles known as quarks. Armadronians can manipulate the quarks and create certain energy. Our atmosphere is mostly nitrogen, but that doesn't really matter because we're channeling this stuff by using the planet's energy."

"How?" Scott was genuinely perplexed.

"Quarks are so small that they don't obey the laws of physics," Seth explained.

Scott was still confused.

"Basically, if you think it, you can do it," Nick explained gruffly, cutting into the conversation.

Sam rolled her eyes. Nick was always so straight to the point.

They all stopped talking and walked toward the plants again.

Almost all the plants that Scott saw in the fields were unfamiliar to him. Most of them had bright, vibrant colors that were very appealing to the eye.

"Let's go!" Sam gave Scott a little push from behind.

Before he knew what was happening, he was immersed in the exotic world of plants. Everyone was explaining all the different varieties and how they tasted, and he could hardly keep up.

"That's a Scranton plant." Nick pointed out a light-blue plant that was bearing large, dark-orange banana-looking fruit. "The Scranton seeds taste really good but have a sour aftertaste. They're good if you mix a Bixtoan plant with them. Also any plant in here instantly fills you up. I don't know how the overgrows do it, but it saves time. All you have to do is eat the whole thing."

Scott pulled a Scranton seed off the plant and almost dropped it. It was *heavy*.

He took a bite and almost sighed in relief. It had the crunchiness of a crunch bar, but the softness of a banana.

His face suddenly squeezed up like it was in a vice, and his eyes became intensely dry.

Ohmygodthisissour! his brain screamed. *Water!!!*

—Use your curse, he heard Claire say inside his mind.

Without any time to think, he put his right hand up to his mouth and thought of having a mouthful of water. He got one.

Water shot out of his hand like a fire hose. He was thrown backward about five feet, his hand still streaming water.

—*Stop it,* Claire told him.

Scott concentrated on his hand and successfully shut off the flow of water.

His sonar vision was going ballistic though, because he had just accidentally Accelerated.

"There you go!" Nick grinned at Scott, who was almost completely drenched. "Are you full?"

Scott stood up, his jaw aching, and looked at Claire. He Decelerated, returning to normal almost immediately.

"Thanks," he told her.

—*No problem,* he heard in his head.

"What are you thanking her for?" Nick asked.

"She told me to use my power," Scott answered.

"Yeah, she was trying to teach you," Sam cut in. "Most infants on Armadron take years to master their curses, but we don't have that long for you—"

"She just called you an infant," Seth joked.

Scott smiled good-naturedly and motioned for Sam to continue.

"Still, we wanted to teach you control. Your body was full of adrenaline just now. That makes it easier for you to access your curse, but harder to use it in small portions. You could have just blown your head clean off if you activated your curse to your full potential."

"That would have sucked," Seth added. "And I'm not eating you, no matter how hungry I get!"

"Speaking of food, now the rest of us gotta eat," Nick concluded, bored with their exchange. "I'm hungry too."

CANNIBALS

They were seated on a wooden bench in a big smelly hut. Around them were perhaps a dozen other people in various seating areas in the room.

A big man, about half the size of a sumo wrestler and dressed in dirty, worn-out clothes, emerged from a room toward the back and headed their way. On Earth, Scott would have put him at about forty years old.

As the man drew nearer, Scott could smell him. He had an overpowering stench that reminded him of pigs.

"Ernie! How goes it with the kids?" Nick stood up and the two shared a quick hug.

"They're alright. Tommy's a little crazy, though. Just got the wind curse. The wife's doin' alright too," Ernie looked at Scott. "Who's your friend?"

Scott got the sense Ernie wasn't too pleased to see him.

"Joseph," Nick lied easily.

"Huh," the big man huffed. He kept staring at Scott. "You ain't from around these parts, are ya, Joseph?"

Nick's eyes pleaded with Scott from behind Ernie's back.

"What makes you say that?" Scott asked, faking confidence.

"You ain't got no scars, boy," Ernie accused. "You ain't been through nothin'."

"He lives in the Balrean Village. The one on the Sea of Sand on the other side of the world," Nick cut in. "He's part of a clan of

Sandboarders. They don't fight each other," he lied further. "Peaceful meditation and all that crap."

"I see." Ernie eyed Scott a moment longer. Suddenly he shrugged and turned to the others. "So what'll it be, kids?"

He took out a yellow notepad and a thing that looked similar to a pen. He smiled at them.

Scott looked around, completely baffled. The man's personality had just changed like the wind!

"I'll have some thigh fat. Rare," Sam answered Ernie.

"Can I get the bicep muscle with about eight percent of fat? Raw," Nick spoke from behind Ernie.

"And I'll have some buttocks fat this time, also raw. With some Hevxita soup, please," Claire added.

Ernie wrote it all down, then looked at Scott.

"And what do you want?" he asked.

"Uh . . . I already ate," Scott answered sheepishly. He felt like he was going to throw up.

"Okay." Ernie turned to Seth. "What about you?"

"I'm a vegetarian," Seth answered. "Could I just have some Hevxita soup and some Nammionbal seeds, cooked lightly?"

"Sure. I'll have it all ready in a coupla minutes."

Ernie walked away, and Nick sat on the bench next to Scott. Claire, Seth, and Sam were seated on the opposite side.

"Nick, why did we have to lie to Ernie?" Scott asked.

"Outside the walls of the Cavern, Armadron's a savage place. We're less than a mile from the entrance right now. Maybe it's Ernie, maybe he's a shape-shifter or something. Anyone could be. It's only safe to trust yourself," Nick said in a hushed voice.

"Rriight," Scott nodded. "So how come we haven't seen any other Icranu like us?"

"There are hundreds of teams of protectors all around Armadron. Probably thousands. We're a secret order dedicated to preserving this planet and stopping Terminus. We formed four years ago. You'll see more of us soon." Nick's brows furrowed. "Do you remember Thaught, the man in the Library?"

"Naaaah, I forgot," Scott answered sarcastically. He was still a little shaken from hearing his friends order lunch. It felt good messing with Nick.

"He and Artam are the heads of our order," Nick finished proudly.

"So they tell you to go on missions and *everything*?" Scott said with mocking wide-eyed wonder.

Nick looked like he wanted to punch him. He almost did.

"Yes," Claire answered seriously, cutting in. "And our next mission is to get you to the first checkpoint in the route that Thaught gave us."

"Okay, then I think I'm ready," Scott said energetically. "I mean, it's been like a day, right? I'm freakin' set to go!"

Everyone laughed.

"You still have to take on the Path of Ascension," Seth told him. "It's what every Icranu has to do before he or she becomes a member. You have to go to the Infinite Cave and face your demons. Once you're done with that, we can get started."

"Path of Ascension?" Scott threw his hands up. "Can't we just skip it? I thought we had less than five days left. Now you're telling me about some frat-boy initiation thing?"

As often happened when Scott made Earth-references, everyone except for Seth looked confused.

"Yes," Seth answered for all of them. "You gotta do it, man. We all did. Everyone does. No one is going to rally behind you if you don't go through with this. We need the other Icranu on our side."

—*Quiet!* Claire's voice hissed inside their heads.

"Here's your food!" Ernie was suddenly beside them, setting four trays of food on the table. "Enjoy!" He clapped his hands together merrily and left them.

Nick took his raw bicep muscle from the tray and held it out to Seth. Sam and Claire did the same with their thigh fat and buttocks fat.

Scott stared at the plates and was about to say something else when Seth rubbed his hands together faster than normal.

Smoke started to come out of his hands, and Seth blew it away. He touched the bicep muscle and the thigh fat with his hands and closed his eyes. The air around the food looked like it was shimmering. Slowly, the pieces of meat started to turn golden brown from the inside out. As soon as the golden-brown color reached the edge of the bicep, Nick tugged it out of Seth's hand, who didn't seem to notice.

"Thanks," Nick said between bites.

"Anytime," Seth answered.

Sam waited a lot longer. She waited until the large chunk of thigh fat turned completely brown, and then took it out of his hand.

"Thank you, Seth," Sam said, winking at him.

"You're welcome." Seth blushed awkwardly.

What? Does she do that to all the guys? Scott wondered.

Sam started eating immediately, even before Claire handed Seth her piece. The funny thing was that as soon as their meat was cooked, it didn't make smoke and it didn't look hot. Still, when Nick bit into his piece, he mumbled something about it being a little fiery on the outside.

"Could you please implode the heat to brown on the outside but golden brown on the inside?" Claire asked Seth politely.

"Sure."

Seth held the piece of buttocks in his left hand while he flexed his right. The right hand instantly was covered with red fire. He made a slight pushing motion with his hand, and the meat was covered in flames. Then Seth curled his right hand into a fist, and the fire seemed to burn inward through the meat, without actually catching it on fire. A couple seconds later, Seth closed his eyes and there was a slight hissing sound that came from inside the freshly cooked buttocks meat.

Nick and Sam had not looked up through this entire process. Claire started eating as soon as she said thank you.

"That was actually pretty awesome!" Scott cheered loudly.

"Thanks. It's a little trick I—"

"Shut up, both of you. Don't draw attention to yourselves," Nick interrupted Seth and glared at Scott.

"Sorry," Scott whispered sarcastically. "I'll try to not exist."

"I'll help," Nick growled between chews.

Everyone ate silently for a while until Scott asked another question.

"What do you guys do?"

Everyone at the table paused and looked at each other.

"We are Protectors," Sam answered, confusion creeping into her voice regarding Scott's question. "We are Icranu."

"Nooooo." Scott almost chuckled. "I know that part. What I mean is . . . what are your curses?"

"Oh!" Seth laughed.

Nick, Claire, and Sam smiled.

"You'll find out," Nick replied.

"What? Come on!"

"Scott," Sam explained, "your curse is highly coveted. Never tell anyone the extent of your true potential. With every curse that has ever existed, there is a way to beat it with another one. Knowledge is power. Protect the true nature of the exact way that your curse works."

"Sure, I guess. So what did Ernie mean when he said that his son just got the wind curse?" Scott questioned.

"That," Seth said between slurps of his soup, "I can answer. Elemental-type curses—like what Nick and I have—are usually the most powerful, and the most dangerous. People like Nick and me got our curses around the same time that you did. We went through qualiph—Armadronian puberty—and got them. Focal curses, like what Claire and Sam have, are inherited when you're born, but that's dangerous too, and babies often don't survive because they levitate and fall, or they die by telekinetically lifting something heavy on top of themselves."

Seth paused long enough to swallow another spoonful of soup, then added, "And Conjurers like Artam get their curses after their parents die, because their power is inherited to them magically."

"Alright," Ernie said as he came to a stop at their table, "time to pay. I will take exchanges or favors, as per usual, unless if any of you are lookin' for a job."

Scott realized with a start that Armadronians didn't have any sort of money. They were still using the barter system, and he didn't have much to trade. He suddenly felt the weight of his dead cell phone in his pocket, along with Jared's blue inhaler.

Seth was doing something, though, so he turned to watch with the others.

He had his elbows on the table and was cupping his hands together, holding a large imaginary ball. Sparks were coming out of his hands that made Scott's hair stand on end. After about five seconds a blue ball of electricity filled up the space between Seth's hands. His brow furrowed in concentration, and the ball got considerably smaller. Then Seth dropped his left hand, and the energy, about the size of a golf ball, levitated less than an inch above his right palm.

Ernie stood staring in amazement.

"This will power your restaurant for one year," Seth told Ernie.

Seth got up and walked over to the back room. He came back about ten seconds later without the ball.

"Where's the ball?" Ernie asked, bewildered.

"I put it under your power box. Don't worry," Seth added, seeing Ernie's terrified face. "It won't release all the electricity at once. I made it so that it only releases electricity into the box when it's needed."

"Alright!" Ernie cheered. "I guess that pays for all you guys! That's a hell of a lot of energ—"

He made a gagging sound, and a lazy stream of blood leaked out of his nose. He wiped at it, blurted, "Excuse me for a moment," and rushed into the back room.

"We're leaving," Claire told everyone suddenly.

"But I'm not done," Nick whined, still holding his nearly-finished meat.

She got up quickly and power-walked out the door. The group followed behind her, with Nick begrudgingly in tow.

Scott took a moment to look behind him before they left. His gaze caught the eye of a woman in the restaurant who was staring at something out of his line of sight.

Scott Accelerated, activating only his eyes. He focused and manipulated his sonar vision until he could clearly see the image reflected in her eyes. He took in a terrible sight.

He saw Ernie reflected in the eye of the woman. He was lying on his back in the kitchen without moving. There was a pool of blood surrounding his face.

"Come on, Scott!" Nick called from outside.

Scott left the restaurant and caught up with the group. As soon as he was with them, they all switched to a fast jog. Once they were hidden deep in the plant fields, they stopped.

"He died in the back room," Claire told them sadly. "I felt his life force crack at the table, his brain popped, and his nose started bleeding." She shook her head.

"Why did we leave, though? We didn't do anything!" Scott cried. "And we could have gotten someone to help!"

"No one could have saved him. And as for getting the hell out of here, we didn't do anything, sure, but no one knows that," Nick pointed out.

"Think about it, Scott," Seth added. "I pull out a ball of intense electrical energy and Ernie dies less than a second later. How might that look to people? Look, Nick knows Ernie's son; the whole thing sucks. Believe me. But we've got more important things to worry about, like a freakin' world catastrophe in just a few days."

"Yeah, I guess it could look bad," Scott admitted slowly, thinking it through.

"Yeah. Not only that, but when he died, I had a vision of him falling on the cooler. He broke it," Claire told them.

Nick and Sam both groaned in unison.

"What!" Scott shouted, incredulous. "You're talking about a cooler when—"

"That's a shame—"

"So much damaged meat—"

"When a man just died?!" Scott finished his sentence.

They all looked at Scott. That's when it dawned on him.

"Wait. People are . . . gonna . . . eat him?" Scott felt dizzy.

"Yes," Claire answered. "Every person matters."

"We have to provide for each other, Scott," Sam said.

He fell on his side before anyone could reach him and threw up for the second time on Armadron.

"I'd say he's ready for the Infinite Cave," Nick said, grinning, in between Scott's heaves.

17

THE INFINITE CAVE

"Is this the way in and out of the Cavern?" Scott asked, looking ahead.

They were standing inside the Cavern on the familiar hard-packed black soil. About half a mile in front of them, the vast walls and ceiling that had surrounded Scott since he arrived in the Cavern came to an end. Jagged rock on both sides formed a gigantic eerie doorway. Beyond the opening, Scott could see only mist.

"I don't get it. That's a big entrance. What's stopping Terminus from coming in here and annihilating everyone?" Scott asked.

"What's stopping Terminus from entering Cavern Pass?" Seth said. "The Invisible Telemine Blockade."

"The Invisible what now?"

"The Invisible Telemine Blockade," Nick answered impatiently. "Telemines are little mines that teleport you to a different part of Armadron. Sometimes they can teleport you through a wall and the result will kill you. Other times you are teleported thousands of miles away. Occasionally you're teleported only a few feet from where you started. They're remnants of ancient tech from a time when Armadron used to be a thriving planet."

"How many of them are there?" Scott asked next.

"Thousands. Hundreds of thousands," Sam answered. "They're invisible, too, so stay close."

She began walking. Claire fell in step behind her, and Nick pushed Scott in front of him. Seth brought up the rear.

"I'm getting a strong World-War-Two-landmines vibe, Charlie," Scott muttered nervously.

"Me, too," Seth agreed.

"His name is Seth," Nick corrected Scott. "And stop the Earth-talk. Focus."

Seth rolled his eyes.

Soon they reached the beginning of the mist. As they were about to go through, a boy stepped toward them from the side.

He was a younger kid, maybe Jared's age. He had long brown hair with a tiny patch of white on the top of his head.

"May I help you?" the boy asked pleasantly.

"Yes." It was Sam who answered. "It's been a couple months since we left . . . could you be our guide, please?"

"Sure. That's what I'm here for."

The boy took up the lead, and they fell in line behind him.

"I can't read his mind," Claire whispered to Sam, nodding toward their pint-sized leader. "I don't know about this. Are you using your curse right now, Sam?"

"No, I'm not," Sam frowned. "Should I be?"

"Aww," Nick crooned to Claire, overhearing. "You scared that he's smarter than you?"

"No, I'm scared that he's—"

"Come along, you're falling behind," the boy called back to them.

They were almost through the mist when Scott heard a very light ping somewhere in the distance.

"What was that?" Nick asked.

"Probably someone stepping on a mine," the boy answered nonchalantly.

—*I don't like this, guys,* Claire projected her thought to the team.

They walked about ten more steps and the boy stopped.

"What are you doing?" Sam said apprehensively.

The boy leaped to one side, and the ping that Scott heard earlier now sounded like a hundred angry bees.

—*They're poachers! Duck!* Claire mentally shouted.

Scott had just enough time to duck before something flew over his head. Surprisingly, he recognized it. It had three large fruits attached to three strings, all joined at the center with one string larger than the other two. It was a bola, and there were a lot more hurtling their way, spinning around and around like propeller blades on an airplane.

As Scott lay on the dirt, he watched Claire, who was now at the front of the line. She stood up and threw her arms out. A thick wall of shimmering energy wrapped itself like a cocoon around the team.

Scott gazed at it in admiration.

—*It's a force field,* the voice of Claire echoed throughout his mind. *It'll stop the bo—*

Three bolas came out of the mist and went right through her force field.

The first one wrapped itself around her feet before she could move. The second came from the side and tethered her arms. Even before Claire dropped to the ground, a third shot out of the mist and violently coiled around her neck. One of the fruits at the end of the bola hit Claire in the face with a sharp crack. She dropped to the ground, completely knocked out and immobilized.

For a second, the bolas stopped.

"They're Carcan fruits!" Nick bellowed. "Everyone, stand next to me!"

Seth ran next to Scott, and they both stopped when they reached Nick, Sam, and Claire, who was now draped across Nick's shoulders.

Scott heard what sounded like hundreds of angry bees again. More bolas were coming. A hell of a lot more.

"What do we do?" Seth screamed.

"We stay together and step on a telemine," Nick answered calmly.

"What?! That could teleport us anywhere! We could wind up in Terminus's castle for all we know!" Sam cried.

"Or dead!" Seth added.

Scott could hear the bolas getting closer.

"Ummm, guys," he said.

Nick repositioned Claire on the top of his left shoulder.

"We'll be dead if we stay here! We gotta go! Now!" Nick yelled.

"You're not the team leader!" Seth argued.

"Claire's out cold, so, yeah, I am!"

"There's no time!" Sam screamed.

The bolas were rocketing toward them, now less than forty feet away. Sam reached for Seth's hand, and Seth squeezed it nervously. Nick stood in front of everyone and threw up a ten-foot high wall of metal. Seth put a hand on his shoulder.

"You guys run! I'll hold them ba—"

Nick's hero speech was shoved back into his throat. He, along with Seth, Sam, Claire, and Scott, were thrown about ten feet sideways. Scott instinctively grabbed Sam's other hand. Just before they crashed against the jagged surface of the Cavern wall, they all vanished into thin air.

* * *

It was like being whipped around and around in an endless tornado.

Seth tried to hold on to Sam's hand, but he just couldn't anymore. He let go and immediately put both hands on Nick's shoulders.

Scott felt as if his face would peel from his body at any second. He tried to scream, but his throat felt like it was on fire. He wasn't sure if his eyes were open or not. He saw only darkness.

He reached out and brushed against someone's hands. He reached for them again and was whipped around by the vortex. Scott's body accidentally knocked the hands aside, and he reached for them blindly. He didn't find the hands, but he did find what felt like a metal-made elbow or a shoulder. It had to be Nick in his armor again.

Just at that second, everything halted.

Realizing his eyes were shut, he immediately opened them. The first thing he noticed was a sense of déjà vu. He was lying on hard-packed pure-black dirt. The sky was also black and streaked with bright-purple lightning. Scott had seen this when he had first entered Armadron with Sam.

He stood up and looked around. Nick was less than two feet away from him. His body was indeed now covered with metal, and he was buried up to his shoulders in the black soil upside down.

Just as Scott started to assume the worst, Nick's body gave a little kick.

He quickly stepped over to Nick and clawed at the dirt with his bare hands. It barely gave way, it was too hard! Nick would run out of air and die if Scott didn't do something. Already Nick's feet were lashing back and forth.

Scott would have laughed if the situation weren't so desperate.

What can I do? he thought.

—*You can grow some balls and use your curses!*

—*What?! Claire? Is that you?* Scott looked around but didn't see her.

—*Yes. Focus. Save Nick.*

He stopped looking for Claire and concentrated on the soil in front of him. He willed it to move, but it didn't budge. Nick's feet stopped kicking.

"Noooooooo!"

Scott Accelerated and the soil blasted Nick into the air with a loud *boom*!

The metal ripped off his body, and he flew like a rag doll. He went about a hundred feet upward and began to fall back down.

He still wasn't waking up. Nick was going to fall on his head in the small crater that Scott had just created.

Without even thinking, Scott shot out his hands. The air as far around as Scott could see fizzed, and the crater rapidly filled with water. Nick splashed into the newly made pool and came up gasping for breath.

"Are you okay, Nick?" Scott called to him, coughing. It suddenly was a little hard to breathe.

"Help! Help!" Nick was thrashing around, terrified.

"Nick, just swim!" Scott yelled.

"I can't!" he screamed, kicking his arms and splashing in a completely counterproductive way.

—*Scott,* Claire thought to him, *Armadronians don't have hybrid lungs like you. We can't really hold our breath, and our pores are used to just separating oxygen from the abundant nitrogen in the air.*

—*Ohhhhh,* he thought, *my bad.*

Instinctively, Scott raised his hand and water surrounded Nick in a bubble and deposited him out of the crater, splashing everywhere.

"Did you do this?" Nick asked incredulously once he stood up, looking back at the crater filled with water.

Scott nodded his head.

Scott's vision went black on the edges, and he would have fallen to his knees if Nick hadn't caught him.

"You okay?" Nick looked Scott in the eye.

"Uugggh . . . yeah," Scott replied dizzily. "I feel like a pile of crap."

"Hmmm." Nick pursed his lips. "You've been using too many of your various curses. I think you should rest for a minute while I figure this out."

"'Kay."

Nick flicked his eyes up behind Scott and said something. Scott was too tired to turn around, so he just closed his eyes and listened to what was going on. After a couple seconds Claire sighed and said, "Thank you."

Scott groaned and painfully turned around. He was too curious not to want to see what was happening behind him.

Nick had an arm under Claire, who was lightly rubbing her neck, and she was leaning on him while they walked toward Scott. She didn't look too good. Sam was behind them holding the three sets of bolas that had attacked Claire.

As the three of them reached Scott, he saw the dark-purple marks and the tortured, raw skin on Claire's neck, arms, and legs where the bolas had been. Each mark looked painful. Coupled with her left pointer finger and thumb that she had apparently broken a while ago, she looked like a mess.

"How are you feeling, Scott? Nick just told us what you did. Are you okay?" Sam asked kindly.

"I'm good."

"He's gone," Claire said in a deadpan voice, looking at the ground.

"What d'ya mean, gone?" Nick was baffled.

"I can't sense Seth's mind anywhere. He's either gone or in a very powerful place that's blocking my curse."

"What?" Sam cried. "I thought he stepped on the same telemine that we did! He has to be near us!"

"Not necessarily," Claire muttered, then spoke louder. "Were any of you holding on to Seth when we were transported?"

Suddenly Claire flinched, and her eyes turned completely white as she dropped to her knees. Nick rushed over to her and put his arms around her. Claire thrashed wildly about, muttering random things. She didn't react to Nick's touch. She didn't seem to see any of them anymore either; it was like she was in a whole different place now.

"Sam," Nick half yelled between Claire's spasms, "do you think you should turn her power off? This looks like a powerful one. It might hurt her."

"No," Sam answered breathlessly. "No. She needs to do this. Let the vision play out. It might help us find Seth—and maybe it'll show us something about the next few days."

"Easy for you to say," Nick muttered as Claire continued to twist and throw her arms around.

Scott took an involuntary step back. *Is this what my seizures look like?* he wondered. *This is . . . it's horrible.*

Nick gritted his teeth and kept holding on to Claire as she twisted around like a snake. She moved in every direction, her spine looking like it wanted to snap. She Accelerated, her red eyes burning with the crazy intensity of a supernova.

Nick Accelerated in response and they both grew to their full sizes, looking like scary urban legends. He wrapped his long, thick arms and legs around her body, trying to keep her from hurting herself.

She continued to writhe wildly for several minutes, then went limp.

After what felt like a very long time, Claire blinked her eyes, and they returned to normal.

"It's okay, Nick. You can let go of me now," Claire reassured him, though her body was still weak.

Nick released Claire slowly. Decelerating, she sat up and collected her thoughts a moment before speaking.

"I know what kind of questions you're going to ask, but I don't have a ton of answers. So please bear with me."

Sam and Nick nodded their heads eagerly. Scott just sat down, watching everyone closely.

"Scott, pay attention. Most of this is about you." Claire glanced at Scott before continuing. "Seth is still alive. He's too far away for me to sense him, and he is in a place of great power. I learned that in order to find Seth, Scott must go into the Infinite Cave . . . with Nick. Apparently, the two of you together must face a creature so powerful that it has the ability to tear my vision apart. It's fuzzy but . . . I think that this creature is going to help us. Somehow."

"What?" Nick shouted. "You want me to go in there with Scott?"

"No, but what I want doesn't matter. You need to do this. I saw it in my vision, and you know how powerful they are."

"No way. I went in there when I was thirteen. There is no way I'm going again! Plus, every Armadronian is supposed to find themselves in there—by themselves! Scott shouldn't be denied that chance."

"Nick," she said quietly, "you know that my visions don't lie. You have to go in there with him—or we will have no idea how to find Seth. Do you really want to risk that?"

"Hold on." Nick raised a hand, then reached into his pocket and pulled out a small device, pressing buttons.

Scott realized with a start that it was a Bastum.

Nick looked at the device. It lit up red and started blinking. He grunted disapprovingly, then collapsed the device and put it back in his pocket.

"Out of range," Nick explained to everyone, then added, "and I'm not going with him."

"Are you scared?" Scott asked.

"Yes," Nick said, staring him down, "and you would be too if you were smart. You have no idea what is in there."

Scott looked away, and Claire continued speaking.

"In my vision I saw you picking up a sword in front of Scott. He was on his knees screaming at you, saying, 'Kill it! Kill it!' Doesn't that kind of sound like he needs you?" She stopped talking and waited.

"No."

Claire dipped her shoulder and put her hands on her hips, glowering at Nick.

"Alright, fine. I'll babysit him," Nick faltered, looking away.

"Good." Claire smiled.

"Did you see anything else, though? Anything?" Nick pleaded.

"Nothing."

"Let's go. There's no time to lose!" Sam cried. "Let's get to the cave and deal with this. We need Seth."

"We would if we knew where to start looking." Nick turned in place, taking in his surroundings. "Oh."

The entrance to the Infinite Cave was right there, about a hundred feet behind them. It was a slanted hole in the ground with a set of old stairs running down.

The rest of the group turned around and saw the cave.

"The probability of us being dropped here of all places is so astronomically low that it's hilarious to even think—"

"Who cares?" Nick interrupted Claire. "We're here. Let's just get this over with."

"Nick, we should stop and think about this," Sam said.

"Stop, Schmop," Nick waved his hand at Sam.

They all walked over to the entrance without another word.

The opening was just big enough for one person to squeeze through at a time.

"Cheery," Sam said with a nervous smile.

"All right, Scott. Let's go. The faster we find Seth and get outta this place, the better," Nick said. "See you guys in a bit." He waved at Claire and Sam.

Suddenly, Nick twisted his body to look back at Sam.

"What about you, Sam? Where did you end up when the telemine dumped you out?"

"I was . . . um . . . like ten feet from Claire?" she answered oddly.

"Was that a question or a statement?" Nick asked, crossing his arms.

"Yeah," Claire confirmed. "She took the bolas off my neck."

"Oh. Okay," Nick said. "Just checking."

He took the first step, then turned around and looked at Scott.

"Don't worry, I'll protect you," he joked.

"That's what I'm worried about," Scott replied.

"Oh, come on," Nick said. "They don't call me an Icranu for nothing."

"Remember," Claire said to Scott, who turned around, "mind over matter."

She tapped her head and winked at him.

"Wow. That was random and weird," Nick interjected. "Thank you for your words of wisdom. Can we go now?"

Nick didn't wait for a response. He just looked at Claire's appalled face and turned around.

They entered the Infinite Cave with Nick's chuckles ringing against the walls.

18

INTO THE HOLE

Seth had never felt so helpless in his entire life. He had been walking for hours through lava spurts, and now Inno Mountain was only about three miles off in the distance. He recognized it because he had seen pictures of it in books. The active volcano emitted a never-ending slow flow of molten lava, so that much of the mountain remained engulfed in liquid fire.

Not all of it, though. There was an overhang that diverted the fiery flow right and left, and below the overhang was a possible entrance into the mountain—and shelter until Seth could figure out his next step.

Seth's problem was that Inno Mountain was on the other side of the planet from where he and the others had teleported, and he had no idea how to get back to his friends in time—even if he had the slightest clue where they had landed. With every grueling step, he turned over in his head the details of his trip through the telemine as well as many other mysterious things that had happened in his life.

While telemining, someone in their group had accidentally shoved Seth's hands off Nick's shoulders, and a second later he had ended up here. That meant that wherever everyone else was, they were probably together. That was good.

Still, he was alone.

But he believed Claire would find him. She could locate him with her curse, and the team would track him down. Unless the rest of the gang had somehow teleported to Terminus's Coliseum. Or worse, his castle. But the odds of that were low.

Seth pulled out his Bastum and tried contacting Nick. It was the third time he'd tried since they'd teleported. Still no luck. He'd hoped that, as he gained elevation closer to the mountain, he might have a better line of sight to the other Bastums so he could contact his friends. And if not them, perhaps another nearby team of Icranu. According to Thaught, there were teams all over the world. For now, he put the Bastum back in his pocket and kept walking.

He was nervous, too. He hadn't been topside in a while. Being above ground on Armadron was risky business. Poachers, blockers, and Conjurers could nab him at any moment. Not to mention sickness, if he were exposed to too much radiation directly beneath the never-ending purple storm clouds. Then there was Terminus's Coliseum and, even worse, his castle.

Seth had been told stories about Terminus's castle. He had heard that since no naturally-born animals from Earth could survive on Armadron, Terminus was in the process of creating new species. He'd also heard from Artam that Terminus wanted to combine Armadronian DNA with Earth animal DNA. That would not be good. There were already rumors that Terminus had created a monster and released it into the Unknown Waters. Other rumors were that he had released not one but dozens of these things all over the planet. And according to Artam, there were even more on the way.

A random, loud fizzing sound came from the ground right under his feet. He looked down and saw that he was standing directly over a four-foot-wide lava spurt.

Sweet Jesus, help me.

The lava erupted from deep inside Armadron and rose to the surface in less than a second. With no time to waste, Seth Accelerated and shot out his hands, slowly stepping back. He was keeping the lava down with his curse, but the pressure was growing.

The back of his head started to buzz and he felt faint.

When he was as far away as he needed to go, he released the tension. The second that he did so, the lava was sucked back down into Armadron.

INTO THE HOLE

Weird, last time it—
Boom!
Craaaaaaackk!

A lava spring just a few feet behind him exploded. Lava shot up higher in the air than Seth had ever seen. It was even higher than the lowest black cloud.

He started screaming and running for his life. He ran as fast as he could, digging his heels in. If even a small splash of lava landed on his clothing, he would have to stop and strip down before it burned through. He didn't have that kind of time.

He ran from the fiery furnace as fast as he could. Inno Mountain was only about a thousand yards away now. He looked up behind him for a split second and instantly wished he hadn't. The amount of lava that had been released from that one burst had been enough to burn through all the clouds nearby. Sunlight shone through the break and warmed his skin for the first time ever on Armadron.

He almost stopped to take a break but noticed that he wasn't tired anymore. He felt unstoppable! Before he could question why, he shot fire out of his left hand. It came out much more powerfully than usual. The force of that one burst of fire lifted his whole body about ten feet to the right. Seth extinguished the fire and fell flat on his face.

He twisted himself up and started running again, all in one smooth motion. A fireball the size of a large farm animal landed on the spot where he had just been, marking where he could have died. He turned back around. He was getting closer to cover. He was now close enough to see a place where the slow ooze of lava on the mountain was diverted around what looked like an entrance a little above the base of the huge mountain.

Another volcanic bomb almost got him on the right, this one much larger than the last. Barely having to glance at the sky, he saw the shadows of incoming fireballs covering the distance all the way to Inno Mountain. Who was he kidding? Seth would never be able to outrun the falling lava bombs without being roasted. Unless . . .

Seth aimed his hands behind him. He was about to try something he'd seen on a cartoon on the Nickelodeon channel back on Earth.

Fire exploded from his hands, and he kept the flow going. Now he was running with his hands behind his back, the thrust of the fire streams propelling him forward. It still wasn't enough, though. Fireballs were raining down on him from everywhere, and the noise was deafening.

Seth was still roughly a hundred yards from the entrance. He had a crazy idea, one that could kill him if he did it wrong or save him if he did it right.

Laughing maniacally, he jumped into the air, aiming the streams of fire from his hands downward.

He concentrated on his legs and screamed. They were covered in flames but somehow not burning up. Still unable to land anywhere, he shot his hands out by his sides and soared higher.

Seth was flying for the first time in his life. His favorite pair of shoes burned off and fell to the ground.

"Yes! Ha-ha! Ha-ha!" Seth would have punched the air, but he could literally kill himself by doing that.

His happy mood was cut short when he discovered the entrance he was aiming for was not a real entrance after all. It was just a small crevice that ended a few feet inside the mountain. To make matters worse, the giant lip diverting lava was just an illusion. The lava was diverted, but simply from the naturally-occurring shape of the volcano. The crevice offered no ceiling to protect him.

He paused in front of the false entrance, levitating in the air with fire.

Now what?

His question was answered courtesy of a gigantic fireball falling in a vertical drop straight toward him. It was the size of a big rig! Seth couldn't fly left because the mountain jutted out and blocked his path. He couldn't go right for the same reason. Flying back away from the mountain would mean having to dodge even more fireballs falling behind him.

He flexed his feet and arms downward as far as they would go and blasted into the air. He was headed straight for the falling lava bomb at a speed that would have impressed a rocket scientist. Propelling himself a safe distance from the surface of the lava oozing slowly down the mountainside, he continued his straight shot upward, aiming for the gap between the falling fireball and the lava on the side of the mountain.

He was thirty feet away when Seth told himself he was going to die. The fireball was falling too close to the mountain. He might squeeze through, but not without his body brushing against the lava.

Seth spotted his chance, though. The fireball was spinning slowly as it fell. Rotating toward Seth was a dark spot on the fiery surface of the burning globe. A cool point.

A heartbeat before impact, Seth made his move. He flew upward, just between the fireball and the mountain. He began to doubt himself, then grinned. The patch of hardened, cool lava rotated around on the fireball. A slight indent in the mountainside gave Seth even more room to maneuver. He willed himself to fly higher and just barely brushed the cooling portion of the lava ball with his stomach and knees.

He shot into open air, and the fireball crashed into the side of the mountain below. Seth was forced to keep going up. More fireballs were on their way. He rocketed up the side of Inno Mountain, dodging the flaming lava bombs the whole way.

He soon realized that even though he was going to a higher elevation, the air was getting hotter.

Seth dodged the last fireball as it crashed into the side of the mountain. Flying upward past the peak, he looked down into the mouth and throat of the volcano.

It was one of the most amazing sights of his life. The mouth of the volcano was several miles in diameter and brimming with bubbling molten magma.

Suspended just above the deadly lake of magma were bridges, houses, hospitals, and schools—all made entirely out of jet-black rock. Still, the most amazing thing of all was that Seth saw kids and adults walking around as if the magma didn't faze them. Some people were actually covered in the magma. Or literally walking around on fire.

Personally, Seth didn't feel heat. However, his body did feel pain *from* the heat. If he was close to something hot, he didn't notice. One time his head was on fire, though, and he had felt a nauseating, searing pain. His hands sparked with electricity from the memory.

He looked around and saw people using their abilities. One woman drew purple lightning from the sky and collected it into a ball of energy. She took the ball over to a house, and a man opened the front door. He let the woman in, and the door closed again.

Seth realized he was still hovering above the volcano.

He slowly decreased his fire output, and his body began descending. As he got close to the rocks on the outskirts of the crater, he halted.

"Hey! What is your name, son?" someone called.

Seth turned in the direction of the voice, which had come from behind him.

He immediately saw four Accelerated, heavily built men. In Armadronian years, they each looked to be in their mid-twenties. They were all at his level: ten feet above the rocks below. They were floating like he was, with their hands outstretched and their legs pointed down with currents of fire streaming from them. In short order, all four had covered the distance to Seth, effectively surrounding him.

Seth looked up and down for a way out—and saw two more men. The one above had strong pulses of lightning keeping him in the air. The one below was the scariest of all. He was standing on a four-foot-wide, thinly layered disc. It was made entirely of shriveling, hissing blue fire.

Seth gulped.

"Hi. I'm Seth. I'm new around here." He let the statement hang in the air awkwardly.

"Hello, Seth."

Seth looked down to see the man on the blue-fire disc talking but not looking up at him. "We are the guards of Inno Mountain.

I am sorry to inform you that just yesterday we had an encounter with a rather nasty shape-shifter. Tensions are high, and due to these recent events and increased security protocol, we must bring you in for questioning. Will you come quietly?"

The other guards tensed a little, and their eyes shifted to one another.

"Yeah, but I have a question," Seth said.

"Ask it," one of the guards said.

"You said that you're gonna bring me *in* for questioning. Where exactly is *in*? Scientifically speaking, the magma should run through the entire mountain. So how can there be more than one level here?"

"Exactly." The man above him grinned wickedly.

"What? That doesn't even—"

"Seth"—it was the man below him again—"may we continue this discussion on foot?"

"Yeah, sure."

Seth let his curse die down, and soon enough his feet touched down on solid rock. Three of the guards instantly landed in front of him, and three of them landed behind. They all Decelerated, as did Seth.

"Let's take a walk," said the guard closest to Seth.

Seth felt nauseous, but he nodded his head.

They walked on a pathway made of stone that appeared suspended over the magma. It was about three feet wide, so they walked single file. One false step and Seth would experience a quick and painful death.

The guards walked in perfect sequence. Seth felt clumsy and childish among them. He looked down at his feet just when the guards stopped. He walked right into the guard in front of him, almost knocking him over.

"Oops, sorr—"

"Watch where you're going!"

Seth looked up and saw that they were standing on the outskirts of the village. He now saw that the village had been built on a huge circle of rock connected to other circles of rock by stone pathways like the one they had just traveled. There were plenty of people from all walks of life up here, all staring him down.

Something was going on with the guards. He noticed that several had Accelerated again and had their palms turned toward a particular spot in the boiling magma. The guards tensed at the exact same time, and the magma parted like the Red Sea to reveal a flight of black steps leading down into the volcano.

The guards began walking. Seth did too. As they descended into the stairwell, Seth gazed at the beautiful walls of suspended magma on either side of him.

At the bottom of the stairwell was an alcove. In the floor before them appeared to be a dark hole, or perhaps the entrance to a vertical shaft. Seth looked up and saw that the magma was floating high above their heads.

"Keith. Gurner. Go up and work surveillance. We've got it from here," one guard barked. He appeared to be the leader of the group.

The guard directly in front of Seth turned around and flew up the stairs, propelled by streams of fire from his hands and feet. Seth turned his head and saw the guard at the back of the line do the same thing. Ten seconds later, he heard a shudder from above. He looked up and saw the magma drop into the mountain a little bit.

Now there were two guards behind him and two guards in front. The remaining guards walked toward the hole in the ground, and because he was sandwiched between them, Seth went too. The lead guard placed his palm on a square panel on the rock wall of the alcove. It lit up red.

"Back up!" he called.

They stumbled backward. Seth could hear something coming up the hole. It sounded like the heavy rustling of feathers, or maybe the sound of crackling fire.

The shaft lit up with light. Yup. It was fire.

A little boy flew out of the entrance at a fast speed, laughing. He saw the guards, stopped laughing, and landed with a hiss as his fire went out. Another little boy about the same age flew out even faster and couldn't stop in time. He was about to smack into Seth when a guard stuck out his hand. The boy's fire was killed midflight, and he flipped through the air with a surprised yell. The guard caught him with astounding agility and set the boy down abruptly.

"Martin! Curtis! What the hell do you think you're doing?!" the lead guard yelled at them as soon as he set the boy down.

"We were, um . . . coming up here to get something for—"

"Don't lie to me, Martin," the guard warned. "I know your mother."

The boy shut his mouth. The other boy, Curtis, didn't.

"Mr. Cameron, sir," Curtis said, "um . . . we were kinda playing a game of tag. We're sorry that we . . . um . . . flew too fast." He lowered his head.

The guard whose name was Cameron walked between the boys. Martin ran around him in order to stand next to Curtis. Cameron turned around in Seth's direction with his eyes ablaze. Literally.

"You're sorry you flew too fast?" he spat, his eyes shooting blue flames.

How is he doing that? Seth thought, completely amazed. *I've never seen that before.*

The boys cowered so much that they seemed to shrink.

"You're not supposed to fly without an adult with you! You could have seriously hurt someone. Now I'm going to have to tell your mother, Martin," Cameron warned.

"Noooo! Pleeeaase! Don't—"

"Nelson!" Cameron interrupted Martin's pathetic cries and looked behind Seth. "Take your son home and take Martin to his mother. Tell her what he did. They will need to be supervised. I'll reach you when I need you."

"Yessir!" said the guard behind Seth.

Nelson came forward and grabbed the boys by their arms.

The boys instantly started screaming and whining. They tried to pull away, but Nelson wouldn't have it. His brow furrowed, and an electric jolt escaped from every one of his fingers. The boys were instantly knocked out. In two fluid motions, he plucked the boys onto his shoulders and jumped into the air about five inches. Lightning crackled under his feet, and he flew up the stairs.

Now there were two guards in front and one guard behind Seth. He would have tried to escape, but he was too curious at this point. He had to see more.

There was a beeping sound, and the panel next to the hole turned green.

"Let's go," Cameron urged. "Seth, you're next to me. Come on."

Seth stood next to Cameron and looked at the shaft entrance. He couldn't believe his eyes.

The top of the hole was filled with a thick layer of blue fire. Seth looked over and saw Cameron with his hand outstretched.

"Step on it, Seth," Cameron told him.

Seth was pushed a little by the guard behind him. He turned his head and glared at the guard. The guard glared back.

"Come on, we haven't got all day!" Cameron shouted. "Just get on the damn disk!"

Seth leaned his body back and carefully stepped on the large disc of blue fire. It felt like he was stepping on stone. He took another step, and before he knew it, he was in the center of the fire.

The three guards joined Seth on the flaming disc. Without warning, they began to descend into the shaft. "How"—Seth coughed as they were going down—"um . . . deep is it?"

"Deep," Cameron answered.

"What's the stone made out of? How come it doesn't melt from the magma?" Seth asked.

"It's solid Armitranium," Cameron answered.

Wow, Seth thought. *That stuff's ten times stronger and more resistant than the diamonds they have on Earth! But how the hell do they have so much of it?*

"I'm a little curious here . . . how do you guys have so—"

"No talking," the guard behind him cut in smoothly.

They played the quiet game the rest of the way down.

19

PROBLEMS, SOLUTIONS . . . AND MORE PROBLEMS

"Can't you just find Seth so we can get out of here?" Nick asked for the millionth-and-a-half time.

"If I knew how, I would. But I don't," Scott answered, clearly annoyed.

"Hey, don't get annoyed with me!" Nick growled. "You're the reason we're here in the first place!"

Scott groaned, and something deep in the cave groaned back. He could feel Nick tense next to him. Both of them halted their steps. The thing sounded big. King Kong big.

"Did you hear that?" Nick whispered.

"No. I must have missed it," Scott whispered sarcastically.

"Man, I wish Seth were here. He could light up this place so we could actually see more than two feet in front of us."

They had just descended the steps into the Infinite Cave. As far as they could tell, the cave really *did* go on forever. The cave was pitch-black, but tiny white flecks on the walls lit their way dimly. Up until now, the cave had been utterly quiet, except for the sound of Nick and Scott arguing.

"Hey, Nick."

"What?"

"How come we can't see in the dark right now, or use our sonar?"

"Something about the cave makes it so that we can't Accelerate well. It runs interference."

"Interference?" Scott repeated. "Like, it jams us or something?"

"Something like that."

They walked on in silence for a while. Often one of them would stumble or trip on a rock jutting out and a stream of muffled curses would ensue.

"Hey, Scott," Nick said, "how long did you know Seth on Earth? He said that you guys were, like, best friends or something."

"Seth went by the name Charlie McEntly on Earth. I knew him for about two years. We went to high school together and became best friends there."

"Wait," Nick said. "You said his name was Charlie McEntly. Why wasn't his name just Charlie?"

"Because that was his last name," Scott said, rolling his eyes.

Nick didn't respond.

Something dawned on Scott. "Nick, does anyone have a last name on Armadron?"

"No. What are you talking about? A last name? Why would you need another name? One is good enough."

Scott smiled to himself in the darkness. "Nick, have you ever been to Earth?"

"No."

"Really? I kinda figured that you would know someone with a curse that could take you there."

Nick grunted in reply.

"You've never seen any animals before?" Scott pressed.

"No."

"Airplanes?"

"Whatever those are, no."

"Submarines?"

"Again, no."

"Cars?"

"N– actually, yes. I made one with Seth a couple years back when we couldn't find a teleporter."

"Cool." Scott nodded.

A random shiver went down Scott's back. He looked behind him and felt the hairs on the back of his neck stand on end.

It was almost like the cave floor and walls suddenly made him afraid.

I should tell Nick.

"Hey, Nick, do you think the cave might be—"

"Look, Scott, I may not know much about your world, but that doesn't mean anything now. From what I've heard, I would be nearly powerless there, and confused and helpless too. I'm just fine here. I can use my curse here."

"Oh, please," Scott huffed.

"What? Nick said defensively. "What now?"

"Nick, if you knew what Earth was like, you wouldn't want to stay on this planet another second. Yeah, you wouldn't be able to use your curse—but it would be worth it! Think about it. Wouldn't it be great not to have to eat other humans to survive? Plus, the variety of food is almost unlimited—and there are grocery stores and restaurants on every corner. You wouldn't have to worry about fighting for your life every day or keeping people safe either. You wouldn't have to trade things in order to have a warm cot; you would have a nice giant bed for free! You could get a job; you'd have money to spend on girls, on yourself, on your fam—"

"Family?" Nick finished for him. They both stopped walking.

"I didn't mean to say that," Scott said.

"But you did. Thanks a lot, Scott. What a nice thought."

"I'm sorry, Nick. I didn't—"

"You didn't what, Scott? You didn't know? You didn't remember?" Nick viciously replied. "Do you remember Ernie? From the restaurant? You remember how he died?"

Scott nodded. At that very moment, he had the ominous feeling that the cave . . . laughed a little.

"Well, take a good look, 'cause that's gonna be me in ten years or so, just like my mom and my old man!" Nick practically spit the next words at Scott. "You know, Scott, you've got it all. You've still got parents somewhere back on Earth, and you're gonna live until you're a hundred years old, at least! Not to mention, you're the golden boy who's gonna save us all, the Mediator who can create peace wherever he goes."

"But I didn't ask for any of this. I don't even have much to—"

"Come on, Scott! What don't you have going for you?"

Nick had a vein bulging out of the side of his neck. Scott suddenly had the feeling that it was the cave that was getting Nick so worked up.

"What do you mean?!" Scott demanded. "I don't have anything. And I know this sounds crazy, but I think that the cave is messing with—"

"You have everything!" Nick bellowed.

The cave shook wildly. The floor moved and vibrated at an intense speed.

Scott was thrown off his feet, but Nick remained standing.

"Nick, stop! You're overreacting! Calm down!" Scott cried desperately.

"Shut up!" Nick screamed, and the entire cave felt like it was going to give way. Pieces of rock fell from the roof with a deafening roar.

There was an ugly twisting sound, like bones snapping. A yell was heard not far off in the cave, and then all was quiet.

The floor stopped moving. The walls stopped too. There was only silence.

"Nick?" Scott called as he hoisted himself off the cave floor. "Nick!"

Scott heard deep, quiet laughter from the depths of the Infinite Cave.

He reached out and grasped at empty air. Nick wasn't there anymore. Scott waved his arms around frantically and darted from place to place.

"Nick! Nick!" Scott screamed. "Nick! Come back! I need you." He whispered the last three words as he dropped to his knees.

PROBLEMS, SOLUTIONS... AND MORE PROBLEMS

"Aaaaaaaahhhhh!"

He whipped his head around and stared into the darkness of the cave from which Nick had just screamed.

Scott ran toward the sound as fast as he could. He ran so fast that Armadron felt like it morphed with him under his feet. Only darkness loomed ahead, but Scott kept running anyway.

Hold on, Nick! Just hold on.

* * *

Things weren't going so well *above* the cave either.

Claire paced around the entrance for an hour before she finally decided to take a breather. The sun had already set, and it was almost completely dark. They were going to have to sleep there for the night.

"I told you." Sam smiled. "They are going to be a while. It is best to sit."

Claire groaned, then sat on the ground.

"Sam, why are you talking like that? You've been talking like that ever since we landed on the telemine. You sound like a damn computer." Claire stared at her. "Is there something wrong?"

If it had been anyone else, Claire would have just gone ahead and read his or her mind. But Sam was her best friend. She deserved to tell Claire on her own.

"Yes," Sam answered calmly. "The Sam you know is nearly dead."

Claire jumped to her feet and backed away from Sam, all the while trying to read her mind. She couldn't.

"Sam, why are you turning my power off?" Claire asked, fighting to stay calm.

Sam was still sitting on the ground, totally relaxed. She began laughing, and her whole body shifted like an eel in the water. The laugh became deeper, and her body became longer. Most of her hair shrunk back into her head to reveal a man's head. The laughing continued, morphing into an evil, maniacal sound that sent chills down Claire's spine. Finally, the transformation was complete, and Sam was no longer sitting on the ground. It was someone else. It was someone muscular with slicked-back, raven-colored hair and sunken eyes. Someone dressed in a sleeveless dress shirt, silk tie, and sleeveless jacket worn over a pair of black dress slacks. It was someone Claire did not want to see.

"Hello, Claire. Do you remember me?" the man asked nonchalantly.

"How could I forget," she said with disdain.

The man sighed. "Oh, Claire. There's no need for these harsh feelings toward me. What did I ever do to you?"

"You killed my parents." She fought to keep her voice steady.

"I've killed a lot of people. But their deaths shouldn't concern you. You probably didn't even like them. You were just a child."

Claire flinched.

"Even if I had spared them, they would have eventually died anyway. Probably sooner than later. The way I see it, I was doing you a favor. You're welcome." The man continued to sit comfortably on the ground.

"I swear," Claire growled, "I'll kill you."

"Oh, I wouldn't do that. If you attempt anything, your little friend Sam will die," the man said, chuckling.

"She's alive?!" Claire gasped, then clamped a hand over her mouth, instantly hating her weakness.

"Yes, I can personally assure you that she is very much alive. However, should you be inclined to try any funny business, I will kill her. Slowly." The man smirked.

"Okay." She shook her head, her thoughts racing for a way out of this. "Okay. What is it that you want?"

"What I want is for you to let me search your mind. When I am done—if there are no complications—I will let you and your friend go. If there *are* complications . . ." He made a slicing motion with his hand across his neck.

Claire swallowed. "You swear that you will let Sam and me live if I let you do this?"

"Yes. However, being that you are a vastly powerful intellectual, you know how to erase memories or completely block them when someone is in your mind." He bit off the nail from his index finger and spat it out. "I am approximately thirty-seven percent more powerful than you are. If you try this, I will force you to live the rest of your miserable life as a vegetable. What say you?"

The whole time he had been talking, Claire had been trying to project thoughts to Scott and Nick.

—*Scott! Nick! It's Claire! Get outta there and help us! Sam and I are about to die! I'm being forced to get my mind read by*—

She couldn't think anymore. She was too busy being suspended three feet above the ground with pressure around her neck.

"You think I can't hear you project your thoughts?" The man, who had yet to move from where he lounged on the grass, looked coldly at her and made a *tsk* sound. "You insult me, my dear Claire."

"Why?" Claire choked. "Why are you doing this?"

"I wanted to have a little fun." The man smiled as she squirmed. "It's been a while since I've had some fun." He dropped the false smile and replaced it with a dead stare. "Now, hold still and let your mind go blank. Or you will be sorry."

"Wait!" Claire gasped. "Where's my brother?"

"That is no concern of yours. Now follow my directions, or Sam *and* Billy die."

Claire went limp. The man let her go, and she fell to the ground, landing hard on her knees. She coughed violently as he stretched his palms toward her face.

She gasped. There was a slight knocking feeling in her forehead. The feeling shortly moved to the back of her head, then to both sides of her head in less than thirty seconds. She let him invade her mind, calling off her defenses.

She felt his presence leave her mind after a minute or so and immediately hated herself.

Claire dropped to the ground and curled up in a ball. She felt violated. The only place she was safe was in her mind, and he had taken that away from her. She shed a single tear out of her left eye and just left it there.

He had figured out everything there was to know about her in less than a minute. Everything. Now he could just go back on his word and kill her if he wanted to.

"You know, Claire," he said in an oily voice as he walked around her in a circle, savoring his victory.

She didn't move from her position.

"I just wanted a way into the Cavern so I could wipe out the rest of those filthy inbreeds. Instead, you gave me Scott, Artam, Thaught, Seth, and Nick. That bit about Faranger being able to use his abilities on Earth, that is very useful. I just *knew* we would find him with your team. We've already searched dozens of other teams across the planet. Thank you, Claire."

She tilted her face up and spat. The spit made it to his slim dark shoes, which he then used to kick her in the stomach, knocking the breath out of her.

He continued talking while Claire was gasping for breath and wheezing.

"Now, that wasn't very nice, Claire. I said thank you. You should have said, 'You're welcome.' Did your parents not teach you manners before I killed them?" He looked at her as if he was asking a real question.

"G–go . . . to h–hell." She struggled to breathe. It had been a strong kick.

"I said," he growled, "say thank you."

Claire felt a pressure rising in her chest. All her other senses were blocked out. She only felt the pain. It was the worst pain she had ever experienced. Blood began slowly coating the front of her shirt.

"Thank you!" she screamed helplessly.

The pain stopped, and Claire spat up a mouthful of blood.

I'm going to die. I'm really going to die. I will never see my friends again. No more Nick, no more Scott, no Seth. No Sam either.

"Hmmm. Now, I wouldn't think that, Claire."

PROBLEMS, SOLUTIONS . . . AND MORE PROBLEMS

He read her mind effortlessly and grinned evilly. "You'll see Sam again. Maybe even sooner than you think."

He snapped his fingers for show, disappearing as Sam appeared in his place, very cut up and very bruised, right in front of Claire. Sam had a gag over her mouth and ropes tying her hands and feet together behind her back. She looked awful, to put it in the best possible terms.

As soon as she saw Claire, Sam rolled a little in place and tried to yell. With muffled words, she urged Claire to try to escape, but Claire knew doing so would be suicide. Claire looked back at her, frozen in fear.

In the meantime, Kane had reappeared behind the two girls. Now he spoke. "You have a choice, Claire," he said congenially. "You have the opportunity to live . . . and the opportunity to die. As I gazed inside your mind, I found that you are aware of the disgraceful magic that has been placed on me to stop my entrance into the Infinite Cave. So, regrettably, I must wait out here for those two monkeys to exit on their own accord. Which leaves me with nothing to do in the meantime. So I thought that we could all play a little game."

"A game? What's it called?" Claire asked quietly.

"Right now, the pregame is called 'take Sam's muzzle off.'"

"You could have gotten your answers from Sam. Why do you need me?" Claire asked, hoping to prolong the conversation and buy some time.

"I need you because Sam's curse makes it . . . nearly impossible."

Claire nodded. Moving as slowly as she could, she moved toward Sam. As she put her hands on Sam's gag, Sam was trying desperately to say something, but her words were garbled by the gag.

"Stay calm. I'll get us out of this," Claire whispered to her friend.

As she pulled the gag off, Sam instantly started screaming at the top of her lungs.

"Kane! Let me go! Let Claire and me go! Why are you doing this?! You're a monster! You're evil! You have no *soul!* Someone should just kill you already! Aaaarrrrgggghhh! Let . . . me . . . go!"

"The game is—"

His next words were drowned out by Sam's continued yelling. "You're evil! Evil! You kidnap and kill children just for the hell of it and—"

Suddenly Sam froze, silent, her mouth still open. While she had been yelling at Kane, he had stated something to them in a quiet, calm voice.

"What did you say?" Claire whispered, her face white.

"I said," Kane replied, "the game is called 'kill Sam with this sword and you're free.'"

Kane held out his hand, and a sword about three feet long appeared out of nowhere. It was jet-black on the serrated side and pure white on the smooth, deadly sharp side. The girls' petrified faces reflected off the white side.

"Do you know why I like this body the most?" Kane asked no one in particular.

Both girls numbly shook their heads.

"It's because I do not have a curse of my own, per se. Whenever I shift into a person that I have personally killed or for whom death is near, I acquire their gifts. Typically, the person has only a run-of-the-mill curse, but the man who used to be in possession of this body had a doozy. Do you want to venture a guess as to what it was?"

Both girls shook their heads again, watching the sword that had been created out of thin air.

"This man could, on a medium scale, imagine anything in the cosmos. He could then create what he was imagining using nothing but the quantum particles around us. He was a god. And I killed him."

20

THERE'S NO PLACE LIKE HOME

Seth had just taken the coolest elevator trip of his life. He had been in elevators on Earth, but this was a whole 'nother ball game.

On the way down into the volcano, everyone had been silent. Now they got off the disc of fire, and it dissipated into the air with a hiss.

"Follow me," Cameron ordered.

Seth walked behind Cameron and another guard. The guard behind him fell into step. They walked for a couple seconds down a short hallway and took a left.

Seth and the guards were now standing on the top level of the complex. He looked down, and far, far below in the volcano he saw chambers of molten magma. Above those—but below the top level where Seth stood—were at least fifty stories of living space. Stairs coiled on the walls throughout the entire volcano. They ran all the way to the magma below. Thousands of people could be seen on every level.

Every level had a platform that extended to its corresponding stair level. Each level also had a sort of mini-village in which people interacted with each other. All the levels looked the same—except the uppermost one. The top level was made of purple rock instead of the black rock of all the other levels.

Seth noted that each level was held up by a support system. From what he could see, every level had four bracers, also made of rock, that jutted from the side of the volcano to the underside of each level. It was these support systems that were supposed to keep Seth from dropping to the level underneath him. He kept that in mind as the guard behind him pushed him in step behind Cameron.

He walked down the three steps that brought him onto the topmost level of living space. Seth took a tentative step onto the purple rock. He didn't die.

Phew! He kept walking behind Cameron and the other guard.

"So what are your guys' names?" He directed his question at the two guards.

"We are almost there," the guard in front said.

Seth was about to ask again—just to be annoying—when a little girl with red pigtails skipped in front of them.

"Cameron! Josef! Tim!" She hugged each of them in turn. "Thanks for saving my mommy yesterday! You guys are the best! I told my daddy that you guys are heroes, but he just says that you're doing your job." The little girl looked at each of them and then realized Seth was there too. "Who's he?!" She pointed at Seth.

"He says his name is Seth," Cameron answered shortly.

"Okay! Bye, guys! Bye, Seth!" The little girl immediately lost interest and skipped away.

They took another step before Seth opened his mouth. He was grinning like an idiot between Josef (the guard in front) and Tim (the guard in back).

"Hey, Igor. Oh! I mean, hey, Josef." Seth grinned. "You're walking with a bit of a hunchback there."

Seth expected the guards to laugh, but they didn't.

Oh, that's right! They don't know who Igor is! Seth thought. *Earth stuff.*

"Very funny, kid," Josef said, clearly not getting the joke, "but I'll be the one who's laughin' when you get kicked out of the mountain, and I get to do the kickin'."

"Josef, stop talking." Cameron looked back at him. "Don't give him anything. Just stick to protocol."

"Right," Josef agreed.

"Um, Igor?" Seth mocked. "I think it's pronounced *yes, master!*"

Seth exploded into laughter at his own joke.

"We have arrived. Do not speak unless spoken to," Cameron said. He kept walking right through a big white door.

Seth looked up at the building he was about to enter. It was a huge, white circular building unlike any of the other buildings, which were all square and black. This building looked like a circus tent compared to all the others.

The first thing Seth noticed as he passed through the doorway into a large, ornate room was a massive orb of pure energy floating in open space. The orb crackled, sparked, and occasionally erupted with flames.

The second thing he noticed was that, beyond the orb, thirteen people sat around a semicircular table. The woman in the middle of the table, sitting in the highest chair, was in a direct line with the orb. On her left side sat six men. On her right, six women. It reminded him of a courthouse on Earth, sort of.

"Greetings, my Guards," the woman said. "What business have we tonight?"

"Council, we believe that this boy may be the shape-shifter," Cameron announced. "However, if we are wrong, then it is not a total loss. He has shown considerable talents in either fire-starter or ozone abilities. He may be of use to us."

There were murmurs through the council; then one of the other councilwomen spoke.

"What do you advise?"

"I submit to the council that we use the Etherfire to look into his soul." Cameron didn't bat an eye, but Tim and Josef tensed.

Some men and women in the council gasped, but others just sat there, stock-still.

"Lieutenant, stay. Second and third, leave," ordered one of the councilmen.

Tim and Josef turned on their heels and power-walked out of the chamber. Josef was so fast that Seth felt a light wind as he brushed past him.

Once they had left, one of the councilwomen cleared her throat and spoke. "We cannot use the Etherfire whenever we please. It will diminish its strength."

"If we do not, we all may not make it out of this room," Cameron said calmly.

"Dude," Seth interjected, "I'm not the shifter. It's probably Kane, Terminus's right-hand man. That's what his famous power is."

"And how do we know that the real Seth did not die, and that you are not Kane?"

"Because Kane speaks like a computer. I can use surfer lingo if you want, bruh."

Cameron shook his head, keeping his composure and choosing to ignore Seth.

The woman who had spoken previously nodded her head curtly. "The council shall vote on this matter."

In less than three seconds, everyone seated at the table except for the woman in the center had cast a vote. In total, twelve council members had either red or blue fire coming out of their outstretched hands. It was a tie.

The woman in the middle slowly outstretched her hand. It revealed a red flame.

Someone tell me what that means, Seth thought nervously. *I'm not Sherlock Holmes here.*

"The Etherfire shall be used," the woman in the middle said with no emotion.

Surprisingly, Seth still didn't know if he should be relieved or terrified. What exactly was the Etherfire? Everything was happening so fast, he barely had time to process anything.

"Step forward, boy," she instructed.

As he stepped toward the sparking floating orb he presumed was the Etherfire, he noticed that the twelve council members appeared to reflect different ethnicities. But what really caught his attention was what each of the council members was wearing: white shirts, each of which emblazoned with the Icranu symbol!

Seth had that symbol, too, on the right side of his shirt. He looked down at himself and saw that his clothes were almost completely covered in ash.

Seth concentrated on the ash and, with his thoughts, caused it to implode on itself until there was virtually nothing left. The result was mildly clean clothing that was slightly charred. He could now see his Icranu symbol.

"Ahem!" Someone cleared his or her throat loudly.

Seth looked up and realized that the woman in the middle of the council was no longer there. She was right next to him, and they were both close enough to touch the Etherfire. If the large orb of energy was in fact the Etherfire.

"What you are looking at is not the Etherfire," the woman told Seth.

Oh.

"It is the power generator to this mountain. Every day, we have a ceremony in which the people of this mountain surrender some of their energy to the power ball."

"Like the lottery?" Seth joked. "Mega millions?"

Not getting the joke and refusing to dignify the interruption with a response, she merely continued. "The energy is taken in and used in many ways. For instance, it keeps the magma at the bottom of the mountain from surfacing, it places magma at the top of the mountain to camouflage what is hidden below, it prevents other Energens from entering the mountain, and, most importantly, it provides hope for our people."

Seth nodded.

"The Etherfire is strongest inside me. It resides in everyone seated at this council, but I have the power to use it or to create more council members. In your case, I will use my Etherfire to look into your soul and see who you really are."

"Okay," he agreed after a moment's hesitation. "But why are you telling me this if you think I'm Kane?"

"I am telling you this because if you are not a true fire user, this will surely kill you. And even if you are, you must pass the test."

"Lieutenant!" one of the councilmen barked at Cameron. "Watch the outsider! Do not let him try anything."

Cameron stood behind Seth. The woman in front of Seth reached her arms out and rested them on his shoulders.

"Be still and try to stay calm," she said in a soothing voice.

Seth looked up at her. She was a little taller than he was.

The woman closed her eyes. When she reopened them, they were burning bright gold. Her body shone like the sun, and Seth was forced to look away. He had a strange feeling that if the woman got much brighter, his body would be blown up or something on the spot.

Without any warning, there was a slight pop, and the room returned to its normal glow. He looked back to where the woman was standing, but she wasn't there.

"Where did she—"

His sentence was interrupted by a shrill scream—his own.

He dropped to his knees, then curled up in the fetal position. His head and heart felt like they were burning through his skin.

Seth saw his life in the back of his eyelids as if he were watching it on a movie screen. He closed his eyes, and the images floated across the darkness.

He saw himself growing up on Armadron with his parents and meeting Nick for the first time when both boys were five. He watched himself meeting Claire about a year later; even at the tender age of six, he believed he was in love with her. Seth watched himself, as an adolescent, befriending Sam at the Training Grounds. He watched as Thaught sent him on his first solo assignment when he was eleven, then teamed him with Claire, Sam, and Nick when Seth was twelve. He observed his journey to Earth and his years of friendship with Scott, and got to relive the moment he dove off the side of the cruise ship after the brainwashed Conjurers into the swirling waters. The events of the past few days streamed past until he saw himself standing before the council. Finally, the images stopped, and he opened his eyes.

Cameron was sitting cross-legged on the floor, yawning loudly. The rest of the council members were also yawning.

A member of the council suddenly cried out, "Lieutenant, attention!"

Cameron shot himself into the air with a burst of fire from his hands. He landed smoothly next to Seth, who was still lying on the ground in a fetal position.

Seth noticed that the woman who had been seated at the middle of the council was still absent. That's when he heard her voice from somewhere inside him.

—Seth! Your inner fire is too strong! Put some of your power into the ball so that I may leave you! There isn't much time! Do it now, Seth!

Seth jumped to his feet, raised his hands, and shot fire into the glowing, floating orb.

"Stop him!" the councilman shouted at Cameron.

Cameron took a step toward Seth.

"No!" Seth bellowed. "I have to lose some of my power so she can get out!

"Liar!" the man shouted. "He is probably absorbing our resources! Lieutenant, that was an order! Do it!"

Cameron was confused. He took another unsure step toward Seth.

"Stop it, man! I'm trying to help!" Seth yelled.

"Kill him!"

"Just wait a second!"

"Lieutenant!"

Boooooooom!

Seth was thrown several feet sideways, and another body was flung across the room as well.

He slowly got up and looked around. The woman who had been inside his mind was now on top of Cameron. They both got up looking at Seth in confusion. The rest of the council was equally flabbergasted.

The woman brushed herself off and slowly took her seat again at the table.

One of the men seated at the table leaned out of his seat and asked, "What happened, Abigale? What is the verdict?"

"No. He is not the shape-shifter," Abigale answered. "However, I have seen that he has lived on Earth. He could be helpful."

Seth looked at the council members. They were all nodding their heads and murmuring their agreement.

"No!" Seth stepped forward. "I need to get back to my friends! I can't stay here!"

"Friends?" one of the council members asked.

"He is allied with a powerful group, as well as a half-Armadronian he met on Earth," Abigale told the council. "Team 61."

"Interesting," one of the women in the council mused.

"Yeah, whatever. I need to leave," Seth said. "My team and I are trying to gather people to fight Terminus. If Thaught or Artam have not been here yet, then they will come soon to try to recruit you to the fight, too."

"There is one more thing," Abigale said, clearly not acknowledging that Seth had said anything.

One of the council members asked, "What is it, Abigale?"

Seth stopped mid-speech. These people were totally ignoring him!

I gotta get back to the team, he thought as he took a silent step back.

"Seth's body has consumed and mutated with the Etherfire," Abigale explained. "And not just mine. All of yours too. His body has absorbed some of everyone's Etherfire through the air, although I don't know how. He's been doing it subconsciously since the moment he walked in here."

Every person in the council gasped and rested their eyes on Seth. He looked at all of them guiltily and stopped trying to slink his way out of the room.

"He didn't even have to touch us—"

"Any minute now—"

"He will change—"

"We must answer—"

Okay, *now* he was getting really freaked out.

A small flame appeared on the front of his shirt. He swatted to put it out, and another one appeared on the back of his wrist. Just as he moved his other hand to swat the fire out, lightning seemed to shoot through his limbs. His back arched so much that the top of his head slammed to the floor.

He didn't feel the pain, though. He only felt the pain of the Etherfire as it took over his body. Seth wriggled on the floor like a worm as bolts of lightning shot from his fingertips and flames erupted from his eye sockets. Black smoke covered his body and rose to the ceiling of the council building. His body erupted into flames and his hair burnt off completely.

All the people in the council room except for Abigale were taking cover. Cameron had backed away from Seth and was watching him with horrified fascination.

Seth did not see what the others saw. He only saw fire. Fire in every color anyone could ever imagine. Inside the depths of his mind, the fire rose up and burned through his entire body. The fire would consume him if he didn't do something to stop it.

Cameron and the entire council gazed at Seth as his body began to give off a faint glow. The glow intensified to a blinding light, and soon the room shook as if it were caught in an earthquake. Seth's skin began to peel off his body in some places, and they all watched as he screamed helplessly.

In his mind's eye, he saw the fire grow. Just as it was about to burn through his soul, he thought of Claire. He thought of the time they had spent together and how he would never be able to tell her how he really felt, and how much he would miss her.

The fire instantly halted inside him.

Seth realized his thoughts of Claire had thwarted the fire. He thought of Nick, Scott, Sam, his parents, Scott's parents, Artam, Thaught, and many more. Soon the fire changed direction. Instead of going outward, it fused with his memories and he remembered them more clearly. He no longer felt the pain of the Etherfire. It had turned into a warm glow that made Seth feel happy again. The last time he had ever felt truly happy was when his parents were alive.

He got up and saw the universe differently than he ever had before. As he looked at Cameron, he saw the electrical currents of his brain, nervous system, and heart coursing through his body. He saw and felt the body heat of everyone in the room. Seth could tell who was afraid, who was confused, and who was happy. He could even tell who was tired! Everyone gave off a different inner flame, the color of which somehow reflected the state they were in.

Even inanimate objects looked different. For example, things like the council table and chairs consisted of molecules that vibrated so fast, they gave off electrical pulses that were normally invisible to the human eye. But not for Seth. Not anymore. The pulses of electricity illuminated these objects for Seth in a whole new way. Even scratches and imperfections in the wood seem to glow from within.

Scott's not The One, Seth smiled to himself. *I am.*

"Council, this is it," Cameron announced ominously.

The council members slowly took their seats while nodding to each other. Whatever "it" was, it seemed unanimously understood.

"What are we talking about now?" Seth asked.

"Ahem." Abigale cleared her throat.

Seth gave her his full attention.

"Thought created the secret order of Protectors a half decade ago. I was there. For years, Thought has created teams consisting of Protectors who have similar curses. But your team is unlike the others. I understand that your team represents a wide range of curses. That was the first sign."

Another woman spoke up. "Thought gave us the five signs. He said that a boy would have an inner fire unlike anything we have ever seen. He then prophesied that your inner fire would absorb the ancient Etherfire and your body would mutate to suit a new set of abilities. Thirdly, he stated that you would become that new ability: Otherfire. He also said when that happened, you would lead us to the half-Armadronian, and with his help the Icranu would come together as one driving force. Lastly, once that is done, we will annihilate Terminus and set free his army of Conjurers—and take back our planet."

The woman stopped speaking, and the council chamber was silent.

"You're saying all this is going to happen because I became Otherfire," Seth said, "but there's one thing wrong. My body hasn't changed! The only thing that's changed is that I can see a lot better."

One of the men sitting at the council nodded to Cameron. Cameron walked out of the room and came back a second later. He now had a mirror in his hand, pointed at Seth.

Seth looked in the mirror and yelled in surprise.

"The room's on fire!" he bellowed at everyone.

He turned around but saw nothing.

What the . . . ?

"Seth, the inferno that you see in the mirror is your Otherfire," Abigale explained. "You have to suppress it from your eyes so that you may see what other people see when they look at you."

Seth shut his eyes and tried to subdue the energy surging through him. The Otherfire was so powerful that it only receded halfway down his irises. He concentrated harder. The energy leveled down to the high part of his cheekbones.

He opened his eyes and saw himself the way other people perceived him to be. He looked like hell. Literally.

He no longer had any hair. Instead, there was a thick outcrop of blue, yellow, and red fire in the exact shape that his hair used to be.

I look like Ghost Rider mixed with Bobo the Clown.

He glanced down at his hands next. They were giving off a rich white glow. So was the rest of his body. He tentatively touched his left forearm with his right hand. When he made contact, a jolt of electricity went off, popping the air and releasing a small cloud of white smoke.

"How am I not having a seizure or Accelerating right now?" Seth asked the council, still staring at himself in the mirror.

"You channel your energy from Inno Mountain now," one of them answered, "not from Armadron. You are one with us, and one with fire. You *are* the Otherfire. You no longer need to Accelerate, and this is no longer a curse to you. You are above such things."

Seth nodded. He continued to look at himself and his eyes nearly fell out of their sockets. He wasn't wearing any clothes! They were in a heap at his feet, burned to a crisp.

Well, *technically* he wasn't wearing any clothes. Instead he was wearing a covering of fire.

Red fire coated his legs, his torso, and his arms. It looked like he might have been wearing red shorts and an orangish-red shirt made from moving, hissing fire. They were all the same design as the clothing that he had been wearing; just the color was different. Plus, the fire had structure. If you looked at it, you couldn't see through it like you could with ordinary flames. It seemed solid, in some fashion. Seth's new clothes looked and felt the same as before.

"Your mind semiconsciously thought of clothes, and the Otherfire obviously supplied them," Cameron explained from behind the mirror.

"Cool," Seth said.

He took some time to turn every which way, admiring his new body. He played with the electricity between his fingers, watching how it arced between joints, and he smiled.

What happens when I have to pee, though? Seth thought, dropping his hand.

Seth suddenly realized that the room had become silent.

"Council," he addressed everyone, still looking down at his fire-shorts.

"Yes?" they replied in unison, along with Cameron.

"We are all Protectors, all Icranu, right?" he looked at every one of them in turn.

He heard murmurs of agreement from members of the council.

"So let's get to work."

Nothing can stop me now, Seth thought.

"I agree," someone said, chuckling behind Seth.

All the council members looked behind Seth and gasped. He whipped around, shooting off sparks, prepared to fight with his new power.

"Seth!" The man exclaimed as a spark hit his shirt. "This is a good shirt. Please control yourself."

"Sorry, sir," he said and smiled. It was always good to see Thaught.

"Thaught," the woman in the center called to him. "What brings you to Inno Mountain? This?"

"Yes, Abigale. This. I was on my way here to inform you that I have found a young Mediator who is half-Armadronian, and to tell you that Seth was the boy for the Otherfire. They are both with Team 61. However, it seems that you already know everything." Thaught nodded approvingly.

"We do." Abigale smiled. "But how did you know that it was this boy?"

"I had a feeling. You all knew his parents and how powerful they were."

The council members nodded at Thaught and each other.

"I am not a scientist like Terminus, or an atomizer like Artam, but I know potential when I see it. Seth's father asked me to watch over him."

At the mention of his dead father, Seth teared up. Or he tried to. Mini lava droplets, like tears, leaked down his face but only as fast as molasses.

"At any rate," Thaught continued, "the boy is clearly up for the task. I have seen his curse myself, and even before this he was powerful."

"Indeed," Abigale agreed.

"But why is this fire constantly on?" Seth asked. "Will I die even faster now?!"

"No."

A man with a short black beard seated at the council table spoke up. "Seth, as we said before, you are the Otherfire, which is the embodiment of all of our curses, along with the mountain. You can feel our energies if you concentrate. We supply you with the extra energy."

Seth thought for a second. "Then what happens if one of you dies?" he asked.

"Then you will grow slightly weaker, until we can create a new council member who is worthy."

"In that case," Thaught interrupted, "I take it that you will join us in the battle for our planet? That you recognize the threat and will no longer be a neutral party?"

"Yes," Abigale answered.

"Good." Thaught nodded. "Then I am off to alert the rest of the teams around Armadron. In two days, you must try to meet me and the other Icranu at the Gateway."

"And where exactly is that?" Abigale crossed her arms. "Do we know where the Gateway is appearing?"

"We won't know the location until the wormhole reverses; at that point the Gateway will become visible on Armadron. Keep your Bastums at hand and you will be informed of the location when it is confirmed. I will have a teleporter team try and collect everyone we can."

"Wait, what?" Seth glanced at everyone. Clearly, he was missing something.

"Terminus will strike fast, and he will strike hard," Thaught explained. "It's what I would do. He will attempt to reach the Gateway first, so as not to draw opposition from the Icranu or from civilians who will fight him. We may be outnumbered. It's going to come down to old-fashioned, last minute luck of the draw."

"Geez," Seth raised his eyebrows, "we have a whole freaking planet to cover. And we're relying on Bastums."

"And Terminus has his Conjurers," one of the council members spoke up. "They have a hive mind and can communicate instantaneously. We cannot compete with that."

"We have to try," Thaught set his shoulders. "Or we subject another innocent planet to Terminus's torture. I for one, cannot do that. I cannot do nothing . . . again."

The room was silent as everyone thought of all that they had lost.

"Mobilize your forces," Thaught ordered, turning away.

"Wait!" Seth shouted desperately to him.

Thaught's form shifted, then solidified.

"Yes, Seth?" he asked.

"Before you leave, how many other teams of Icranu have you assembled?"

"Three hundred and seven. I have been to the red continent and assembled many teams while I was there. Artam is working around the clock as well. The last I heard from him, he had convinced some Gravics, Storzals, and many others at Hellhole to heed the call, and he has long been involved in the process of freeing those who are trapped within Terminus's castle. At last count, he had freed seventeen Armadronians. I believe that he is still continuing in that work as we speak."

"Great," Seth said.

They were gathering people and saving lives. This is what the Protectors were meant to do. This is what his parents had dedicated their lives to.

"Is that all, Seth? I really must be going," Thaught told him. "We have less than three days left."

"Yeah, that's all."

"Thaught?" the council leader said.

"Yes?"

"Respectfully, why is Artam not delivering these messages? You are our commander, in charge of all the strategies and training, while Artam is to handle the communications."

"I do not know, Abigale. Perhaps he is too busy. We all are. We must split the work."

"Indeed," she agreed.

He turned to Seth. "I leave you with this: Fight with your new set of abilities. Find your team immediately. You will receive the location of the Gateway soon, and I will meet you there."

"Yes sir." Seth nodded his head of fire.

"As for all of you," Thaught projected his voice, addressing the council members, "be warned. Terminus has now finished creation on a new set of abilities. He calls them Upgrades. We must fight through Terminus's supporters without killing them, and then deal with the remaining Conjurers. It will be no easy task, but I assure you that we will have a strategy in place by the time enough of us arrive at the Gateway. We will rely on guerrilla tactics due to his large amount of assets."

Thaught turned around and shifted into a dragon.

Literally, a dragon.

He was now at least as long as a school bus and had thick red and black scales. The dragon, Thaught, turned its head and winked at Seth with its large, terrifying yellow eyes.

Thaught threw back his head and blew red fire onto the rocks above. Then he flew up the stairs, through the magma without any of it harming him, and out into the sky without hesitation.

He was quiet on the entrance, Seth thought, stunned. *But he sure as hell knows how to make an exit.*

21

ONE DOWN, FOUR TO GO!

"Terrifying, isn't it?" Kane regarded the sword in his hand with mock interest. "I think I'll call it Friendkiller."

Sam cringed. "Kane, don't do this," she whispered.

"Oh, I'm not going to do this. You are." He pointed the sword down at Claire's face. "You are going to kill your friend, and I get to watch!"

Claire looked away. Sam closed her eyes and shivered.

"Kane, if you think for one second that I would—"

"Shut up," he threatened.

"—that I would let you hurt Sam, then you're not as smart as you think," Claire finished, ignoring him.

"Shut up!" he barked at Claire.

"No!" she bellowed. "You're just Terminus's pawn. You think that whatever enhanced power he gave you doesn't come with a cost? You've been living under a tyrant who will throw you aside the second he doesn't need you."

Sam was looking back and forth at them, helplessly struggling against her bonds.

"Lord Terminus is the strongest being on the planet. In the universe. You cannot hope to even touch him. Once he leaves for Earth through the reversed Gateway, he has promised me control of Armadron," Kane explained proudly.

"What do you mean?" Claire asked, buying time. "Terminus doesn't even control all of Armadron. He doesn't control anything past the Unknown Waters. He has experiments in there that prevent anyone—even Terminus himself—from going further. That's a quarter of the entire planet that no one knows anything about!"

"Then I shall explore that side when I become king. Now be quiet."

"Make me, you effing puppet," Claire spat at him.

A wad of spit almost hit him in the face, but he dodged it.

"You insolent little girl," Kane sneered at her and then smiled as he was struck by a sudden thought. "If you will not shut your mouth, then I shall do it for you."

Claire had seen that expression before in the Coliseum. She had seen it when her parents had been killed, too. It was a look of pure lunacy.

"What are you . . . ?"

Claire stopped what she was about to say. Her mouth felt like it was literally getting sewn shut. She would have screamed and pleaded for him to stop, but no words would come out. Blood leaked from her mouth as something cut again and again into the soft skin around her lips.

"Stop! Pleeeeaaase!!" Sam screamed, clawing at the ground, trying to look away from Claire.

Kane glanced at her and shifted halfway into another person whom he had killed. He overpowered her physical will with a simple thought. He forced Sam to look at Claire and locked her eyes into place so that she couldn't look away.

Sam watched in horror as Claire's mouth was sewn shut by a floating needle and a thick black thread.

Sam felt Kane's power release her and she turned to the side and hurled. She sat back up straight and wiped the foul acid from her mouth with the back of her hand.

Claire was now lying sideways in the fetal position.

"Stand up and take the sword," Kane ordered Claire.

She didn't move.

"Kill the dumb animal. Or I will."

Sam's piercing cries banged against Claire's consciousness. Claire stirred, then crawled to her feet and began to walk slowly toward Kane.

"Good. Now take the sword from my hand and kill her," he ordered with no emotion.

Except pure, psychotic joy, that is.

Claire took the sword from him with cold, dead eyes. She walked over to Sam and rested the sword on her neck.

Sam was trying to say something.

"I'm sorry, what are you trying to say?" Kane mocked her.

"Now," she whispered to Claire.

Claire whipped around, sword in hand, and flung it at Kane as hard as she could.

Sam had been trying to save up the energy fueling her curse. She unleashed it now, trying to neutralize Kane's curse for as long as she could.

He faltered for a moment but had just enough time to jump out of the path of the sword. He landed on his side in front of the entrance to the Infinite Cave, morphing again, this time into a thin man with a thick stubble on his chin.

Claire used her telekinetic power to change the course of the sword. It whipped around and rocketed at Kane's heart. He jumped above the sword by pushing up on a pillar, which he'd suddenly built from the earth using the ability of his current body, and the sword shot into the cave.

Kane shifted into a short woman and attacked Sam's mind with a thousand mental knives. Sam went limp and fell backwards, her eyes rolling back. Kane smiled.

He morphed back into his favorite body, which was heavily muscled and stood a couple inches above six feet. With his "Kane" body he reached out with his hand, and something unexpected happened. Green sparks danced across his wrist and palm, and a strong electrical pulse shocked him. He fell to the ground, grimacing at Claire.

"Resourceful, Claire. Very resourceful." Kane clapped, suddenly now only a foot away from her. "Having Sam try to neutralize me long enough for you to kill me? That was very good. I did see it coming, though."

Kane paced around her. Claire tried to concentrate on the sword's energy. If she could only locate it . . .

"Trying to find my sword, are we?" Kane smiled. "Don't worry. My master's curse took care of that. I attempted to teleport it to my hand again, but the cave ran interference due to whatever forces repel him. I imagine that the sword is lost now in the depths of the cave."

My vision, she remembered with a start. *Nick and Scott!*

"Your friends?" Kane interrupted her thoughts. "Ah, yes. We will see them soon. Hopefully they will last longer than that unsightly animal over there." He twisted his head in Sam's direction. As did Claire.

She attempted to scream for Sam, but the thick thread around her lips had them firmly sewn shut. She cringed in pain as the thread stretched when she attempted to speak. Claire limped over to Sam, sat beside her and drew her head into her lap. She hummed soothingly to her friend.

"She obviously can't hear you," Kane explained, examining his clothes for dirt. "She's dead."

Claire glared at him. Dirt and blood covered Sam's face, making her not even look human anymore. He was right, though: Sam had no pulse.

"Look, I'm sorry!" Kane cried, acting like a little kid. "I just got a little carried away! It won't happen again. Well, maybe it won't happen again." He grinned an evil grin. "Maybe next time you and your little friends try to fight me, you will learn to—"

He stopped midsentence.

Claire stared at him.

"Of course!" He playfully slapped himself on the head. "The Coliseum! I can see which one of you survives the longest. Hopefully you'll last longer than the animal." He smiled at Sam's dead body. "I think I'll not make it teams this time. I believe that I will make you face each other individually. I still have a day until my master colonizes Earth and I get control of this planet, so why not have a little fun?"

She started shaking. Usually, Kane would just let people attack each other in the Coliseum, because he generally didn't care. However, Claire had heard of a couple instances where he would bring out opponents—hybrids, unnatural animals, some of Terminus's failed experiments—to battle people if he took a special interest in them.

—*You think right, Claire,* Kane thought to her. *I have a special surprise for you.*

* * *

Scott ran until his feet hurt, but it didn't feel to him like he was getting anywhere. Before, they had just been in what looked like one cave. Now he realized that the Infinite Cave consisted of perhaps hundreds of smaller caves that were all interconnected. All he could see was, well, nothing. The darkness of the cave enveloped everything. Light was not an option.

"Nick!" he bellowed for perhaps the billionth-and-a-half time. "Nick!"

No answer. Great.

"Where are you?" he asked, half to himself.

Scott rubbed his heel on the cave floor, feeling miserable, thinking of Nick. His foot jerked itself to the left on its own accord.

He jogged in that direction, following his instincts. He continued to think of Nick, and as he did, his feet seemed to read the earth like a compass.

Nick controls metal, he thought. *I wonder if that has anything to do with this!*

He ran faster.

He couldn't Accelerate. The cave was doing something to him. Something bad. He no longer had his sonar vision, and he couldn't really see where he was going. His feet seemed to know exactly where they were going, though. He ran through tunnels, and in no time at all he heard sounds of screaming.

It was Nick. It sounded like he was being tortured.

His feet followed the sound to a door that was made entirely out of bones.

Scott backed away from the door, covering his mouth to keep from throwing up. The stench was unbearable! It made his head swim and his eyes blink uncontrollably. The smell was so disgusting that his nose started to bleed.

He took off his shirt and tied it to the back of his neck, spreading it over his mouth like a handkerchief. Then he put his hand on the knob made entirely of jumbled human teeth and pulled at the door. It opened easily. All Scott had to do was barely move the door from its current position, and it swung the rest of the way with a creak.

He was now staring down a narrow, dimly lit hallway that was also made entirely out of human bones. He started walking.

He looked down at his hands and realized that he could see them now. As he approached the end of the hall, the light grew until he could make out another door at the end, made of more human bones. There was a very disturbing theme here.

He realized that the light was coming from behind the door. He put his hand on the knob and stopped.

He had seen too many movies where people would open a door out of curiosity and end up dead. Still, the pressure in his legs pulled him toward the door. Nick was in there. He was sure of it.

"Oh, hell." Scott sighed as he pulled at the door.

It didn't open. He tried again. Nothing.

He hit the door in frustration with his hand still on the knob. The door opened inwards.

Oh. It's a push.

Scott scratched his head. This was one of those times where he was happy no one had been around to see that.

He laughed to himself despite the seriousness of his situation and took a step into the room just as someone slammed the door back into his face.

His nose took the brunt of the attack. It cracked and flattened against his face. He fell down to the ground with blood splattering beneath the shirt covering his face.

The last thing he saw before he passed out was Nick standing over him, holding the door handle.

* * *

Scott awoke to the smell of smoke. He coughed and opened his eyes.

He moved a bit and cried out in pain. Ropes tied his feet together, and another cord bound his hands behind his back. He was hanging upside down about two feet off the ground. His bloody shirt was now tied snugly around his neck.

"Have a look around, boy."

He looked around to see who had spoken, but no one was there. He saw that he was hanging in the middle of a circle of fire. Thirteen candles with blue flames, placed around the circle, lit up most of the room. The only part that wasn't lit up was a dark corner on the far side of the room.

A chill went up Scott's back. He stared harder at that corner until something came into focus.

"Yes, good. You see me. But do you really *see* me?" the voice in the corner asked.

Someone stepped out of the corner. It was Nick.

"Nick? What is this? What's going on?" Scott asked, confused. The blood was rushing to his face, making it hard for him to keep his eyes open and to speak normally.

"Nick? Oh, is that what this body is?" Nick asked, but not in his voice. "No, I am not Nick. I am more. Much more. Or at least I was. I am Plegaborne, the Higher Being of Sacrifice."

"What?" Scott asked, bewildered.

"Did you not hear me, cretin?" Nick's face turned into an ugly sneer. "You mean to tell me that you have not heard the Armadronian tales of the old gods?"

"No. I'm not exactly from around here," Scott answered.

"Interesting. Well then, since we have quite some time, and you are my first willing visitor, I will have to tell you, won't I?" Nick's body paced around Scott. "Where shall I start? Oh, yes!

"I had lived in a Higher Plane of existence, on a planet known as Earth for many millennia. However, some years ago I went to bring death to a man, as I normally did when an offering was presented to me. He was floating endlessly in the bottom of the ocean. I knew something was wrong with the man. He had something different inside him. When I touched him, something strange happened. He awoke from death and saw me even though I was on a different plane! The man grabbed hold of me and somehow—I don't know how—extracted part of my soul. In fact, half of my essence was stolen from me in that moment."

Nick/Plegaborne sighed.

"He injected that part of my essence into himself, which empowered him to travel to the Chaos Dimension where no lesser being in the Six Worlds Complex has ever gone before. That part of my essence acted as a shield against the forces there, and I have never been able to access it since.

"The next thing I knew there was a flash, and we were both transported to this wretched planet. But I was weakened and had a physical body for the first time in millenia, and so the man threw me into this cave and used my own abilities against me. He had a Conjurer lay a powerful spell on me that prevents me from leaving this cave. However, what the man did not find out until many decades later was that his curse backfired. Since he had stolen part of my essence, his body was not in perfect sync with the power. Now, my ability will not allow him to venture into this cave, and anyone to whom he grants power will suffer the same fate."

"Then what happened?" Scott asked, silently stretching his fingers behind his back, attempting to break the cord.

"Then the rest of my essence slowly began to wither away." Plegaborne sighed. "I no longer even have a body, so I have to possess the unfortunate bodies that dare to enter this cave. Each body lasts forever to me, because the man did not take away my invulnerability. However, I eventually grow tired of one body and move to the next. Sacrifice is needed to keep balance," Plegaborne added. "I will never forget that man, and I still wonder how he somehow possessed the power to see the Higher Planes. Still, it is better than being enslaved on that stench-ridden planet Irri again."

"Okay, listen, Plegaborne," Scott said nervously, thoroughly confused. "Do—do you think you could let us go? Just this once? I mean, you could find another body, right? You said that you don't really need us."

—Scott! Nick! It's Claire! Get outta there and help us! Sam and I are about to die! I'm being forced to get my mind read by—

Scott strained to hear more, but there was only silence. He fought back feelings of panic and tried to refocus on solving the one problem keeping him from helping Sam and Claire: Plegaborne.

"Hmmm," Plegaborne answered. "No. I see that you are partly from Earth, just like the man was. That means that you can hold my essence and maybe, just maybe, you can disrupt the stability of the curse long enough for me to get out. However, seeing as how I don't need him, I will let this one die. The one you call Nick."

"What?!" Scott gasped.

He was almost ready to pass out from being upside down for so long.

"Plegaborne," Scott pleaded, "listen to me! You can't—"

"Yes, yes. That's a good idea," Plegaborne mused, scratching his chin thoughtfully.

Nick's body crumpled to the floor, and a deformed, black holographic ball was sucked out of his chest. The ball moved lazily toward Scott in midair. If Plegaborne's spirit had eyes, Scott would have sworn that he was watching him squirm.

"Plegaborne, no! Please!" Scott whimpered.

The ball was almost at his chest.

Scott played his last card, even though he really didn't know what it meant.

"I can make you a deal!" he cried. "I'm a Mediator!"

Plegaborne stopped just before entering Scott's chest.

Scott blew out a breath of relief.

The black ball shot at Scott and disappeared within him.

Scott's body felt a familiar tingling feeling.

—What could you possibly have to offer, halfling? Plegaborne asked Scott from inside the depths of his consciousness.

—I promise that I can find the man who cursed you and bring him back to you.

—You do not possess the power, Plegaborne said, mocking him. *You will be no match.*

—I may not be, but my friends and I will have a plan. If you try to take my body now, then my friends will find you and kill you once they realize that you are not me. There are a lot more teams out there, just like mine.

—Ha! Plegaborne laughed into Scott's thoughts. *I am invulnerable to your petty curses.*

—Not in my body, Scott interjected, going with a gut feeling. *In my half-Armadronian body, like you said about the curse, your powers will be shifted and corrupted. You won't be nearly as powerful.*

Plegaborne remained silent for a while, lost in thought. He then spoke.

—All right, halfling, Plegaborne sighed. *I have thought about your proposal.*

Scott waited inside his own consciousness.

—I have read your mind, Plegaborne said into Scott's thoughts, *and I see now that you are the key to stopping the one known as Terminus. I damn Lezkav for the day that he assumed the role.*

—Lezkav? Scott asked.

—Yes, boy, Lezkav! The Higher Being of Chance! He is the one, after all, who created the Mediators. His infernal meddling in human affairs has caused this imbalance.

—He created me? Scott asked.

—*No, you idiot. The Highest Being created you. Lezkav simply rolled the cosmic dice. Long ago, he randomly selected an inhabitant of each of the planets in the Six Worlds Complex and created a bridge for that person to the Chaos Dimension. Forever.*

—But why would he do that? And what does being a Mediator actually mean?"

—*He was bold and foolish, wishing to empower humans so they would no longer be simply pawns on our chessboard. Now shut up and let me think, human.*

Scott waited, letting the silence speak for itself.

—*All right then,* Plegaborne thought irritably. *I will now merge my essence with yours and take control of your body. I will take my chances and use your memories and knowledge to have my revenge, and then I shall return to the Chaos Dimension and be free again.*

—*No!* Scott thought.

Plegaborne chuckled darkly and attacked Scott's mind. Scott tried mentally to push him out, but Plegaborne was too strong.

—*Give up,* Plegaborne spoke inside Scott's mind, *I have infinite endurance, and you do not.*

—*I have something else,* Scott thought.

When Plegaborne had entered his body, Scott realized that the familiar tingling feeling was the same one he'd experienced after physical contact with people who had curses and abilities other than his own.

I was able to talk to Claire in her mind, even though she has that power and I don't, Scott thought to himself.

—*Are you attempting to solve a mathematics problem? How human.* Plegaborne continued his mental onslaught relentlessly.

I have lightning-fast reflexes, Scott continued thinking to himself, knowing he could be overheard by Plegaborne. *I never had those before, and Sam's neutralizing ability doesn't affect me.*

—*You will die, halfling.*

I found Nick by using magnetism, not by the earth curse that I have. I shouldn't be able to do that. Those abilities are theirs, not mine.

—*I will crush your consciousness forever.* Plegaborne laughed.

I copied what made them special! Scott realized, the pieces finally coming together. He addressed his next thought to Plegaborne directly.

—*So that means I can copy you!*

Plegaborne quickly redoubled his efforts to attack Scott's mind.

Scott merely smiled. He knew what being a Mediator really meant now, and what he had to do.

He focused on Plegaborne and neutralized him by using Sam's ability, making him completely harmless.

—*Noooooooo!* Plegaborne howled.

Scott then copied Plegaborne's own immense powers and merged them into his body. He felt a rush of power that made his limbs tingle.

Plegaborne became silent.

He felt Plegaborne in his mind, but he was harmless to him now. He was now just a consciousness possessing the same power that Scott had just copied. If Plegaborne was inside his consciousness, Scott knew that he himself would remain in control.

After a minute, Plegaborne sent a thought through Scott.

—*What have you done to me, human?!*

—*I'm not a human. I'm a Mediator. And I copied your power from you,* Scott answered. *So we're equals now.*

—*Then let me go or kill me,* Plegaborne said angrily. *You have no further need of me. Do not prolong my suffering in this prison. I am not on Irri. You cannot hold me in this prison.*

—*I made a promise to you that I would find the man who cursed you and bring him back to you. This is the easiest way, and plus, you're a lot smarter than me. I might need your help.*

—*I will kill you the second that you let your guard down,* Plegaborne responded calmly.

"The enemy of my enemy is my friend," Scott muttered.

He suddenly realized that he had just spoken aloud. He opened his eyes but couldn't register what he was seeing.

Nick was alive. He was crawling over to Scott, who was now standing up.

Scott looked behind him. There was no longer any evidence that he had just been hanging from the ceiling. There was no rope, no blood, nothing.

"You okay, Scott?" Nick asked him, slowly crawling closer.

"Yeah," he answered a little shakily. "I can't say the same for you, though."

Nick's right leg was turned at a grotesque angle below the knee. Scott could see bone poking out of the skin.

—*F**k you, Plegaborne,* Scott thought.

—*Such primitive language.* Plegaborne laughed in his mind. *The beast deserved it.*

"I'll live," Nick grimaced.

He kept trying to crawl, but Scott stooped down and hoisted him up. After a couple muffled curses, Nick was back on his feet.

"Let's go find our friends," Scott said.

"Let's go find a fricken healer," Nick added.

There was a low growl from somewhere in the tunnels behind them. They moved faster, and soon they were out of Plegaborne's bone lair and back into the darkness of the Infinite Cave.

—*There are other things besides me in this cave, boy,* Plegaborne said inside his mind. Scott chose to ignore the ancient being, but Plegaborne kept laughing anyway.

* * *

After about an hour of hobbling supported by Scott, Nick stopped to rest.

"Water," he croaked.

"I don't have any—" Scott started to say then stopped. He literally had the curse of controlling water.

—*You are an imbecile,* Plegaborne commented dryly inside Scott's mind.

"Open your mouth," Scott directed Nick.

Nick opened his mouth.

Scott concentrated, thinking of water. Nothing happened.

"Adrenaline," Nick told him.

"Right. Adrenaline."

He thought of running during soccer tryouts back on Earth. That made him think of Molly Clenton too.

God, I miss that woman, Scott thought.

Ugh, Plegaborne mentally threw up.

Scott's heart sped up. He quickly thought of water, and a trickle leaked out of every one of his fingers. Scott held his fingers over Nick's mouth and let the water fall. After a couple greedy gulps, Nick tried to stand up again.

Earlier, Nick had reset his own bone below his knee. It still wasn't perfect, and it had been the grossest, most painful thing Scott had ever watched—but it enabled Nick to walk. Sort of.

Scott helped Nick to his feet, and they stumbled on.

Thud!

Something hit Scott so hard that he flew back twenty feet. Nick spun in place and fell on his butt, since Scott had been supporting most of his weight.

A heavy glowing mass the size of an SUV had landed on Scott, trapping him.

Unfortunately, Scott took the time to look at it.

—*Get up now,* Plegaborne thought to him. *Now.*

The creature looked like a cross between a centipede and an alligator. It had a sandpaper hide with hundreds of legs protruding from both sides. Something that looked like greenish-yellow mucus ran off its body in various places. The tail had a barbed stinger at the end with venom leaking from it. One large red eye gazed at Scott in hunger. Scott did what came naturally: he screamed and punched it.

—*Idiot,* Plegaborne scoffed.

The thing didn't blink an eyelid—well, not that it had one—when Scott hit it dead center in its bulging eye. It just continued to stare at him.

Suddenly the creature was torn away from Scott by a hurled chunk of metal.

Scott jumped to his feet.

"Come on!" Nick shouted weakly. "Before it gets up!"

Scott ran as quickly as he could toward Nick. He almost made it too.

With a wild screech, the ugly creature leaped at him. It hit him in the side, and Scott rolled several painful yards and came to a stop on his stomach.

The creature was about to strike again.

Scott quickly dissolved the earth into quicksand beneath the creature and, with a start, realized at the same time that he had Accelerated. The thing began to slide backward, being sucked quickly into the muck as if into a giant vacuum.

All at once, the centipede-alligator creature rocketed out of the quicksand and landed on the cave floor, looking angrier than ever.

We're dead, Scott thought.

—That is a fair assessment, Plegaborne agreed.

When the monster had propelled itself from the quicksand, most of the mucus that had covered its legs and hide was left behind. Now Scott could see that all over its body, hidden between and behind the centipede legs, were thousands of sharp, thick, jagged teeth.

The creature turned slightly and curled up into a deadly, spiky ball. It somehow propelled itself toward Scott, and he dove aside at the last second.

The creature took a wide turn and began rolling back toward him.

"Nick! We can Accelerate again!" Scott yelled behind him without looking away from the deadly ball in front. "A little help?"

Scott's sonar vision allowed him to see inside the dark cave perfectly. The beast was bigger than he had originally imagined.

"Too . . . weak," Nick mumbled softly.

Scott was on his own.

He quickly jumped in the air above the rolling mass, but his right shoe caught on one of the jagged teeth of the monster, stretching the rubbery material of the footwear. Startled, the creature howled and reversed directions. The momentum freed Scott and flung him to the hard-packed earth. He landed roughly on his stomach, knocking the wind out of him.

—*Get up and fight, or I will die as well!* Plegaborne screamed.

Scott wheezed in and out in a feeble attempt to get air, but it wasn't working very well.

—*Pathetic,* Plegaborne mused.

As he finally caught his breath, Scott realized the cave had fallen totally silent; the only sounds that could be heard were Nick and himself breathing.

The hairs on the back of Scott's neck stood up. He knew he was in trouble. He turned around and used most of his remaining energy to pull himself to his knees.

The creature was right there, savoring its moment of triumph.

The thing flexed its huge tail and was ready to shoot poison at Scott. Luckily, it had completely overlooked Nick, who was now lying directly under the beast in his Accelerated form.

"Nick, kill it! Kill it!" Scott wheezed, staring at the tail that would soon become a murder weapon.

Nick moved his hands pathetically, but no metal emerged from the ground.

"I can't," Nick moaned. "No energy."

The creature shot poison at Scott, but he threw up a rock wall. The poison cut right through the rock like acid and kept on coming. Scott ducked, and the poison narrowly flew overhead. The creature roared like a deranged lion and, with his enhanced vision, Scott got a good look at its multiple rows of serrated teeth.

"Try, Nick!" Scott gasped, unable to look away from the creature. The thing was flexing its tail again.

"I can't—"

A sword miraculously bounced on the ground and slid right next to Nick. Nick stared at it, amazed.

"Kill it!" Scott screamed.

ONE DOWN, FOUR TO GO!

The creature was about to shoot poison again.

Nick broke out of his daze, and by summoning the last of his strength, he picked up the sword and thrust it into the creature's soft underbelly.

The loudest, ugliest, and most torturous scream ensued for about a minute.

Nick stayed under the creature the whole time, slicing the sword up and down into its flesh.

Once it stopped wailing, the beast curled up like a dead spider and black fluid leaked out from all over its body. With one violent shudder, it was dead.

The sword gave a slight shake in Nick's hand, and a cloak of black energy enveloped the centipede-alligator. When the cloak dissolved, the creature was no longer there. It had been absorbed into the sword.

Without pausing, Scott got up and picked up Nick, who was still holding the sword and gazing at it in bewilderment. He half carried Nick in the direction that they had been going, afraid to look back.

—*That sword is from the planet Irri,* Plegaborne thought inside Scott's head. *But how did it come here?*

"There it is!" Nick cried.

They both saw the light. It was the light at the bottom of the steps that would eventually lead them to the entrance.

No, the exit. It was now the exit.

At the bottom of the stairs, Scott and Nick combined their last remaining strength and used their curses to churn the ground up underneath their feet, riding a wave of metal and earth up the steps, destroying the ancient architecture beneath them without a backward glance. When they reached the top and emerged from the Infinite Cave, they fell greedily into the Armadronian darkness and simply lay there.

Nick was the first to speak. "How come we suddenly could Accelerate down there?" he asked. "Did you kill that Higher Being guy who was controlling me?"

"Sort of." Scott looked up at the purple lightening, then closed his eyes briefly. "I trapped him."

—Idiot! Plegaborne yelled at Scott inside his thoughts. *You are the one who is about to be trapped! GET UP!*

"And here is the package I've been waiting for," someone greeted in a mock charming voice. "Lord Terminus will *love* this."

Just before the boot hit his face and knocked him out cold, Scott saw Claire. She didn't look so good. In fact, she looked like a seriously messed-up voodoo doll.

REJOINED! OR . . . MAYBE NOT

"You must go to your team," Abigale told Seth.

"Yeah, but don't I have to lead you into battle and everything?"

"You can do that if we all meet at the correct Gateway," one of the men from the council said. "For now, you must find your team and get them there. They need you more than we do, I fear. We have our own forces to command."

"Are you sure?" Seth asked.

"Yes, I am sure," the man told him, a note of irritation creeping into his voice. "Find your friends. The Otherfire is meant to be shared, not held up in Inno Mountain. Every second you spend here is another second in which they could be captured. Or worse, killed."

"Okay," he agreed. "I'll go and—"

"I will show you out," Cameron smoothly cut in.

Cameron turned on his heels, and with a short "good-bye" from Seth to the council members, they were out of the council chamber. Soon, they were back in the hallway that would take them to the shaft with the blue flaming disc, which they would use to rise out of the volcano.

"Is it weird looking at me like this?" Seth suddenly asked Cameron as they were walking.

"Yes," he replied, glancing at Seth's hair.

They reached the opening to the shaft, which was now in the ceiling above their heads. The panel was already green, but Cameron put his palm on it anyway.

A circle of flickering blue fire appeared before them. Without any hesitation this time, Seth stepped on the disc of fire. As soon as Cameron was on, they shot upward. The ride was a little shorter than the last one, and a little faster too.

When they stopped, Seth jumped in the air and activated his Otherfire. He was now floating high above the floor, his arms and legs streaming fire.

"I guess I'll see you all in a bit?" Seth asked.

"Hopefully you will."

They were both silent for a moment, then Cameron spoke. "Two of my guards are waiting at the top to part the magma for you, so you will not have to stop."

"Thanks." Seth grinned. "I'll see you later at the Gateway."

"Yes," Cameron agreed, "and take this."

He tossed a roll of parchment up to Seth. Seth burned out his left arm and caught it easily. He opened it. It was a map.

"Thanks."

"You're welcome. Now get going."

Seth took a couple more seconds to memorize some things on the map, and then he was gone.

He flew up into the mountain. He reached the magma on top, and it instantly parted for him. Without stopping, he soared through and came out into open air. Seth floated there for a minute, looking down at the peaceful volcano and the people he might never see again.

I want to live here, he thought. *When this is all over, if we win, I want to come home to Armadron and start over.*

He shot toward the direction of the Infinite Cave. Even though it would take him a day or two to get there, it would be worth it. He was about to change the universe.

He just hoped that everyone else was still okay, and that he could find them and get to the Gateway in time.

* * *

He was back in a cage. He was back in one of these stupid, smelly cages that were coated in blood. Scott wasn't too happy.

Hmm. If I'm in here by myself...

—*You are not,* Plegaborne interjected calmly, making Scott jump.

—*Plegaborne!* Scott thought excitedly, *can you get us out of this?*

—*No.*

Scott's shoulders slumped.

—*Normally I could,* Plegaborne explained, *but my powers are trapped with your body now. I fear that we must respect your physical limitations, or we will both die.*

—*Gotcha,* Scott thought to Plegaborne, then began thinking to himself again. *Where are Claire, Nick, and Sam? Where's Seth? He won't ever know where we are now! This sucks! We were supposed to take Terminus by surprise! We were all supposed to come up with a plan and attack him with the other Protectors! I need to get out of here. And where the heck are Thought and Artam right now anyway?*

A headache and a painful throbbing in the crook of his right arm interrupted Scott's thoughts. He squinted at his arm in the darkness, but there was no evidence of any wound or damage. Maybe he was just imagining things in this tiny cage. He couldn't move anywhere, he couldn't use his curses, and he was scared. He was back to square one. Back in the Coliseum probably.

His arm throbbed again, and instantly he remembered what the pain was. It was the pain he always felt after being stuck with a needle!

Someone had taken blood from him! His monster headache and his feeling of being weak told him that it had been a lot of blood too.

—*Yes,* Plegaborne told him. *A man came in and took some blood from you. I tried to wake you up.*

Before Scott could process this, purple light spilled into the small cave as the wall was slid aside. Two of Terminus's brainwashed Conjurers walked in, dressed in their usual black robes. They put their hands on the bars of the cage and pulled. The bars ripped off with a clang, and Scott climbed out.

"Follow us," the guards said, then headed toward the Coliseum.

Without any time to waste, Scott unleashed a huge torpedo of water and dirt at the two men. The first man was knocked down instantly, but the second one dodged to the side.

Scott directed the torpedo back around with his mind and aimed it at the second guard. It looked like it would easily take him down, just like the first one.

Scott looked down at his shoes for a brief moment and discovered a piece of folded paper tucked into the side of his shoe. He picked it up and closed it in his fist while the guards were distracted.

The Conjurer waved a quick sign and a blue symbol glowed in midair. The man thrust his palm through the symbol, and his whole hand glowed a deep blue. He held out his hand and the torpedo disappeared into it. The Conjurer simply continued walking like nothing had just transpired.

Scott realized with a shock that the Conjurer he had knocked down was gone. He started to turn around, but something white hot pressed into his back, making him stop and face forward again.

"Move," the Conjurer behind Scott ordered.

He walked with the Conjurer shoving him the whole way. Once he stepped out of the cave, he was once again greeted by a screaming crowd, the familiar bloody-black soil, and an imminent sense of doom.

He had time to look at the people sitting in the crowd this time. None of them looked like they wanted to be here. Sure, they all were standing and screaming, but none of the onlookers seemed cheerful or genuinely happy about the fact that somebody was going to die. Some people were even looking away while they continued to smile awkwardly.

He also noticed that many of the spectators would occasionally cast nervous glances around themselves. Scott suspected they were looking for Kane, or maybe even Terminus.

This was pathetic. Terminus was so lonely and so loathed that he had to force people against their will to be near him. Disgusting.

—*Focus,* Plegaborne warned him in his head.

The Conjurer stopped shoving Scott forward, and based on the immense amount of blood, bones, and skulls at his feet, Scott realized they were in the center of the battlefield again. It was dim outside too, and Scott had no idea how long they had until the Gateway would open. He looked up and saw someone walking purposefully toward him.

"Nick!"

"Prepare to die," Nick said in a monotone. His eyes were glazed over, and he was looking at Scott as though calculating the best way to kill him. Like a machine.

"Nick!" Scott shouted, realizing what was going on. "Nick, stop it! Someone is controlling you! He's—"

"Be quiet," one of the Conjurers ordered calmly.

"Go to hell!"

"Welcome to my Coliseuuuuuum!"

It was Kane's voice.

"Everyone take their seats and enjoy the show! The time for action is at hand! Today I have a special treat for all of you. First, the only half-Armadronian in existence on this planet, Scott Faranger, will battle one of his dear friends. Watch as this Mediator is ground into dust! And to top it off, our ruler, Lord Terminus, has taken personal interest in the battle. Who will win?" Kane chuckled from wherever he was.

"Come out and fight, Kane!" Scott yelled. "You're a coward!"

"Next, I have a powerful, psychically-inclined female who will battle her own little brother. Can you think of anything more entertaining than that? I think not!"

The crowd grew quiet.

"I *said,* can you think of anything more entertaining than *that?*"

It was still quiet. Scott looked over at the towering rows of benches and saw that almost all the people were gone. There were only maybe a hundred or so left.

Just as he was about to look away, Scott saw him.

He was walking through the crowd slowly, looking for something. As he walked, he whispered something repeatedly to the people nearby.

Some people's hands twitched when he whispered to them. Nobody turned in his direction, and when he bumped into someone, they turned around confusedly.

Scott realized with a shock that he was the only one who could see the man. He was invisible to everyone else!

He continued walking through the crowd and met up with another man, also invisible to the crowd, who had been walking through on the other side, doing the same thing. They joined hands and yelled, "Now!"

In the moment before the rest of the audience was teleported away, Scott saw Claire attempting to smile to him as she sat in one of the seats, holding the hand of a boy who looked like her, except he had no eyes.

After Artam and Thaught teleported everyone away, all of the Conjurers in the Coliseum vanished, beginning what Scott imagined was a deadly game of teleport-tag.

Realizing that this was probably his only shot, Scott quickly opened his hand and read the words on the paper from his shoe.

Scott,

The other Icranu will be assembling where we now suspect the Gateway to be, which is near Terminus's castle. I, along with Thaught, have assembled hundreds of different teams for different tasks. Your task is to get Nick out of Kane's control and distract Kane long enough for us to release some of the prisoners in the castle. There is one boy in there who, with your help, can defeat Terminus. I will explain everything when next we meet.

Claire is secured. However, after I removed the bonds from her mouth, she told me about Sam's death. I am truly sorry. She was an amazing young woman. Now we all must honor her sacrifice and win this battle.

I can only hope that Seth gets to us in time, before he is lost as well. Thaught has told me that he is now the Otherfire. You may not recognize him when you see him.

One more thing, Scott. You must survive for us. We do not have the resources to come get you, secure the Gateway, and take up battle positions all at the same time. We have narrowed the appearance of the reversed Gateway to seven locations around our world. We are manning ours so that we may defend it. Hold on and buy us time to fortify our positions. Kill Kane. You can do this. We believe in you. You are the Mediator of Earth. If you fail, there is no one else who can take your place, and all is lost.

Scott dropped Artam's note in shock. It floated in midair, suddenly consumed in purple and green flames. Then it dropped to the Coliseum floor, no more than a small pile of ash.

Before he could process the details of the note, he heard a howl of rage. He looked up and saw someone standing between him and Nick. The man's six-foot frame was muscled, and he had brown hair and red eyes that glowed in tune with his obvious rage. He was dressed in a sleeveless shirt, sleeveless suit coat, and a silk tie.

"Where did they all go?" the man spat at Scott.

"They left," Scott answered, grinning.

The man moved so fast that Scott didn't even have time to suck in a breath. While in the process of morphing into another body, the man punched Scott dead center in the chest so hard that he flew backward into the Coliseum wall thirty feet away.

Scott crawled to his feet. He felt fine. Well, not completely fine, but the punch hadn't hurt as much as he'd thought it would. Scott looked at the man and grinned madly at him from across the Coliseum.

—*Do not get overconfident. We do not know how extensive my power is in your frail body,* Plegaborne warned.

Scott noticed that when the man's nostrils had flared with anger, the haze over Nick's eyes had lifted. In that moment of clarity, Nick looked pleadingly at Scott. Then the man regained his composure, and Nick slipped back into being controlled.

"I see that your curses are becoming substantial," the man called from across the Coliseum. "When I took your blood for Terminus, he did not tell me that you don't feel pain."

I don't feel pain? Scott thought. *I felt that.* To the angry man he said simply, "You took my blood?"

"Come, Scott," the man called. "Let's finish this. We don't have to keep you alive anymore. We know everything we need to know, and now we've got the blood we required, too."

"Finish what?" Scott yelled. "You're already finished!"

Just as he had hoped, the man fumed.

The haze over Nick's eyes lifted temporarily.

"Kane!" Nick gasped.

Kane turned around and looked at Nick, who slipped back into being controlled, and the man smiled.

"Clever, Scott. You're trying to release Nick so that he may help you fight me. Ask yourself this, though. Whose side is he really on?"

Kane morphed into a five-year-old boy with long brown hair, then disappeared and reappeared as a man again, now sitting in the empty stands with one leg crossed casually over the other.

"Fighting stance!" he yelled as he shifted into a large, barrel-chested man.

So this is Kane, Scott thought to himself. *But why isn't he just fighting me?*

Nick snapped to attention and lowered his center of gravity. He put his palms curled up by his sides and his elbows back.

Kane? Scott thought frantically. *Of all the things he could say, why say Kane? I could have figured that out on my own!*

"Attack!" Kane shouted happily.

"No!" Scott yelled.

Nick did a perfect front flip right onto the ground. The second that his feet touched, his whole body covered itself with metal. The dim Armadronian light reflected off the metal like cheap, deadly glass.

Nick shot a wall of sharp metal at him. Scott dove to the ground, and the metal soared over his head, burying itself in the Coliseum wall.

—*He is very powerful, and we are not completely invulnerable,* Plegaborne warned Scott.

Scott improvised as fast as he could. He willed the black soil to wrap itself around his body.

—*Not enough,* Plegaborne chastised from inside him. *I'm going to have to help, or we are going to die.*

—*Fine, go for it.*

Scott backed off a little bit and felt Plegaborne take control of the curses that he had inside him.

The soil hardened and became a suit of rock, copying Nick's suit of metal. The black soil was thicker and harder than Earth soil, but it was also more flexible somehow and allowed for better movement.

Scott made enough space in the rock so he could see and breathe, and then steeled himself.

Nick hurled a javelin made of metal at him.

(23)

IT ALL COMES TOGETHER

Seth had been flying nonstop for nearly thirty hours. He'd passed over the Sea of Sand, the Telemines, and the Bridge of Fate with no incidence. He had crossed over the Armadronian Equator, and before that he had flown over what people on Earth would have called the polar ice caps. The entire planet of Armadron was about double the size of the United States as far as Seth could tell. He had seen deserts, mountains, valleys, and volcanoes, but no rivers, oceans, or trees. Or animals. It was all very depressing.

He was about to take a rest because he was hungry.

Out of the blue, Seth saw familiar landmarks and knew that he was near the entrance to the Cavern. He thought about the map and realized he was slightly off course. He stopped, landed on the ground, and slumped to his knees, taking a short break. When he looked up, he saw two little kids. They were maybe nine or ten years old. They were both wrapped in Carcan bolos, the same bolos that he and the team had been attacked with before they landed on the telemine.

Dammit.

He shot fire from his hands and legs and propelled himself to the kids as fast as he could. He landed easily and observed them for a second. There was a boy and a girl, both of whom were wriggling on the ground, trying to escape their bonds. The girl was crying frantically for help, and the boy was focusing all his energy on breaking the ropes wrapped around their limbs. Neither of them had seen him yet.

"You guys look like you could use some help," Seth said.

The kids stopped moving and looked up at Seth.

Initially, his appearance shocked them so much that they were utterly speechless. The girl seemed to ponder her situation and either didn't care or was just tired of being tied up.

"Pleeeease help us!" she cried desperately.

The boy just looked at Seth suspiciously.

He stooped to their level and, without touching the ropes themselves, held his finger out. A thin flame the size a welder might use came out of his finger. Seth cut the bonds with the flame without harming the kids.

The girl shot to her feet and went to hug Seth around the waist.

Just before she reached him, he extinguished his fire and pushed all the energy out, compacting it into a flame bracelet around his right wrist.

"Thank you, thank you, thank you!" she whispered, still hugging him. "I thought the bad men were going to take us."

"Are you one of the bad men?" the boy asked Seth, getting to his feet.

"No."

"You look like one of the bad men," the boy pressed.

"Well . . . I'm not."

The boy nodded slowly, dropping his tough-guy persona. "Thank you."

"We're the bad men," someone said, chuckling.

Seth whipped around to find three men in their mid-twenties and a child. He realized with a shock that it was the same boy who had pretended to guide him and his team through the Invisible Telemine Blockade.

"Get behind me," Seth whispered to the kids.

They happily obliged.

"No," Seth shouted at the opposing group. "You're the dead men."

He released a wave of fire at the four people. The man all the way to the left disappeared before the fire could get to him, but the man next to him was not so lucky. He was so surprised that he didn't even move.

The man instantly turned to ash because the fire was so intense.

The man next to him shot water out of his hands. The water connected with the rest of the fire, and the elements canceled each other out, creating steam. The boy who'd appeared with the three men looked frightened.

Seth felt the air get warmer directly behind him. He was feeling someone's body heat in the atmosphere. Someone much bigger than the two kids who were cowering nearby.

He dove to the ground and turned immediately before one of the men slashed a sword through the air where Seth had just stood. The man stumbled, and before he could regain his balance, Seth kicked fire at him. The man teleported away as he had done before.

Seth used fire to get himself back up to his feet.

The man who had shot water from his hands did it again. Seth twisted his body to the right and just barely dodged the water stream. He shot fire from his own hands, and the man was forced to stop releasing water in order to dive to the side. Seth glanced around for the little boy and girl.

He found them hiding behind a rock near the Cavern entrance, about twenty feet away.

Seth turned his attention back to the hydro-powered man on the ground and the boy who had once led them into danger, now standing next to him, frozen in fear. In that instant, Seth felt another temperature spike to the right of him. He turned and melted the sword being thrust at his heart by simply looking at it and focusing his energy. The man didn't see what happened to his sword in time and didn't let go fast enough. The melting process was so hot that the teleporter's hand melted right off. He screamed, and the melting began to slow.

Before the man could teleport away—if he even could anymore—Seth punched a red-hot fist through his heart, melting his internal organs. The man screamed one last time, then died looking like a melted wax candle.

Seth turned to the man who had shot water at him. The guy was lying on the ground about ten feet away. He looked at Seth and gasped in fear. The boy guide shrank away as well. Deciding they were no longer a threat, Seth turned to leave when a powerful torrent of water hit his back. He was knocked to the ground.

Seth regained his footing and was starting to visualize his next move when he stopped and looked at the man's hand.

He couldn't be too sure with his new vision, but there were swirling molecules in the shape of a cube hidden in the man's palm.

"What the hell is that for?" Seth demanded.

The man smiled oddly and threw the cube as hard as he could at Seth. Immediately the boy guide opened his eyes from a trance-like state.

The cube expanded exponentially right in front of Seth's eyes. Watching molecules going haywire, Seth couldn't tell what the cube was made of until it was right in front of him. Even after he figured it out, he couldn't believe it.

It was a solid wall of Armitranium, the toughest metal on Armadron. Nothing could cut, slash, or grind into it. Supposedly.

Seth couldn't find a way out. The wall was flying at him so fast that he didn't have time to run, fly, dive left, right, or under. Plus, even if he got out of the way, the wall would hit the kids.

He made himself become hotter than an exploding star for about a microsecond and directed the heat straight in front of him.

As the wall hit Seth, he melted through it like a hot knife through butter.

The boy guide, or what was left of him, was now about ten feet in front of him. Seth felt the wall disintegrate into nothingness as the boy who had created it died.

He walked up to the kid. The boy had melted so much that his entire body had become thinner than water. His "remains" seeped into Armadron and disappeared.

Seth's shoulders suddenly sagged. He missed Earth. He never had to kill anybody there.

Suddenly he remembered something.

The two kids!

He found them still hiding behind the rock, crying. The rock was slightly melted in the front and steaming.

Suddenly Seth spotted Mr. Hydro out of the corner of his eye. Seth had forgotten about him.

Contorting his face and body, the man conjured up a ball of exploding ice, sending deadly shards slicing toward Seth like shrapnel. Seth flung lightning at the shards, and they broke up into flakes, then melted into water.

Without pausing, Seth hurled a small ball of pure heat at the man.

The guy tried to put up his hands as a shield, but instead his body fizzed on the spot and evaporated out of existence.

Great. Now they're all dead, Seth thought glumly.

He hated having to kill people. He really, really did.

He flew over to the kids, and they instantly backed up and started wailing. The girl ran away, fearfully looking over her shoulder. The boy did the same, but not before having the last word.

"Monster!" he shrieked at Seth.

He watched them go and sighed. It didn't matter. Those kids would understand someday. Actually, hopefully they wouldn't have to if Terminus was out of the picture.

I have to find my team, he thought, and immediately took flight in the direction of the Infinite Cave.

He'd barely gone five feet before he touched back down. Out of the ground, there were dozens of edible plants growing, producing fruits and seeds. They were all growing in the exact place where the little boy and girl had been standing.

They both could grow food!

Seth began to eat with ravenous hunger. The kids obviously hadn't been trained to grow food, so it took a lot of fruits and seeds to fill him up. He gulped down every bite, attempting to fill the hollow pit in his stomach.

Once he was finished, he shot back into the air, still feeling empty even though his stomach was full.

Twenty minutes later, he was finally standing at the entrance to the Infinite Cave. Seth looked down at it in complete and utter puzzlement.

There were signs of a brutal fight. Still, he couldn't discern one pair of tracks from another! It looked to him like there had been seven people, but that couldn't be right. The tracks were probably just overlapping each other.

"Uuugghh!" he growled.

"This piece should be good," someone muttered, not too far off.

Seth walked toward the voice. The first thing he realized was that someone was dead. He could smell it. The second thing was that someone was getting ready to eat whoever had died. A man hunched greedily over the body.

"Hey man!" Seth shouted.

The man whipped around, knife in hand. He glared at Seth, then grunted when he saw the Icranu symbol on his shirt of fire. The man put his knife away by attaching it to his belt.

"'Lo, stranger. Ya nearly gave me a heart attack, lookin' like that 'n all," the man replied. "You off to save another world 'er somethin'?"

"Who died?" Seth asked, not even attempting to explain his new fiery appearance or answer the question. The man didn't seem interested anyway. He had already turned back around to his dinner.

"How should I know?" the man grumbled. "D'you always know the names of *yer* meals?"

Seth was somewhat curious, so he leaned over the man to get a good look.

"What's wrong with you, man? You ain't ne'er seen a grown man eat before?"

No. No way. This cannot be happening. Not now, not ever.

The man looked at Seth uneasily, then said, "Could ya take a step back, mister? You might cook the meat, 'n I wan' it raw."

Seth's anger exploded. He took the man by his shoulders and threw him a good ten yards from Sam's dead body. Then he collected a ball of intense energy in his hand and threw it at the ground right where the guy had landed.

The blast was short but powerful. With a tiny pop, the guy was blown off his feet, far into the distance. He went so far away into the air that Seth couldn't even see his outline after a while. The man screamed the whole way, smoke trailing in his wake.

Seth crouched down next to Sam. Turning off his heat, he carefully picked her up and cradled her in his arms.

"Sam, Sam. Nooo, Sam," he moaned, his mouth against her hair.

He closed his eyes and willed her to respond. Did he have powers he hadn't discovered yet? Could reviving someone he loved be one of them?

"You have to be alive. Please be alive . . ."

Nothing.

Seth shook his head and howled to the sky. He rocked back and forth on his heels for a while, continuing to hold her lifeless body.

"You were closer than a sister to me," he whispered.

Eventually he did what he needed to do. He gave her a proper burial. He called fire out of the depths of his being and burned her to ashes. Then he levitated the ashes and scattered them far and wide into the winds of Armadron.

Once the last of the ashes had blown away into the distance, he looked around for a few minutes for other bodies. Holding his breath . . . afraid to look . . . afraid to hope . . .

Please don't let Claire be here. Pleasepleaseplease . . .

After finding nothing, he took off.

There are only two people who have the power to do this, he thought as he flew toward the direction of the Coliseum. *Kane and Terminus.*

And I'm going to kill them both.

BREAKING BONDS

Scott waited for the right moment. Once the metal javelin was close enough, he intercepted it with a boulder. The boulder knocked the javelin off course, but with a wave of Nick's hand, it made a beeline toward Scott once again. Scott immediately used a constant stream of both water and earth to slow the javelin in its path until it dropped to the ground.

Nick walked slowly to the left while repeatedly punching the air. Every time he did so, a thin layer of metal flew off his suit and sliced through the air toward Scott.

Copying his technique but moving to the right instead of the left, Scott retaliated by quickly shedding a layer of the rock he'd formed around his body. He repeatedly shot the rock to collide midair with the metal, sending it spinning and crashing down.

Nick and Scott were now circling each other, neither of them getting the upper hand.

Scott risked a quick glance at Kane. He was gone from his place in the stands.

Dammit, Scott realized, *this was all just a distraction.*

"Nick," Scott shouted at his friend over the repeated clash of metal and rock, "you're too strong to be controlled like this. You can stop it before you lose yourself."

The attacks continued. They stared each other down, looking like demons in their Accelerated forms.

Scott ground his teeth together. Using one hand, he continued to block the incoming metal by shedding and throwing rock from his improvised body armor. With the other hand, he summoned a huge mass of moving earth and waved it toward Nick, willing it to encase itself around Nick's body. The metal instantly stopped coming because Nick could no longer see. Scott stepped toward him and continued to form the earth and rock around him.

Nick was thrashing in place, attempting to free himself. Scott, walking toward Nick, kept piling it on.

Scott heard a sound behind him. It was most likely Kane, which gave Scott an idea.

The huge lump of earth vibrated, cracked, and fell apart. Nick stepped out of the rubble and mechanically walked toward Scott. Scott was exhausted and fought to keep his eyes open as Nick created a spear of glistening metal out of the earth.

"Nick . . . ," Scott began. He felt like he was about to pass out. Forever.

"Good-bye, Scott Faranger," Nick replied in a hollow voice.

He thrust the spear toward the space between Scott's eyes, just as Scott lost consciousness.

* * *

Seth couldn't believe what he was seeing. Flying toward Terminus's castle, he was above the almost-empty Coliseum when he looked again and spotted his friends.

Seth flew toward Scott as fast as he could. However, he was still about eight hundred yards away when Nick broke out of a lump of earth.

What is going on?! Seth thought.

He saw Scott fall to his knees; Seth figured the overuse of his powers had exhausted him.

Seth was now less than a hundred yards away.

Nick, covered in metal, walked toward Scott and created a spear. He said something, then thrust it toward Scott.

Seth didn't make it there fast enough.

His fire did.

He rocketed toward Nick, firing a bullet of solidified flame from each of the fingers on his right hand. They connected with the spear of metal and wrenched it from Nick's grasp. Scott fell to the ground, completely passed out at this point.

Without moving his body, Nick turned his head around at a grotesque angle and glared at Seth.

Seth landed between Scott and Nick and glared back at Nick. Before he could grasp what was going on, metal rose from the ground and coiled around his entire body.

"Nick, stop," Seth pleaded, the air swiftly rushing out of his pores.

The coils ceased constricting for a moment's reprieve, then resumed crushing the life out of Seth.

Seth let his Otherfire burn through the metal. The metal slowly fell around him in molten pools. He stepped closer to Nick, noticing that something was horribly wrong.

With his new vision, Seth could see that Scott's inner fire was a solid color: dark green. However, when he looked at Nick, his inner fire was a light blue on the inside, but his skin had a dark-red layer that enveloped his entire body. His inner fire was flickering, almost as if it were dying out.

"Die," Nick stated calmly in a robotic voice, and then he attacked.

He came at Seth like lightning. In a nanosecond, long, sharp metallic swords replaced Nick's hands. He jumped and spun like a tilted helicopter blade, slicing the air repeatedly toward Seth's face.

Seth dodged and rolled to the left, attempting to stand while Nick thrust at him with an arm. He instantly reacted by heating up a tiny pocket of air in between them.

The second Nick's "arm" passed into that pocket of air, it fizzed, and instead of the metal melting, it broke off.

Heat expands metal, moron, Seth thought smugly.

His thought was cut short by a sharp blade slicing its way toward his face. Seth ducked at the last second.

Talk about a close shave! Nick's blade would have sliced through his hair except it was made of pure fire now.

He noticed that Nick had two blades again.

"Hey!" Seth cried. "Watch the hairdo! It took me a while to grow all that!"

Nick laughed, moaned, then immediately regained his machine-like composure. During that time, Seth noticed that the light-blue fire on the inside of Nick's essence had flared, diminishing the red glow on the perimeter.

That meant someone was controlling him by redirecting the electricity in his brain. Probably Kane. He wasn't as powerful as Terminus, and mind controlling wasn't one of his abilities, as far as Seth knew.

"Hey, Nick," Seth said, grinning.

Nick resumed his fighting stance and began circling Seth.

"What do train operators and metal have in common?"

Nick stumbled for a moment, then went back to circling. In the meantime, the real Nick on the inside was trying to figure out the answer.

Just as Seth opened his mouth, Nick danced forward and jabbed both of his pointed metal spears at him. Seth jumped back, just out of reach, and made two lightning bolts appear in his hands.

"They conduct!" Seth finished the joke and rammed both arcs of electricity against Nick's metallic arms.

"Aaaaaarrrgghhh!!!"

Nick fell to the ground, and the metal fell off his body in lumps, turning into rust as it did so. Seth instantly saw that Nick's inner fire was burning bright again, and that the red fire that had been controlling him was no longer there.

Nick was now passed out next to Scott, and they both looked like they had survived an actual train wreck.

Suddenly Seth heard a sharp noise behind him. Diving, he threw his left shoulder into the dirt and fired an electromagnetic pulse at the spot where the noise seemed to be coming from. The noise sounded like nails on a chalkboard reverberating through the air.

He rolled to his feet and stood protectively in front of Scott and Nick. He looked for his attacker.

Before him was a floating speck of green light.

"Meet everyone at the Gateway. Now. The battle is nearly at hand." The floating speck spoke with Artam's voice of authority. "You have three hours. Our Gateway area is the correct one."

Once the message was given, the green speck dissipated into the atmosphere, leaving the scent of a freshly mowed lawn in its wake.

Seth wasted no time. He lightly touched both Scott and Nick on the shoulders and focused his energy.

He tried to control the electricity in both of their brains to wake them up. Seth wasn't having much luck, though.

Nick suddenly shot up, took Seth by the wrist, and threw him over his body and to the side.

Seth stood up and willed a fiery bomb of lava to form into his hand. He hesitated for a second.

"What the hell is your problem?!" Nick stood up and glared at Seth.

Seth was dumbstruck.

"I—I . . . um . . . ," Seth stuttered.

"You what?" Nick continued to stare at Seth accusingly, only breaking eye contact for a second to dust himself off.

"I—I thought your mind was still under control," Seth answered.

"Well, it's not," Nick said.

"Oh." Seth lowered his ball of lava, then raised it again with a sudden thought. "Why did you throw me then?"

"I was testing your reflexes." Nick grinned.

"Funny."

"*I* thought so."

Seth dropped the ball of lava.

"What did I miss?" Nick asked nervously, looking around.

"Well," Seth said, "a lot."

"Tell me."

"Not right now," Seth said, shaking his head. "Right now we have to get to the Gateway."

"Our location is the right one?"

"Yep."

"I can help with that, then." Nick nodded.

He forced a huge lump of metal to rise out of the ground, then molded it into the shape of a small car. It had curved seats on the inside, with no seat belts or steering wheel.

"Aaaah, this again?" Seth whined.

"Just like last time," Nick said with a mischievous grin.

Nick picked up Scott from the ground and laid him in the backseat. Nick sat in the front driver seat, and Seth sat in the front passenger seat.

As soon as everyone was comfortable, Seth formed a constant flow of combustion behind the car with a thought. Nick, however, was doing the steering. Together, they drove the car out of the Coliseum, onto the barren landscape, and sped toward the Gateway with twin trails of fire propelling them.

Seth hesitated, terrified to ask the next question. "Where is Claire? Is she okay?"

"I dunno. I know he didn't kill her, though, because the bastard would have been laughing about it," Nick answered. "You seen Sam?"

Seth's heart dropped into his stomach. "She's dead."

The car pulled to the left, and then Nick got it back under control.

"What did you just say?" Nick's voice was suddenly hoarse. "That can't be true. Are you sure?"

"I'm sure."

"How? What happened?"

Seth shook his head, eyes closed. "I don't know how. But I stopped some dude from turning her into his dinner."

They drove in silence for a couple minutes.

"Did you light him up?" Nick finally asked.

"Hell yeah."

Scott groaned in the backseat. They both turned to look at him, but he was still asleep.

"I hope for our sake that he wakes up very soon," Seth stated glumly.

"Yeah, me too. Did you try electrocuting him a little like you did to me?"

"I tried," Seth said, shaking his head, "but it's almost like a part of his brain didn't want me to wake him up yet."

25

A NIGHTMARE IN A NIGHTMARE

The first feeling that came to Scott was that he was surrounded. He felt like he was in a small glass box at the bottom of the ocean. He could feel pressure coming at him from all sides, compressing his body.

He slowly opened his eyelids and looked around him, trying to find who had just yelled.

He was utterly alone, at least as far as he could see, which wasn't far. He was in a dark place with a strange gray light filtering through the air—except that it wasn't light. Whatever it was, it pulsated through the air, coating everything in a kind of haze.

—*Hello?* Scott called into the gloomy haze.

—*Hello, Scott,* a familiar voice answered.

He turned around and around in circles, looking for the ominous voice. No one was there.

—*Who are you?* Scott asked.

—*Who are you?*

Scott continued to peer into the darkness, but it seemed that the more he looked, the darker the atmosphere became.

—*You just said my name. You know who I am!* Scott said.

—*Yes.*

He was confused. He kept trying to look into the darkness to see who was talking to him, but he couldn't find anyone.

—*I am not on the outside,* the voice said.

Scott felt a low humming sensation. It took him a second to realize where it was coming from. *It's coming from me,* he thought.

Scott could feel another presence occupying the same space that he was, which he figured was pretty much—

—*Impossible?* The voice completed his thought mockingly.

The voice was so clear and powerful that it nearly made Scott jump out of his skin. This felt different from when Plegaborne first shared his mind. Stronger. More integrated. He felt a cold shiver run down his spine. Just then he had a fleeting mental image fly behind his retinas. He knew who it was now.

—*Plegaborne?*

—*Yes.*

—*Where am I? Am I dead?* Scott asked.

—*No. You are in the Chaos Dimension.*

—*The what?*

—*You and I are one now, so now when your human brain sleeps, your unconscious mind can travel to the Chaos Dimension, as mine does,* Plegaborne explained.

—*Why do you call this place the Chaos Dimension? It's quiet.*

—*It is quiet because I am making our presence unseen,* Plegaborne explained slowly. *There are Higher Beings in this place to whom it would not be wise to reveal our whereabouts.*

—*So why are we here?* Scott asked.

—*We are here because when you locked me in your primitive human brain, you placed me in the area that also deals with your unconscious mind. Now, whenever you sleep, I will gain control, as I stated previously.*

—*Well, that's shi—*

—*I am speaking to you now for the sole reason of helping you. Well, for the sole reason of helping us.*

—*Really?* Scott asked suspiciously.

—*Yes. I am here to tell you that you need to copy Terminus's curses.*

—*I've never seen Terminus. I don't even know what he looks like.*

—*I know that. But when you see him, that is what you must do.*

—*Fine,* Scott agreed. *But it won't change anything. It'll just mean that he and I will have the same abilities, and he's had hundreds of years to hone his skills.*

—No, Scott, Plegaborne explained. *You will be able to use numerous abilities at a time, while I believe that he will have to switch between them.*

—I wish I could just absorb his curses now, instead of copying them, so that I could just take them from him, Scott said.

—No. That would kill us both.

—Why?

—Terminus has too many curses now. If you were to take his abilities, your body would tear itself apart.

—But I'll be taking them anyway if I copy them! Scott argued.

—No. What you do and what absorbers do are different. Absorbers take the energy to use the ability, which means that the power to use that ability is stored in their own body's energy supply, or life force. When you, however, touch someone, you reconstruct your genetic code to vibrate in order to fit a new ability. That means that you should be able to have an infinite number of abilities, and still hopefully retain control.

—That's very awesome. And extremely useful.

—It is very useful, Plegaborne agreed. *Now you must wake up and cripple him, and then release me.*

—Release you?

—Yes. You must wound him and then release me into his body. I will kill him from the inside out . . . and, in doing so, finally have my revenge. It is settled then. Now that we are done with our discussion, you must wake up!

* * *

"Finally!"

Scott opened his eyes slowly to find Nick staring at him from the front seat of a . . . car?

He immediately sat up and prepared to shoot Nick in the face with one of his curses.

"Whoa, whoa!" Seth yelled from the other front seat. "Calm the hell down! He's alright now!"

"What?" Scott asked.

"Seth brought me back," Nick explained.

"Oh." Scott sat back and slumped in the seat.

"Wait!" Scott leaned forward again. "Seth!"

"You look tired," Seth replied as a form of greeting.

"I'm *very* tired."

Scott looked at the car. It was made entirely of metal, and there were no gears, brakes, steering wheel, or windshield. Scott guessed there probably wasn't even an engine.

The metal in the front of the car was so thin that they could see through it, so that was kind of cool too.

"Are you done admiring her yet?" Nick asked.

"No." Scott grinned through his exhaustion. "What the hell is this?"

"A car. I made it," Nick answered shortly.

"Alright, I'm done now," Scott replied, rolling his eyes.

"Good," Seth said, "'cause we all have some catching up to do."

"Yeah we do," Scott agreed in amazement, staring at Seth's new form for the first time.

Seth turned around in his seat.

"You like?" Seth joked.

"You look like Ghost Rider," Scott said admiringly.

"That's what *I* was thinking!" Seth agreed.

They both erupted into laughter, but Nick didn't.

"What's a Ghost Rider?" Nick asked.

Scott shot him a puzzled look.

"It's an Earth movie thing." Seth waved him off.

"What's a movie?" Nick asked, still confused.

"It's an Earth thing," Scott said.

Seth and Scott laughed again, and Nick began to get frustrated.

"We're only an hour away," Nick cut in. "We need to catch up."

"Sure," Seth responded.

After Nick and Scott shared what had happened to them since the Telemine, it was Seth's turn. When Seth shared his discovery of Sam's death, Scott closed his eyes. A repressed memory of Sam's death mentioned in Artam's note reared its ugly head.

The three young men in the car fell silent.

Eventually, Seth cleared his throat and broke the silence. "Do you have a ton of curses now?" he asked Scott.

"I guess so."

"So why didn't you neutralize Kane with Sam's ability and kill him?" Nick wanted to know.

"I tried. He didn't even blink."

"Didn't even blink?!" Seth and Nick said at the same time.

"Yeah."

"What about when Nick was trying to kill you?" Seth asked.

"I forgot," Scott admitted. "I was too busy trying not to hurt him. Plus, it's hard to . . . you know . . . use her abilities. It just doesn't feel right."

Seth nodded, looking confused.

The sorrow and remorse were almost palpable.

They were nearly there. They were just fifteen minutes away from . . . well, no one really knew.

"This doesn't feel real. Everything is happening too fast," Scott said.

"I know," Nick agreed. "And now, in about an hour, Terminus is going to try to get to Earth through the reversed Gateway and take an army of Upgrades with him."

A moment later he added, "We're here."

The car stopped as Seth withdrew his arm from the window opening, stopping the flow of combustion. Without a moment's hesitation, Nick and Seth climbed out.

Scott didn't move. *Do I really want to do this?* he asked himself. *What happens if I can't beat him?*

—Then you will never see your family again, and you will lose, Plegaborne whispered from a corner of his mind. *And you will always have me in the wings of your mind, waiting for you to fall asleep so that I may take control. So get on with it.*

Scott thought of Jared, his mom, Molly, and his friends. They would all be dead or enslaved if he failed.

He felt his pockets. The Bastum was gone, but Jared's inhaler and Scott's cell phone were still there.

He stepped out of the car.

(26)

POTENTIAL

Scott looked around as he exited the car. There were hundreds of people everywhere.

They came in all colors, shapes, and sizes. Most of them had the Icranu symbol somewhere on their bodies or clothing, and they all stopped whatever they were doing and looked his way. He felt like the lead guitarist at a rock concert, the person everyone had been waiting to see appear on stage.

Someone stood in front of him in a flash of light and held out a hand. It was Artam.

"Hello, Scott," Artam said as they shook hands.

"Hello, Artam."

Artam turned to the hundreds of eager faces surrounding them.

"We are here for two reasons," Artam said, his voice suddenly amplified so that everyone could hear him. "We are here because Terminus will destroy our worlds if he is not stopped."

There were murmurs of agreement all around them.

"We are also here because of Scott and the role that he plays in our destiny." He nodded at Scott, who remained silent.

Artam continued. "Kane is now wandering the Roots of Metali, past Inno Mountain, searching for us. Earlier today we freed many individuals, and because of our actions, Kane is now very angry. Good. He and Terminus have killed many, *many* innocent people. They have enslaved my brothers, and they have experimented on your children. They are done doing what they want."

There were approving nods and expressions of relief throughout the crowd. Scott spotted Nick and Seth standing next to Thaught, Claire, and a boy with no eyes.

"Furthermore," Artam continued, "I will share with you this: Kane allowed us to break free from our enemies today."

He let the statement hang in the air, and the crowd instantly became silent.

"Our intel has relayed to us that Terminus wishes to use his Conjurers and his loyal, misguided Armadronian followers to keep us busy while his new race, the Upgrades, moves on to Earth past us. He thinks that we are only a minor military exercise for him."

Many people shook their heads, spat on the ground, or cursed Terminus's name.

"We will exercise them to death then!" Thaught was speaking now.

He had morphed into a fly and flown across the field, and was now standing next to Artam, having reassumed his regular Armadronian form.

The crowd cheered, and Artam stepped back smiling, letting Thaught finish the speech.

"We will combine our curses and do what they cannot," Thaught spoke with authority and passion. "Terminus has never taught them the one fundamental concept of battle: teamwork! We will stay in pairs, we will work together, and we will win!"

Everyone cheered, and Thaught held up a hand to silence them.

"Things have changed. Until this point, only Artam and I have ever laid eyes on Terminus. Some of you believe him to be a myth." Thaught sneered. "Well, he is not a myth. He is a cruel, twisted demon who has taken our once-rich planet and turned it into a battleground for his own amusement. He has pillaged our environment. Darkened our skies with radioactive cloud cover. Sent us scurrying underground for security and survival. And as if that weren't enough, he has taken your loved ones indiscriminately from your homes and experimented on them! You may not want to kill someone you once loved if they are under Terminus's control, but they do not remember you, and we must stop the Upgrades from getting to earth, no matter the cost. If Terminus is allowed to cross the barrier, then our world is lost. He will colonize Earth before finding a way to return to Armadron. We will not allow the innocent people of Earth to be killed because of our world. Because of our mistakes."

The crowd hushed as Thought paused for a moment.

"Now we get to the plan," he announced in a commanding voice. "Icranu teams one through forty-seven, along with Scott and myself, will be stationed next to the Gateway, engaging in battle with Terminus to keep him distracted. We believe that when his mind is focused, Terminus has a harder time keeping his Conjurers in check. However, when a Conjurer is killed, that means one less for Terminus to control, and remaining Conjurers will become stronger, faster, and more intelligent than ever before; for this reason, we must not kill them. Let me repeat this: coordinate your attacks so that you don't kill any Conjurers. Our goal is to free them first—and then to use them on our side in the battle."

Now Thought pointed at Seth. "Seth will lead teams forty-eight through eighty-one. You will stay at the perimeter and take out the first wave of Upgrades as they try to reach and secure the Gateway."

Seth nodded.

"Next," Thought continued, "Icranu teams eighty-two through ninety-five will take the east sector, and ninety-six through one hundred nine will take the west. We've sent teams ahead to dig fighting positions for guerrilla tactics. East and west teams are to join them, get in position, and stand by."

—*Ineffective plan,* Plegaborne commented dryly from within Scott. *What about the air?*

"As for Icranu teams one hundred ten through one hundred eighteen, you will cover air attacks. Kill every enemy on sight that is not a Conjurer."

The crowd roared in approval.

"There are about a thousand of us here today," Thought said, raising his voice, "and Terminus will use all of his Conjurers, as well as his followers and Upgrades, to battle us, giving Terminus an advantage over us by several hundred."

The crowd grew silent again.

"But as the humans say, quality over quantity!"

The crowd roared in approval, and Scott could tell that they were ready for anything.

Thought held up a hand to silence the excited crowd, then lowered his voice.

"How many of you have a family member or friend who has disappeared in the last several years?" Thought asked.

The crowd fell silent.

"Who do you think Terminus has been using to do his experiments on?" Thought softly asked. "How do you think he finally got the Upgrades to work, after all this time?"

"We have to kill our family?" a woman in the crowd screamed. "Can't we try to free their minds or something?"

"No," Thought said and sighed. "You cannot, because Terminus is not actually controlling their minds. Terminus is powerful, but he cannot control all the Upgrades' minds as well. We have reason to believe that their new powers have taken over and are creating alterations that even Terminus could not conceive, nor that he can control. That makes them very unpredictable."

"So why are they doing this? Why are they fighting for him?" Scott spoke for the first time in a while.

"They are fighting for him because he has promised them a new life on Earth. A new beginning. And he has manipulated and tortured them for years with the help of his right-hand man, Kane." He once again addressed the Armadronians gathered around him. "They will not know who you are, and they will be unnaturally vicious. Do not hesitate."

A man in the crowd created a pillar of earth that rose from the ground beneath his feet, elevating him above the hordes so he could make himself heard. "So why are we fighting this battle?" he bellowed. "If we can't even save our own kin, why are we trying to save the humans? What have they ever done for us? They don't even know that we exist!"

The Armadronians started to mumble amongst themselves, but Artam stepped forward and spoke.

"We must help them because if Terminus leaves Armadron, he will eventually destroy life on Earth. And when he has done that, he will return to Armadron more powerful than ever. He will be even more unstoppable. We cannot let him leave."

The crowd fell silent again.

"Now, we have spent too long talking," Thought interjected. "It is time for action. Everyone, take your positions near your section leaders. Stand by for my signal and be ready for the fight of your lives. After the battle begins, we may get more reinforcements from Icranu teams as they arrive. They are getting here as fast as they can. We are going to take our planet back, today. We are going to let the fight come to us."

"And the fight has just arrived."

Scott turned and saw a man standing behind Thought, a mocking sneer still on his lips.

It was Kane.

Everyone froze with fear. No one moved an inch.

Kane circled Thought, grinning from ear to ear.

Why is no one moving?! Scott thought.

That's when Scott realized he wasn't moving either.

In fact, he couldn't move anything, not even his eyes.

"But how will you take action when no one can move? My master has you all stopped," Kane jeered.

Suddenly Scott saw the hundred Conjurers flash into existence. They surrounded the Icranu crowd in a giant circle, or at least as far as Scott could tell.

"Let's see . . ." Kane chewed his lower lip, contemplating something. "We still have an hour until the Gateway is operational. Looks like I have time for a little fun."

Kane walked over to Scott, who felt chills go down his spine.

Kane reached out his hand and pointed at Scott, his finger inches from Scott's chest.

"This is the boy who is supposed to defeat us?" He mocked.

Just a little closer, Scott thought. *If only I could—*

"Copy my abilities?" Kane said aloud.

Scott would have gasped if he could have moved a muscle.

"You cannot without touching me." Kane laughed. "How useless you are."

Kane sat back in a sitting position and levitated six feet off the ground. He leaned toward Scott slowly and spoke into his ear. "I will kill all of your friends now."

Scott's heart dropped.

"But do not worry. I promise that I will savor every scream, every terrified whimper, and every pathetic plea for mercy, as I did with Sam."

Come on! Focus! How do I get out of this? Scott thought.

"I understand that you formed a bond with Nick in the Infinite Cave. He feels to you like a brother now, yes?" Kane taunted. "What is it that the humans say again? Love can overcome anything? Let's test that bond, shall we?" Kane disappeared and then reappeared next to Nick.

"Now, I am going to kill him right before your eyes, and we shall see if you can do anything to stop me. If you cannot . . . well, then love just does not exist, does it?" Kane gave an evil grin.

It came to Scott then. The thoughts began entering his mind in quick succession.

How does Terminus have so much power and not die from overexertion of his abilities? Why was he able to control all those Conjurers? Why does Terminus want to colonize Earth when he could do whatever he wants with Armadron?

Plegaborne had told Scott that the man dying at the bottom of the ocean had darkness inside him. Scott realized that man had most likely been Terminus, and Kane was his pawn.

"I think I will kill him with his own weapon," Kane continued.

Scott saw something that resembled a cross between a gun and a sword appear in Kane's hands. The weapon was about three and a half feet long and had knives and a gun barrel at the end of it, its functionality enhanced by a variety of levers and buttons, the purpose of which Scott couldn't begin to guess. Kane pressed a button at the base of the sword, and tip of the blade shot out twenty feet and then sprang back. The sword was now a type of whip, with three deadly knives attached to the end of it. Kane pressed the button again, and the weapon returned to normal.

"Your friend built this," Kane said, looking at the weapon with disgust, "for people whose abilities are not sufficient enough to protect them. He calls this crude machine a Bastum. You see, folks, Nick believes that we should all have a fair chance at survival." Kane waved the weapon in front of Nick's face. "I disagree."

—*Something is wrong,* Plegaborne thought.

—*Yeah, no duh,* Scott agreed. *Everyone's about to freaking die.*

—*No,* Plegaborne responded. *Kane is not the one holding everyone suspended in motion. This is the work of a much more powerful enemy. Kane is merely a distraction to take us away from the real threat. Without Terminus's powers that have been given to him, he only has his own curse.*

Before Scott could grasp what Plegaborne was talking about, Kane moved.

He brought the sword up faster than Scott would have thought possible and sliced downward toward Nick's immobilized head.

—*Take me there!* Scott screamed into the far recesses of his mind.

—*You will not survive with your conscious mind. Only Terminus has done that, and it has obviously corrupted him,* Plegaborne warned.

The sword was almost at Nick's neck.

—*Just do it!* Scott screamed into his thoughts.

THE JOURNEY

The world was burning, and the world was flooding. The world was a black hole and a blinding light. There was death and rebirth everywhere, and Scott felt as if he had been here his entire life.

Or was it a second ago? he thought to himself.

—*Shhhhhh!* Plegaborne thought to him. *The power of the mind controls everything in this Dimension! You must silence your thoughts, or we will be noticed.*

—*Are we back in the Chaos Dimension now?* Scott asked quietly into his mind.

—*Yes.*

—*How did we even get here? I don't remember . . .*

Scott could see giant, unfathomable monsters and beings far off in the distance. He could feel pure, unimaginable power coursing through the air, making the atmosphere vibrate and crackle with energy.

—*Or are they right next to me?* Scott thought, feeling fearful.

—*There are no laws of physics here,* Plegaborne whispered in Scott's thoughts. *There are only the laws of thought.*

—*Wow.*

—*Do not think that,* Plegaborne warned.

—*Think what?!*

—*You were just pondering whether you could open your eyes or walk around. Do not do it. You must use your sixth sense in order to navigate this place.*

—*Okay.*

—*You also must hurry. You came here in order to stop Kane and Terminus, yes?*

—*Yes.*

—*Then you must figure it out quickly, or your feeble human mind will be ripped apart by the Higher Beings.*

—*Geez,* Scott thought, *that's comforting.*

Scott knew what he had to do. He had to find Kane's power source and trace it back to Terminus.

—*Power source?* Plegaborne questioned.

—*You said that Terminus used you as a shield in order to enter this place, like how I'm doing right now,* Scott explained. *I realized that if he knew about you, then he wouldn't stop there.*

—*Go on.*

—*He would want more power. I can see that in this Dimension you guys are all-powerful and whatnot. Terminus is all-powerful on Armadron supposedly, so he must have gotten the power from here somewhere, seeing as how no one else has ever become this powerful.*

—*Where would he have gotten his power?*

—*Well...,* Scott thought. *Where do you get your power? How did you always go back and forth from Armadron and the Chaos Dimension?*

—*Of course,* Plegaborne said, something dawning on him.

—*Of course what?* Scott pressed, growing excited.

—*Terminus must always have a portal open inside himself, so that he can take the infinite energy from here and use it on Armadron.*

Mind over matter, Scott remembered Claire saying to him before he had entered the Infinite Cave with Nick.

—*He's been lying!* Plegaborne exclaimed. *He just takes the power of thought from here, and on Armadron he can do almost whatever he wants to do with it! And he gave some of it to Kane so that he can hide in the shadows and no one will ever know!*

A loud noise that sounded like a wild animal screaming reverberated through the Dimension.

—*However,* Plegaborne noted, ignoring the sound, *on Armadron he is tethered by the laws of physics. He cannot create new matter per se, he cannot create or destroy energy, and his thoughts are only as powerful as his limited imagination. He has thrown aside the part of my essence that he had been using as a shield. Now, the gateway to his power is in his mind. He is unstoppable as long as his mind is connected to the Higher Planes.*

—*Where can we find him in here?* Scott asked.

—*It could take millennia to find him.*

—*But we can't get to him on Armadron either!* Scott cried.

—*Then we shall get to him on Armadron from here,* Plegaborne said.

—*What are you talking about?*

—*Right now, Terminus exists in two places at once. I shall show you.*

Scott felt a buzzing sensation in his head, and then he saw a familiar sight.

He was once again standing by the Gateway. All the Conjurers and Icranu were by him, and Kane's sword was just an inch away from Nick's neck. Scott gasped when he took in this sight, and he suddenly realized that he had control of his body, not just his mind.

—*Do not worry,* Plegaborne thought, *he cannot hurt your friend in this place. But we must hurry before Terminus realizes that we are here.*

—*What do I do?*

—*You must kill Kane. Quickly. That will get Terminus's attention.*

Scott no longer thought about how gruesome it was to kill someone. He was way past that, and Kane had already killed Sam and countless others. Instead, he used one of his many curses and shot a bolt of lightning out of his right palm. It came out slowly, trickling toward Kane.

Something in the corner of his vision moved.

He looked at the spot but saw nothing. Scott looked back toward the lightning and saw a man standing in front of Kane, blocking the bolt. The man had blond hair and was of medium height. He didn't even look scary. He just looked like an everyday normal guy. He was even wearing a plain brown cotton T-shirt and simple black shorts.

Aaargh! Scott cried out in his mind.

The man crossed his arms, annoyed. His eyes moved, and the bolt of lightning disintegrated into electrical dust.

—*Uhhh, Plegaborne?* Scott asked fearfully. *Can he see us?*

"I can see you, Scott," the man said out loud, straightening up. "And if you were wondering, then yes—I am Terminus."

Scott remained silent, backing up a little.

"Are you afraid of me?" Terminus laughed pleasantly.

Scott kept quiet, continuing to inch back.

Suddenly, Terminus grew impatient.

"Why are you walking away from me?" he questioned. "I want to talk."

Terminus extended an arm, and a giant wave of water more than a hundred feet high rushed toward Scott at a breathtaking speed.

I am about to die, Scott thought, accepting his fate. *I failed, and now he's—*

—*You can do what he can do!* Plegaborne yelled. *This dimension is controlled by thought alone!*

Scott acted on instinct. He extended his arms, and the wave evaporated into nothing.

"I see that you have found the secret," Terminus said, smiling and walking slowly toward Scott. "But that's no issue. The comet that will reverse the Gateway is an hour away at most, and you don't have what it takes to challenge me."

"Why are you doing this?" Scott suddenly asked, catching Terminus off guard. "This doesn't make any sense. You're already the ruler of Armadron. Why do you want Earth?"

Terminus stopped mid-step and smiled.

"You haven't guessed?" he said.

Scott shook his head no.

"I want to rule Earth because I—"

Terminus choked back his words, and his eyes nearly popped out of his head. His voice took on a deep, scratching tone that sounded older than the universe itself.

"I'm bored. I have grown tired of the Higher Beings."

Scott didn't know what was going on.

—*Acoadis?* Plegaborne thought aloud.

—*Who's Acoadis? Is he a Higher*—

"Ahh, Plegaborne," the being that was Acoadis said through Terminus's form. "I knew it was you. You have the stench of the dead."

—*I did not know it was you,* Plegaborne admitted. *You hide your form well.*

"I've had a couple years of practice," the Higher Being answered through Terminus.

—*Years?* Plegaborne asked.

"Yes." Acoadis smiled. "This Armadronian has been getting his power out of the Chaos Dimension for quite some time, and he did not realize that once he entered the Chaos Dimension, he might not exit alone."

—*I see,* Plegaborne muttered. *Well, then you and I have a problem, Acoadis.*

"Oh?" the demon asked. "What sort of problem?"

—*I wish for revenge on that man. He enslaved me and stripped me of some of my powers. I wish to make him pay.*

"Hmmm . . . ," Acoadis mused, scratching Terminus's chin with his hand. "I shall let you have your revenge after I take control of Earth. You see, this man has created new powers in these Armadronians and, once they travel to Earth, they will still be able to use them! This means that, perhaps for the first time, a Higher Being such as myself will also be able to use my full abilities in their dimension!"

—*I see,* Plegaborne projected his thoughts. *A good plan, even without the technology that we need from Zwaetaru.*

"Yes, yes, it is," Acoadis agreed. "And once I have seen that I can use my abilities, I will call other Higher Beings to Earth, and we shall all reap the benefits! No more will we be physical abominations, like we are on Irri. No more will a mere fraction of our power be called upon when needed. No more will we be just a Conjurer's plaything."

Acoadis raised a fist in the air and brought it back down in triumph.

"Get out of me!" Terminus screamed, momentarily regaining control.

Acoadis remained still for a second, fighting with Terminus. Acoadis regained control, sliding back into Terminus's form wearing a smooth, triumphant grin.

"Terminus has grown weak," Acoadis explained. "I lent him my power for him to sustain his influence over the Conjurers that I enslaved, so that we could take over this planet. He was slipping, and so I let him stand upright again, for a short while. Now it is my turn to control this form." His eyes blazed with fury. "No longer shall our breed of Higher Beings reside in the Chaos Dimension. I have grown tired of the power of the mental. I wish to feel the joys of the physical!"

"You can't," Scott said simply.

"Why not, little half-Armadronian?" Acoadis mocked.

"Because I won't let you."

He looked at Acoadis and imagined him crushed up in a microscopic box with an unbreakable lock on the outside.

It didn't work.

Acoadis pointed a finger at Scott and laughed at him uncontrollably, doubling over in Terminus's body.

"That will not work on me, boy!" Acoadis said. "I am all-powerful! I have lived millions of years! There is not a thing that you can imagine that I cannot counteract. Whatever you can throw at me, I will throw back tenfold."

That gave Scott an idea. There were currently two mental portals open. One inside Terminus's mind and one inside Scott's. The first time that Terminus had come into the Chaos Dimension, he had used Plegaborne as a shield.

"Give me your most powerful attack. I will not be harmed," Acoadis goaded Scott, bracing himself.

—I know what you are thinking, boy, Plegaborne thought. *Do not do it. You promised me my revenge.*

—I lied, Scott thought.

He thrust out a hand and placed it on Acoadis's chest.

"What are you doing, boy?" Acoadis laughed. "Does this form please you?"

Scott concentrated harder.

He pushed with all his thoughts, using Plegaborne's essence as a shield. Scott pushed against Acoadis, forcing him out of Terminus's body.

"Stop this!" Acoadis screamed, attempting to push back.

Scott continued to push, and Plegaborne tried to wriggle out from between them. Scott kept Plegaborne's essence in place with his mind and kept pushing.

Acoadis was almost out of Terminus's body when Scott started to lose strength. Acoadis pushed on the barriers of Scott's will until Scott was the one who was going to be pushed out of his own body, and Plegaborne would assume control.

Don't give up, kid. We need to beat them. Scott was surprised to hear Terminus's voice in his head, and he persevered.

He pushed harder than ever, and this time he succeeded in forcing the demon out of Terminus's body. He once again forced Plegaborne into the center, using him as a shield.

The second that Acoadis and Plegaborne were completely separated from them, Scott created a portal and mentally jumped into it, taking his and Terminus's minds back to Armadron.

(28)

THE FINAL BATTLE

Scott blinked and heard someone yell. He looked up and saw Nick standing up, levitating a sword with his mind.

It was pointed at Kane's heart.

Kane was standing still, dumbfounded.

"This is for killing my parents "This is for coming into *my* home, on *my* birthday, and killing *my* parents before I could even blow out the candles." Nick stared Kane down with all the anger in the universe. "And for messing with my head."

Nick mentally pushed the sword, and it went clean through Kane, killing him instantly.

Kane dropped to the ground and landed next to another figure.

"He can't hurt you anymore," Scott said to Nick, walking over to him.

Scott came to a stop next to Terminus, who had appeared and was now lying motionless on the ground next to Kane.

"Yeah, I know," Nick said, not taking his eyes off Kane. "He's dead."

"No," Scott replied, pointing at Terminus. "*He* can't. I'll explain later."

Scott looked around. Everyone surrounding them had unfrozen, and they were all looking at him. Even the Conjurers were slowly coming out of their stupor.

"There doesn't have to be a battle. He doesn't have any power anymore," Scott said, pointing again at Terminus.

Even as Scott watched, flakes of skin slowly began to fall off Terminus's body, and his face turned as white as a sheet.

"Is he dying?"

"Yes," Artam said. He had suddenly appeared next to Scott.

"What is going on?" Nick asked. "What about the Conjurers?"

Hundreds of Icranu were gathering around them now, watching Terminus die.

"Their minds are still interconnected with his. I believe that they will die as he dies," Thaught commented sadly.

"What about the Upgrades?" Seth interjected hopefully. "Will they die too?"

"No." It was Claire who spoke. "Terminus convinced them to go to Earth. He couldn't control their minds. He just . . . twisted them. Same as his loyal followers."

As Terminus was crumbling away to nothing, he whispered something, and part of his ear blew away in the wind.

"What did he say?" Nick asked, now holding the sword to Terminus's neck.

Scott knelt and put his ear next to Terminus's mouth.

"What was that?" Scott asked.

"Tell Jared I s–said hi, k–kid."

Scott's heart stopped.

He pulled his head back and looked into Terminus's eyes. They were now his dad's eyes. Terminus was saying something else and was smiling.

"You and J–Jared were . . . my gr–greatest experiments in the Six Worlds C–Complex."

"What do you mean?" Scott asked numbly, but he felt like screaming. Nothing in the world made sense anymore. *"What do you mean?"*

Nick put a hand on Scott's shoulder. Everyone else was silent, straining to hear.

"Earth, Ar–Armadron, Zwaetaru, G–Ghorn, Byaeter, Irri . . . did you r–really think . . ."

Terminus slowly smiled at him, and his eyes became glassy.

The self-proclaimed ruler of Armadron took one last final breath, and then he was gone.

The crowd was silent for a couple seconds, and then . . .

"Yes!" someone screamed. "Yes!"

The crowd roared in approval, and everyone was suddenly cheering. Their entire little army from all around the planet was cheering. It was the happiest day on Armadron.

Scott had never felt so empty and alone in his entire life.

Out of nowhere, all the Conjurers dropped to their faces, dead in the dirt.

Suddenly someone screamed.

Scott heard a slight rustling noise in the once-again silent crowd.

Claire quickly stretched her hand out just in time.

A girl was approaching Scott. She must have been running *extremely* fast, but now she was slowly running through Claire's force field, stretching it like a balloon.

The girl had a fierce scowl on her face, and she was holding a bloody knife. When she was just a few feet away from Scott, she raised the knife in slow motion and pointed it at Scott's neck. Claire promptly closed her force field and crushed the girl like used aluminum foil, killing her instantly.

Seventeen people in a straight line as far back as a quarter mile dropped to the ground in the same breathtaking moment. Scott noticed as they fell that their necks were slit open.

"They are here!" Thaught bellowed. "Battle positions!"

Everyone scrambled to his or her battle groups. Scott and Thaught immediately moved toward the Gateway to stop anyone from getting through. Seth assumed command of his section, Artam disappeared into the crowd, and the other teams got into their foxholes and covered their sectors.

Scott took a second to look around as he got to the place Thaught had described where the Gateway would appear. He stood next to Thaught before something large was thrown at his face.

He looked at the boulder that was about to strike him, and it fell to the ground, knocked away by Thought, who had taken a giant lizard-bear form.

Scott turned toward him and stared.

"I've got your back!" Thought yelled. "Take him out!"

He looked around for who had thrown the boulder, and he caught the eyes of a boy standing less than a hundred feet away from him.

The boy suddenly ran to him, and Scott shot fire at him. The boy ran straight through the fire, not even batting an eyelash.

Scott tried water next, expecting the boy to get blown off his feet.

The boy kept running, completely unharmed.

"Terminus is dead!" A lot of the friendlies were screaming now, trying to get some of Terminus's followers to turn around.

Thought looked around and noticed that they were down to about six hundred already and were up against nearly eight hundred enemies. Some enemy forces were turning around and running away, but not nearly enough of them.

* * *

Scott threw lightning at the boy, but the boy shook it off and kept coming.

The boy reached Scott and threw out a fist.

Ohhhhh, sh—, Scott thought.

Suddenly he found himself twenty feet behind the boy. The boy wheeled around, angry that he had missed his target.

Then Scott remembered: he had touched Terminus and copied some of his curse from him!

Scott tried a new tactic this time. He focused on the curse from Claire and used his mind to try to read the thoughts of his attacker.

His mind was flung off an impenetrable barrier. He staggered back just as the boy started to run forward again.

He's unstoppable, Scott thought.

* * *

Others were having trouble as well.

Nick was in the middle of the field, throwing metal knives at a man who stretched his body out of the way like rubber. The man was taunting Nick and getting closer.

I'm gonna beat the freaking snot out of you, Nick thought, creating a large metal bear trap that erupted out of the ground.

The trap clamped shut just as the man stretched his body horizontally and narrowly escaped.

"Bravo," the man said, clapping his elastic hands enthusiastically, "but not good enough."

* * *

Claire was next to her brother, Billy, standing defensively back to back. They were each battling someone. Claire was using her telekinesis to hurl imaginary walls at the girl she was fighting, who seemed light as a feather and was incredibly fast. Claire suddenly wrapped her in a force field, and the girl's eyebrows furrowed. Claire yelled out, released the force field, and the girl dropped to the ground extremely fast and hard. She created an impact crater at least six feet deep and then came out a half second later.

What the hell kind of curse is that?! Claire thought.

"How ya doin', sis?" Billy suddenly asked her over his shoulder.

"Not good. You?"

"Uh . . . okay," Billy summarized. "Some family reunion, huh?"

Billy was blind, but he was using his enhanced precognition to fight hand to hand against an Upgrade who was just as fast as he was, if not faster.

"You can't keep this up," the brown-haired boy attacking Billy said smugly. "I memorize physical movements and copy them instantly. It's only a matter of time before I kill you."

Billy just gritted his teeth and relied on his curse to tell him a second early what the boy's movements would be.

* * *

I can do this, Scott thought as the boy attempted to land another punch at him.

This time, he dodged the punch by angling his jaw in a different direction. The boy continued to try to punch Scott at an alarming speed, but Scott had lightning-fast reflexes now.

"Hey, Scott!" Nick called from somewhere. "A little help would be nice!"

Scott lost focus for a second and was awarded with a heavy blow to the face.

He felt the familiar tingling feeling in his limbs. He had copied the kid's ability when he got punched.

He was flung back, and the boy immediately rushed forward, pressing his advantage.

Scott let this second punch hit him, but this time the boy's hand was flung back.

Scott didn't waste any time. Nick needed help.

He swallowed his disgust and thrust his fist into the boy's open mouth. Scott's fist punched through the back of his throat, as expected.

"I guess you're not as tough on the inside as you are on the outside," Scott said as the boy dropped to the ground, dead.

"Scott!" Nick yelled. "Anytime!"

Scott teleported to Nick using Terminus's curse and immediately saw what the problem was.

Nick was facing three people now, and he only had one other ally fighting next to him.

Scott immediately acted and punched through the back of the boy he was sneaking behind.

There was no blood, no hole, and no wound. His hand just disappeared and came out the other side like a portal.

"You see what I mean?" Nick said as he flung a piece of metal at someone who simply bent their body around it. "That's a problem."

Scott pulled his hand back out, and the boy whipped around. He smiled at Scott and thrust his hand inside him.

The boy somehow solidified his hand, and it stopped being intangible for a second.

Scott would have been dead if he hadn't subconsciously copied the boy's ability and become intangible himself.

The boy's hand harmlessly passed through him, and Scott stepped back.

As an experiment, he punched the boy in the face as hard as he could while remaining intangible.

Just as he predicted, the boy became intangible as well.

Scott's fist connected with the boy's jaw, and he combined both his intangible power and the unstoppable power that he had just copied from the other boy.

Apparently, if two people are intangible, then they can cause bodily harm to one another. Which is why Scott's fist plowed straight through the boy's face, this time spewing blood everywhere.

The boy dropped and didn't get back up.

A man flew through the air, and Scott ducked, looking around. Everywhere, people were killing other people. From what he could tell, every Upgrade had a completely new, never-before-seen ability, and they were killing a lot of Icranu.

Scott looked at Nick. Nick had killed a girl, and now, with the help of another Icranu with the metallic curse, he was finishing off the boy who looked like he was made of rubber.

—*Scott!* Claire yelled to him in his mind. *Help us!*

He was about to teleport to Claire when Thought yelled to him from the Gateway.

"No! Scott, get back here! We have our own job! Claire and Billy can take care of themselves. We cannot allow these Upgrades to get through the portal!"

"But—"

"No! We need you for this!" Thought yelled, turning into a gorilla-spider combo and attempting to punch a boy who was extremely flexible and acrobatic.

—*Sorry, Claire,* Scott whined. *I have a job too.*

—It's okay, Claire immediately responded. *We've got this. Help Thaught.*

He teleported next to Thaught, and the acrobat boy jumped up, aiming a kick at Scott's face.

Scott shot a torrent of water at him, and the boy twisted impossibly in midair, completely dodging the attack. He landed lightly on his feet, closer to Scott, and punched this time.

Scott hardened his face, and as the boy's fist connected, Scott heard his opponent's bones crack all the way up to his shoulder.

The boy cried out, and Thaught changed into a mammoth. While the boy was in the fetal position, Thaught stepped on him and made sure that *every* bone in his body cracked, effectively turning the kid to pudding.

They fought for hours like that, leaning on each other for help. They killed so many Upgrades that Scott lost track, and he didn't even care anymore. The faces of his enemies just blended together, and all Scott could remember at any given moment were a few important phrases:

Throw him. Save her. Teleport there. Go intangible! Use water. Jump! Tell Nick to move. Holy crap, Claire's brother can fight.

* * *

"The Gateway!" Artam screeched from somewhere. "It's opening!"

"There are still seven more Upgrades!" Thaught yelled.

Scott looked around the battlefield again with fresh eyes. About fifty Icranu were left, when there originally were hundreds. It was a slaughter.

"Hey," Scott called to Thaught. "How do we—"

Thaught turned to answer Scott, and someone came up behind him. Before Scott could say anything, the boy behind Thaught put his hands on Thaught's shoulders.

The boy grinned, and Thaught grimaced in pain. Thaught somehow wriggled out, turned into a falcon, and flew weakly into the air.

Scott immediately teleported in front of the boy and shot lightning at him. The boy just stood there grinning, as his body somehow absorbed the blast from the lightning.

The boy continued to walk toward Scott.

Scott threw a boulder at the boy, and the kid was hit dead on.

The boy flew thirty feet back, away from the active wormhole that was now behind Scott. He was obviously dead now.

Scott went to turn around when he saw a familiar face. It was Claire, and she was stepping next to the body of the dead boy.

Suddenly, the boy's hand shot out and grabbed her ankle. Claire gasped and crumpled to the ground.

"Claire!"

It was Seth. He flew in like a rocket with two other men behind him.

He knelt and punched the boy through his chest, burrowing straight into the ground.

The boy was still holding on to Claire, grinning. His chest started healing rapidly, right before everyone's eyes.

Seth took his hand out of the boy's torso and saw, along with everyone else, that his wounds were closing.

Someone came out of nowhere and sliced off the hand that the boy was holding on to Claire's ankle with.

The boy didn't utter a sound. He just used his other hand to grab Seth's wrist.

Seth felt deathly cold. His mind shriveled, and he saw his life flashing before his eyes for the second time that week.

Scott saw this and teleported there next to him. The boy looked at him, grinned mischievously as his wrist began to regrow, and grabbed Scott's wrist instead.

Scott felt like death was coming for him, and then he felt the familiar tingling feeling in his body.

He copied the boy's ability and grabbed his wrist. He forced the dark energy of death back into the boy.

The boy screamed uselessly as all his teeth fell out of his mouth, and he turned to a skeleton in less than five seconds.

Scott stood up and looked at Claire and Seth.

Billy was kneeling over her, cradling her in his arms.

"Is she . . . ?" Scott swallowed nervously.

"She's alive," the boy muttered. "But really weak."

The boy looked up, and Scott remembered his face from the Coliseum. It was the boy with no eyes.

"Who are you?" Scott asked, dazed.

"He's Billy," Seth groaned, standing up. "Claire's brother."

Oh, Scott thought. *I knew that.*

"Finish this," Billy told Scott. "Please."

Crrrraaaaccccckkkkk!!!

Scott whipped around and examined the appearing Gateway for the first time.

It was a blinding flash of all sorts of colors. It floated two feet in the air and was about four feet wide in diameter. It was a perfect circle if he ever saw one.

"Three more Upgrades left!" Artam screamed.

Thaught landed next to the wormhole in bird form and then transformed back into a regular, Accelerated Armadronian.

"A few have already made it through!" Thaught screeched. "Don't let anyone else get past us!"

Scott took a quick look around and saw that now there were fewer than twenty Icranu left standing.

"Excuse me." A teenager with short brown hair and a thin build suddenly appeared in front of Thaught. "You mind? I'm trying to get to Earth, mister."

Before anyone could react, the guy moved faster than a hummingbird and created a mini sonic boom, perforating everyone's eardrums.

Ten seconds after he crossed through the wormhole, they could all still hear his childish laughter.

"I'll be going next," someone said in a pleasant voice.

Nearly all the remaining Icranu were standing in front of the wormhole, guarding it.

They all looked out to a young girl who looked about fifteen. She had long brown hair and a cute smile, or at least Scott thought so.

"No. You're not," Nick threatened, stepping up in front of everyone.

"Oooh, big muscles," she said, flirting with Nick, stepping closer.

She was ten steps away.

Five Icranu rushed to stop her. She started running, and all their attacks went through her and came out the other side.

She's intangible, Scott realized.

Scott stepped in front of her and became intangible as well.

He jumped to tackle her, but as he came in contact with her, he felt immensely dizzy.

One second, he was in front of her, and the next he was behind her.

She stopped a couple steps before stepping into the wormhole and winked at Scott as he lay on the ground.

"Boys," she commented. "Always wanting what they can't have."

She ignored the dozen or so people who were flinging attacks through her.

"Walton!" she suddenly yelled. "What's taking so long?"

"Shut up. I'm right here!"

There was a large guy charging for the wormhole about fifty feet away.

Ten Icranu, including Nick and Seth, ran up to the guy going for the wormhole.

Four Icranu were literally flattened, punched, swatted aside, or kicked effortlessly as the large boy ran.

Nick covered himself in metal and punched the guy as hard as he could in the face.

The sound of bending metal filled the air. Nick fell to the side, got up, and ran after him, pissed. His punch had no effect, other than to bend the metal on his own fist.

Scott noticed Seth nearby shooting extremely hot fire at the kid. The boy, running with his mouth open, began swallowing the fire.

As he ingested more and more fire, his body grew even larger until he was the size of the Incredible Hulk.

Walton reached the wormhole and then jumped through with the girl.

Suddenly everything became silent. Everyone put his or her senses on overdrive, looking for anyone else. They couldn't let any more through. Enough of the Upgrades had already slipped by.

Scott saw Artam out of the corner of his eye, backing up toward the wormhole, looking around.

Scott started to walk toward him, and Artam beckoned to him.

Scott bumped into something—or someone—next to the wormhole, but he saw nothing. He felt a tingling feeling in his limbs and stared at the spot.

Suddenly, clear as day a boy appeared. He was a little younger than Scott, and with his hands outstretched, he pointed at the wormhole. He seemed to be concentrating very hard.

"Hey," Scott asked, "who are you?"

The boy ignored him.

Wait a minute . . .

Scott remembered something Seth had told him about a kid named Brandon who could manipulate and even create wormholes. But if this was Brandon, why was he here? Whose side was he really on?

Artam suddenly appeared next to Scott and spoke quietly. He muttered words in a language that Scott did not understand.

Scott felt his limbs grow heavy. He slumped to the ground, but Artam caught him.

"It's okay, boy, I have you," Artam said soothingly.

Artam lifted Scott easily and took a step toward the wormhole.

"Hey!" someone called to Artam. "Where are you going?!"

Artam ignored the question and stepped toward the wormhole again.

Suddenly Nick stepped in between Artam and the wormhole.

"Where are you going, Artam?" Nick asked.

Scott saw some form of green energy build up in the fist that Artam was holding behind his back. He tried to warn Nick about it, but he couldn't speak.

Mind over matter, he remembered Claire saying to him.

—*Nick! Artam's going to hurt you!* Scott projected to him. *Put up a shield!*

Nick reacted just in time. He raised a wall of metal up from the ground as Artam jabbed his fist at him.

The fist connected with the metal and warped it, turning it into molten pudding.

Artam turned his hand through the metal and waved his hand. "No!"

Nick flew backward through the wormhole.

Scott saw the look in his eyes. He had never seen Nick look so afraid.

Artam took another step toward the wormhole, still dragging Scott. Suddenly Artam was shot aside by a blast of fire.

Seth now stood in front of the wormhole, glaring at Artam, as were the twenty remaining Icranu.

—*Nick!* Scott yelled in his thoughts.

—*I'm okay. I'm on some kind of floating island, I think,* Nick thought from back on Earth.

Somehow Scott could still pick up Nick's thoughts.

—*Claire, are you picking up on this?* Scott asked.

—*Yeah, but . . .*

Artam stood up and left Scott limp on the ground, unable to move.

All of the other Icranu just stood by. They didn't know anymore who the good guys and the bad guys were.

"I had my suspicions about you," Seth said, staring down Artam.

—*Come back to the wormhole,* Scott projected to Nick.

—*I can't get through. The Gateway has reversed, remember? It's one-way only.*

—*Just do it!* Scott thought.

"But no one ever believed you," Artam said with an evil grin.

What are they talking about? Scott thought.

"I always knew you were the traitor. I just knew it," Seth said. "Terminus never killed you when he could have, you brought Scott here, and someone knew that we were going to the Infinite Cave. The real Artam *was* connected to the other Conjurers with a hive mind like he should have been, and you killed him and morphed into him before Terminus enslaved them all five years ago. Also, that fake death that you pulled, Kane? I know that you were controlling Nick with one of the curses that you stole, making him your puppet. You would never be taken down so easily like that."

"Seth, what are you talking about?" Thought questioned, stepping up next to Seth.

"Kane. He's Kane," Seth said, pointing at Artam.

After hearing this, several Icranu rushed forward with weapons, intent on killing Artam.

Kane, in the form of Artam, made a rapid symbol in the air with his hand, and the rest of the Icranu, except Seth and Scott, suddenly looked like they were in a time warp, including Thought. They were all now moving slower than a snail's pace.

"Well, good for you," Kane said, smiling. "You figured it out. I killed old Artam long ago. But I must be going now. It's time for me to rebuild."

"Rebuild?" Seth asked.

"Yes." Kane grinned. "I will assume control of the Six Worlds Complex. You see, I never really needed Terminus. Even though he was more scientifically inclined than I, I am a Mediator like Scott. My abilities are diverse and will allow me to manipulate the Upgrades and go from world to world, changing history as I see fit. I will look like everyone, be no one, and yet influence all."

Scott, immobilized on the ground where Kane had dropped him, realized that he no longer had the energy to project his thoughts to Nick.

"I'll find you and kill you," Seth growled.

"How?" Kane challenged. "You are useless on Earth, and on Zwataru—"

Seth fired a blast of lightning at him as fast as he could.

Kane held out a hand, and Seth dropped to the ground, convulsing. The lightning died away in pathetic sparks.

"Time to go," Kane said happily to Scott. "Bernard, kill them for me. Kill them all."

From the ground Scott looked around at the remaining Icranu and saw a familiar face.

Bernard, the absorber Scott had faced in the Coliseum, was walking toward Billy, who was in suspended animation at the back of the group.

He walked right behind Billy and stretched his hand out, grinning.

Kane picked up Scott, and he lost sight of Billy.

Kane stepped toward the wormhole, and Scott just hung there on his shoulder like a sack of useless Mediator potatoes.

I need to freaking move! he shouted inside his head. *But I don't have any power!*

Then the craziest thought occurred to him.

Kane was two steps away from the Gateway when Scott opened a portal to the Chaos Dimension with his mind.

RECHARGING

The first thing that he felt was the power. Secondly, he felt *him*. Acoadis sensed the Gateway and was mere seconds away from him.

Scott absorbed the power that he needed and closed the Gateway.

"Nooooooooooo!" Acoadis screamed, tearing apart that section of the Dimension as Scott snuck back into Armadron.

—*We will kill you!* Plegaborne screamed behind him. *We will see you soon, boy!*

* * *

Scott returned when Kane was only one step away from the wormhole.

He felt the rush of energy and kneed Kane in the face. Kane fell to the ground, dropping Scott in the process.

Scott rolled quickly and prepared to end the traitor's life.

"I wouldn't do that," Kane said, smiling. Somehow, he was on his feet again and holding a glowing purple knife up to Seth's neck.

Scott's shoulders dropped. Kane was levitating Seth slightly off the ground, holding him in front of him. Seth also had lost all his new fire look, likely from Kane's attacks.

"Grrrraaaahhh!"

Scott looked over at the sound. It was Billy. His mouth was wide open, and he was turned toward a different scene.

Scott followed Billy's gaze and saw Thaught holding a sword that he had just run through Bernard's back. Bernard dropped to the ground, dead.

"Everyone who allied with you is dead," Scott announced. "It's over, Kane."

"Never! A dozen of my Upgrades are already through the portal. Now, come with me through the wormhole, or Seth will die," Kane ordered.

Scott thought about going to the Chaos Dimension again. If he went there, then he could kill Kane faster.

He knew that Acoadis and Plegaborne were waiting there for him, though. He couldn't risk it.

"Put him down," Scott said evenly, racking his brain for a curse that could get him out of this mess.

"I will if you step with me through the wormhole," Kane said.

"I will go with you after you put him down," Scott replied.

"You will go with me now," Kane corrected. "Start walking."

Scott slowly walked toward the wormhole, looking at Thaught out of the corner of his eye. Thaught was the only one not in suspended animation anymore besides Scott and Seth.

Seth funneled all his remaining energy into his eyes to send Scott one message: *Don't do whatever it is that you're thinking about doing.*

Scott nodded his head slightly and glanced at the other Armadronians. They were all pleading with him in suspended animation to save them.

"Thaught," Kane said.

"Yes?" Thaught replied.

"We both know that Artam's powers didn't work on you, but they work just fine on Scott and Seth. Do not move or I will kill them. Do you understand?"

Thaught remained where he was.

"Good"—Kane smiled—"Now—"

"Don't black holes dice people into a million pieces?" Scott asked.

"This is a wormhole," Kane explained quickly. "It is safe."

RECHARGING

"It is?" Scott looked at it fearfully.

Seth shot a confused look at him.

"We do not have much time!" Kane argued. "Look. It is safe. You see?"

Kane stuck his arm through the Gateway to prove his point. Suddenly something or someone from the other side pulled on Kane's arm, and he teetered, about to lose his balance.

Scott used telekinesis to fling Seth away from Kane, and then he teleported next to him.

Kane tried to make a symbol in the air, but Thaught was faster. He turned into a large octopus with scales and wrapped his tentacles around Kane's arms and legs.

"Aaaarrrggghh!" Kane screamed like a madman, thrashing about wildly.

The Armadronians ran forward, finally free of the spell.

They all ran up to Kane and—

"Wait!" Scott yelled.

Kane's stomach and head were shrinking, causing his body to fold like a paper airplane. He tried to move, but his body looked completely stuck between the two worlds, likely from standing near the wormhole for so long.

Thaught let go, and Kane continued to scream for at least another minute.

Suddenly Kane made eye contact with Scott. He thrust out his hand and muttered something, hitting Scott in the chest with a gray light.

Scott had the sinking feeling that he had just lost something important, and then Kane smiled an evil smile. Then there was a flash of light, and Kane disappeared.

Scott stepped back and wiped his hands on his shorts.

"Is it over?" Seth asked, standing up. "Is he dead?"

Scott looked at Seth.

"Yeah, it's over," he said. "And I don't think so."

"Good. Now you have to go home," Seth said.

"Does he have to?" Claire interjected, staggering up to them.

"Yes," Thaught answered shortly. "The Gateway will close sooner than anticipated. We've been messing with it unnaturally, and it is now unstable."

There was a long silence and some muttering from the crowd. The rest of the Icranu teams congratulated each other and started to carry off their wounded. They left Scott, Thaught, Seth, Claire, and Billy alone near the wormhole.

"Will any of you come with me?" Scott asked.

Seth thought about it for a couple seconds.

"Not this time, buddy."

"Why not?" Scott asked.

"Because a dozen Upgrades escaped through the wormhole and are now on Earth. You have to find them, and I have to stay and make sure things here are safe. Plus, I think I've sorta got to help rebuild this place."

"Why?" Scott asked, stunned.

"Because I noticed, when there was a break in the clouds," Seth told all of them, "this planet has light and warmth, and I want it to be like Earth. I want money and cars and trains and stuff like that. I can help with that, since I know where to start. No, not like Earth. Better. We'll make our own way."

"Who's gonna be the king or whatever?" Scott asked.

"No kings or monarchs," Thaught said. "We will have a council, and we will take advice from the residents of Inno Mountain. They have schools, hospitals, and a self-sufficient life there. They are withdrawn from the world, but with Seth as our liaison controlling the Otherfire, we can bring them back into the world, and bring our world into theirs. Everybody wins."

"I'll go with Scott," Billy suddenly declared.

"What?!" Claire asked. "I just got you back! And you won't have any curses there to help you. And you're blind!"

"Thanks for reminding me, sis," Billy huffed. "Terminus and Kane did some experiments on me, though. I'm even better with tech stuff now that I can't see, and I'm kind of in the future constantly. I'm basically living two steps ahead all the time."

The others shot him quizzical looks.

"I know it's weird," he admitted, somehow sensing their expressions, despite his blindness.

They all were silent after that one, imagining the horror of being treated like an animal. Going through what Billy had to go through. Being experimented on. Having your eyes taken away.

Wait a minute . . . Scott was remembering.

He looked over next to the Gateway. The boy was there, still invisible.

"Hey, show yourself!" Scott yelled to him. "Or I'll make you."

The boy jumped a little but stayed crouched.

When his friends reacted and stared, Scott knew the boy had just made himself visible. Seth, especially, was staring at the kid.

"Brandon?!" Seth asked, incredulous.

"Seth?" the boy responded, looking at Seth's changed appearance and finally recognizing him. "That you?"

"Yup." Seth grinned, then addressed the group. "Brandon's the dude who created the portal to send me to Earth in the first place, before he got captured."

Brandon thought about waving, but he was busy calibrating the portal.

Seth thought for a moment, then said, "Brandon, why are you here?"

Brandon nodded in Thought's direction. "He freed me from Terminus, and I've been working to keep the wormhole calibrated and stable so if any Upgrades slipped through, at least we'll know where and when in history they landed on earth. So we—I mean, so Scott—can find them."

Brandon sounded exhausted. Then he added, "But Thought's right—it's becoming unstable. And it's sucking up all the available energy—I won't be able to create a new portal until Halley's Comet has completely passed, days from now. Scott, if you're going to go, you have to go fast."

Scott took this all in and nodded silently, thinking of what he was leaving behind and what he had to do. If he went back to Earth, then he wouldn't have another chance to see Armadron, or Seth, again.

"Yes, you will," Claire said aloud. "We'll have Brandon when we need to reach you."

Everyone else looked slightly confused, but Scott nodded in agreement.

"Go to your family," Thought told him. "See your mom and your brother. Find those escaped Upgrades and take them in. Teach them that there's more to life than killing. We've killed enough, and I think it's time we put that behind us." Thought smiled. "We will take care of things here. You have Nick and Billy as well to help you. Now go."

"Wait," Seth interjected. "You still have your Bastum?"

Scott checked his pockets, but it wasn't there. He pulled out his Smartphone and Jared's blue inhaler instead.

Seth took Scott's phone and shot a little bit of electricity through it. He gave Scott back his smartphone and smiled.

"Not sure if it'll work," Seth said, grinning, "but it would be sick if we could talk. That electric frequency I just shot into your phone is the same that is in my Bastum. It's how we talk here. We don't have cell towers, so Bastums access our own bioelectric frequencies."

Scott just laughed and rolled his eyes, pocketing his dead cell phone.

He looked at each of his new friends, trying to memorize their faces.

"I guess this is good-bye for now," he said.

"For now," Thought said and winked.

"Wait!" Seth yelled.

"What?" Scott asked, suddenly anxious to get back.

"Tell my . . . parents that I fell off the side and drowned in the confusion. Please."

Scott looked at him for a long minute, thinking about how that would go down. He would cross that bridge when he needed to.

"That's messed up," Scott said.

"Be creative then," Seth told him.

"Okay."

Scott and Billy gave everyone hugs and stepped through the wormhole. Claire was not happy. She had her arms crossed and was looking away, trying to keep her tough persona.

"I love you, Billy!" she suddenly yelled. "Be safe, little brother!"

Scott and Billy both stepped through, and Brandon immediately threw down his arms, exhausted, and collapsed to the ground on Armadron.

On Earth, the first thing that Scott heard was yelling. It sounded like Nick and a hundred terrified cruise passengers.

He opened his eyes and saw that he was on the deck of the cruise ship again. People were running everywhere, upturning chairs and furniture in a mad dash for safety.

Scott looked around and Accelerated, instantly sighting Jared and his mom in his mind. They were still in their room, hiding with a crew member.

"What the hell is going on?" Nick was yelling.

Nick came over to Scott and Billy, who stood by the bow of the ship.

Alarms rang out. *Beep! Beep! Beep!*

"Attention all passengers and staff! Attention all passengers and staff! We are now in full lockdown mode. Go to your cabins and lock all doors immediately. Do not come out until you are instructed to do so. This is not a drill."

No freaking way, Scott thought.

"Guys, come on!" he yelled.

Billy and Nick followed Scott to the edge of the ship. Scott hid along the side of the pool house and instructed the others nearby to do so as well.

"What the hell are we hiding for?!" Nick cried, standing up. "The Upgrades are out there, and I owe that guy Walton a freakin' beating."

"Nick!" Scott said, trying to get his thoughts in order, "I think we went back in time before I left, by about ten minutes."

Nick chewed on this new piece of information.

"So what do we do?" Billy asked the question on everyone's mind.

"I don't know—"

Crack!

Gunshots, and lots of them, were getting closer.

Suddenly, from their hiding spot, Scott saw himself and Sam break out from the lower decks and sprint across the ship, dodging bullets.

I look terrified, Scott thought, seeing himself cowering at every little sound.

He watched himself and Sam get to the edge of the ship and look down at the vortex that would surely take them to the wormhole below.

The Conjurers in black robes were not far behind them, and they had guns. The deck of the ship was clear now. Everyone had run to their rooms for safety.

Scott saw the Conjurers start to take aim with their guns, as his past self and Sam talked frantically by the edge of the ship, oblivious to the threat.

"Stay here for a minute," Scott told Nick and Billy.

He teleported behind his past self and telekinetically threw him off the ship and into the vortex, using Claire's power.

"Hey, you can't be here!" Sam cried.

"But I am," Scott said.

"But how . . . ?"

"Sam. Leave. Now," Scott said. "If you don't go to Armadron with me—the other me—right this minute, I don't know what's gonna happen. But I'm not going to let you die again . . . I'm going to find a way to save you, Sam, I promise."

He tapped into Claire's power and delved into Sam's mind. Without really knowing what he was doing—and only following his instincts—he erased the memory of this meeting from her mind.

She instantly lapsed into unconsciousness from the shock, and Scott caught her. He looked at her for another second and then pushed her over the side, just as another bullet clipped her in the leg, narrowly missing him.

When Scott turned around, all five Conjurers formed a semicircle around him, guns at the ready.

In the blink of an eye, Scott suddenly realized what he had to do. He couldn't hurt them: he had to let them go. He had to make them go after his past self so that all that had happened on Armadron could still occur.

Nick crept up behind the Conjurers with a broken chair leg in his hand, with Billy in tow behind him.

Scott waved him off.

Just before the Conjurers opened fire on him, he teleported behind them and called up a torrent of water. It didn't come.

He tried to make metal from the ship attack them.

Nothing.

Scott wrapped them all in his telekinesis and threw them off the ship. They felt much heavier than normal, and he felt exhausted as they went over the side.

As they descended into the sea, one Conjurer turned around in midair and fired at Scott.

Scott immediately called upon the curse that he had gotten from the boy with enhanced strength.

The bullet flew through his left bicep and he screamed, falling to the deck.

Nick ran over to him and propped him up.

"Scott," Nick said, shaking him. "Heal yourself or something. You copied the curse from that kid who tried to kill Claire and Thaught."

Oh, Scott remembered. *Right.*

He tried again and again. But nothing happened.

Next he tried to go intangible, Danny Phantom-style. It worked!

Ping!

The bullet fell through his body and hit the deck of the ship.

Billy walked over, waving his hands out in front of him. Here he was completely, truly blind.

Scott barely heard Nick saying something to him.

"Scott! I said, what curses do you have left?"

Scott thought it all through quickly in his head.

No more water. No metal. No strength. Controlling earth is gone too, I can feel it. No more healing power either.

"I'm left with telekinesis, telepathy, teleportation, and phasing," he told Nick. "And I think that I'm losing those too, but slower than the rest because they have to do with my mind or something."

"Good," Nick said. "Now get up. We need you."

"Why?"

"Because we're on Earth, with no curses and no idea where we are on this floating rock, and Billy is actually blind."

Oh.

Scott stood up and looked around. Everyone was off the main deck, presumably hiding from the gunfire. Everyone who was still alive, that is.

"I guess we should go find my family then," Scott said cheerfully. "Apparently I haven't seen them for a whole ten minutes."

WAIT! THERE'S MORE!

Are you ready to get a head start on what happens next? You can read the first chapter of Book 2 in The Otherworld Series for free. Download the first chapter by visiting: **www.coreytatebooks.com/zwataru**.

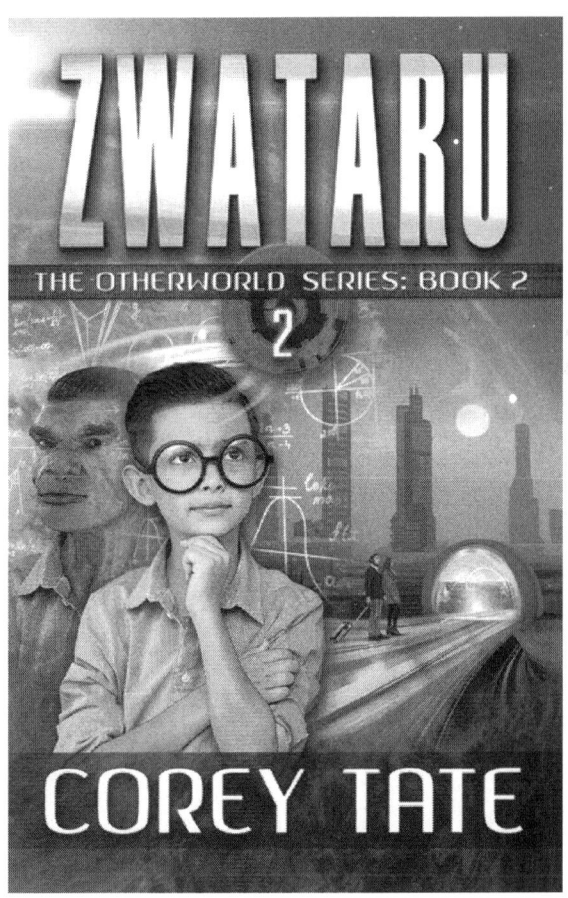

ABOUT COREY TATE

COREY TATE is the creator of *The Otherworld Series*, a series that drops readers smack in the middle of a fast-paced intergalactic conspiracy spanning six planets. The series follows a small group of savvy young people with supernatural abilities who must stop the inhabitants of the Chaos Dimension from their malevolent schemes—or die trying. The author, who is active duty Air Force and a martial artist, weaves psychological and military tactics into the actions of his engaging heroes—and those of their diabolical enemies—in the battle to save the Six Worlds Complex. Learn more about Corey (and read sample chapters for free!) at **www.coreytatebooks.com**.